The Cabine

By

Jack Rollins

Dark Chapter Press

Dark Chapter Press
Apartment A, Henderson Apartments,
Bondgate Within, Alnwick, Northumberland, NE66 1HZ

www.darkchapterpress.com

This edition collects three seperate Dr Blessing novellas:

Dr Blessing's Curse, Or, The Baby In The Bell-Jar first published in 2011

Dr Blessing's Rapture, Or, The Beast And The Bell-Jar first published in 2012

A Christmas Blessing first published in 2013

The Cabinet of Dr Blessing first published in 2014 by Rob McEwan

References to De Omori and Owen McEwan made with the kind permission
of David Basnett

978-0-9930620-2-5

A CIP catalogue record for this book is available from the British Library

Cover art © Mark Kelly, Grim Ventures

About Jack Rollins

Jack was born and raised among the twisting cobbled streets and lanes, ruined forts and rolling moors of a medieval market town in Northumberland, England.

He claims to have been adopted by Leeds in West Yorkshire, and he spends as much time as possible immersed in the shadowy heart of that city.

Fascinated by all things Victorian Jack often writes within that era and his period gothic horror works include The Séance and the Dr Blessing series.

The Cabinet of Dr Blessing

Also By Jack Rollins

The Séance: A Gothic Tale of Horror And Misfortune

Anti-Terror
featured in the anthology
Carnage: Extreme Horror

The Cabinet of Dr Blessing

By

Jack Rollins

Part 1:

Dr Blessing's Curse, or, The Baby In The Bell-Jar

In which we are introduced to Doctor Blessing, and learn of his most unusual, and horrifying predicament.

One.

Margaret and I were entertaining a group of friends one evening in July 1859, these being the accountant Francis Flanders and his wife Annie, the catholic priest Father Haddon, (a recent acquaintance who was blissfully unaware that I was completely aware of his hopeless addiction to card games in various nefarious dens in our grey city) and finally the art dealer Edward Summerscale who was joined by the latest muse of his latest victim (that is to say, client), a French girl by the name of Dominique.

The dinner itself was given for no particular reason, the guests largely unremarkable in that they had become our regular company. Francis had tended to my finances for six years. Edward was always hoping to shift paintings and prints at the various dinners he attended but relaxed the selling at dinner in this particular company and with good reason. This reason being, chiefly that myself and Francis were only too aware of the "brand new works by the fine artist Alexander Pond, fresh from Paris" that Edward had been shovelling onto collectors in London, Manchester and Newcastle a year after Pond was stabbed to death in a robbery on the street in Paris.

It seems wise to point out at this stage that, at the time of this dinner, Margaret and I had been married for a little under five years and remained childless, and of equal note is that in all of those five years, and all of the gatherings, dinners and parties we have held, not once have I invited another doctor. That is to say that by day, I, Doctor George Blessing, am a general practitioner, but in my leisure time I do not care to consort with others of my kind nor discuss in any great detail the activities engaged in, while ministering to my duties.

As the maid of all work cleared away downstairs, we retired to the drawing room. After half an hour, Edward and Dominique, Francis and Annie took their leave. I had noticed that Father Haddon had been particularly struck by Dominique. I suppose some would consider her beautiful, some as ravishing, but I have long since had my desire for the pleasure of a woman's thighs dampened. At my age of thirty-one this might seem out of the ordinary, especially given the lack of children and at the risk of sounding self-satisfied, Margaret's considerable beauty.

Margaret dismissed Lily, the maid, for the night. Lily stayed down the hall from Margaret and I, in the room that would, in any other home, perhaps be a nursery. Then Margaret took herself off to bed. Her hand had lingered at the doorframe; her eyes had taken on a longing, a deep sadness, and I knew that she would slip into a laudanum-induced sleep before long at all. Her health had held during the dinner, but the truth of the matter was that she had become a deeply troubled, melancholy woman.

This left Father Haddon and I alone in the drawing room. I poured us each a heavy measure of brandy and took to my chair. Father Haddon considered the drink. He seemed phased, almost a little frightened by it as though afraid that upon drinking it, he might be reduced to some base, drunken monster to be cast out on the street. It occurred to me that perhaps he hovered about us so in the hope that should Margaret and I bring a child into the world, the family might be a further addition to his parish. Then again, I thought, Father Haddon had never seen me so much as set foot in a church, so would he expect me to raise a child with such ties?

I took a deep, burning swallow of brandy. I wondered if upstairs, Margaret would be making ready another attempt at seduction, trying to lure me from the fascinations of my study. Poor Margaret, if only she had seen the things that I have seen, then she might understand. It is not the lice and the discharges, not the pustulous dribbling sores, the slobbering madness of diseased whores, nor the liquefying, tumour-knotted breasts that have made a monk out of me. I have seen horror such as would make a surgeon, battle-hardened in the Crimea, turn out his guts.

I got to thinking of that night, and it seemed appropriate to talk about it, looking over at that hypocrite with his white collar and crucifix. Perhaps he might like my story. I drained my glass.

"Quite a drinker, eh?" Haddon muttered.

"What's that?" I asked him, snapping out of my reverie.

"I say, you must have been thirsty."

I nodded. Yes. Yes, Father Haddon would like to hear the story. Yes, he would like it. He might even have some theological insight, some angle or notion that my science can not detect. Perhaps my pragmatism is insufficient to free me from the slavery and wonderment of the gruesome marvel that has burned all desire and lust from me. "Drink," I told him. "Drink, Father. We shall have another, but in my study."

"Pardon me, George, but I don't usually drink brandy. I'm not accustomed to drinking it quickly," Haddon protested.

No, I thought, cheap gin in the slums is your tipple. "I have no communion wine, Father. I recommend you drink that brandy, however, to steady your stomach. I'll find an alternative for you in my study for the next charge."

I detected then a nervousness in Father Haddon. At first I had mistaken it for wounded religious sensibilities at my communion wine comment. Was he afraid of what I might tell him? Had my tone changed? Had I flushed? Was I becoming overly-belligerent? Was I bordering on the aggressive? I made for the door, empty glass in hand, and looked back over my shoulder. Haddon took two big gulps of the brandy and contorted as though struck in the abdomen.

"It's good drink, eh Father?"

"I-I can appreciate the quality of the liquor, George. But as I say... it's not really my tipple."

I led the priest to my study, which was locked, the lock to which I alone held the key. We entered the room in darkness, the gaslight from the drawing room enough for me to find the safety matches on the side table with which to ignite the gas jets to either side of the mirror behind my desk. The bulk of my study now suitable illuminated, I motioned for Haddon to take a seat while I closed the door.

"Does whisky take your fancy, Father?"

Haddon's smile was sudden and broad, his eyes glistened in the gaslight. "Now that I can drink."

"I have no water in here, Father."

"No, to water it down's a sin," he replied. Did I detect a hint of a Scottish accent? I wondered if this particular notion of a sin had been handed down to him by a father or grandfather.

Haddon cast glances around the study, the walls mainly hidden behind bookshelves, the corners and wall behind him still dark where the active gas jets could not throw their light. The bookshelves he could see closest to him were stacked with medical texts, old copies of the Lancet and such. Those shelves closest to me, to my left, contained far less conventional literature. One book from that collection sat open on my desk, but Father Haddon did not appear to observe it for more than a moment. I wondered then if he wondered at my interest in "The Anatomy of the Blood-Fiend", by Dr Samuel Brown, III. Then I wondered at his lack of wonder, given the nature of the diagram that would have greeted his eyes.

Haddon's attention then shifted to the various bell-jars he could make out on top of the bookshelves. I could see that the contents caused him no little discomfort. His jaw firmed, his eyes moving from one jar to the next, I then had the notion that he might have been looking for something rather than being interested in the collection in general. Perhaps he had heard tell of the shrunken head sent to me from Peru, or the lamb, born inside-out, perhaps the iguana, possibly the monkey foetus. I considered telling Haddon of the inverted lamb, which was still considered living when the veterinarian plunged it into the brine.

I resisted that urge, but was forced to assess my loose-mindedness. Why did I want to horrify Haddon? Had I the urge to tell because of the drink, or had I drunk so much to drum up the courage? How to frame the tale – ask for help or wait for help to be offered? Could the priest offer help and advice on such matters, or would I be causing him needless discomfort? And could he keep a secret? And what if he couldn't?

Haddon seemed trustworthy, seemed nice. Well, as agreeable as any other fellow.

Then again, I thought, he is a priest.

Two.

Three years ago, I was indulging in a guilty pleasure with a friend of mine, Henry Burton. Both of us enjoyed 'roughing it', as we used to call it, which involved, chiefly, our going to various low-class drinking and gambling dens around the city.

On that particular night, we had selected Charlie's Gin Palace, one of the more tame establishments, but still one where fights over between whores were commonplace.

Henry was a practical man, a man of business and trade. It was his line of business that rendered him something of an outcast in polite society, and it was not considered normal for a doctor to fraternise with a trader frequently, without my being attached to his business in a practical way. Our friendship was all the more controversial as various parties became aware of our 'rough' trips. There were many married men who tutted in judgment and sensationalised our behaviour over tea in various parlours with their wives, while secretly wishing they were out in the darkness with Henry and I, drinking heavily and talking at length about subjects avoided in polite company.

Henry and I had developed a business together, long after our friendship was cemented. I was chief of the staff at a hospital that he and his wife had helped me to create.

Other friends of mine would ask probing questions to gather intelligence on his means. I knew for certain the fear in their enquiries – for Burton had started out with nothing, and was now a man whose fleet of clippers were making handsome returns for his investors. The wonder was where that first clipper had come from. Some said he had mutinied and seized a ship and begun a lucrative opium run. Others say that the pirate known as the Bilbao Devil was none other than Henry Burton, stealing ships, cargo and silver only to leap into legitimacy and, (Heaven forbid!) polite society. He was a man who made his own waves, and who had every chance of seeing his children or grand-children firmly established in the upper class.

His wife Charlotte was a delight and managed his house well, however, she was a source of amusement to society too, for no other reason than she had been a housekeeper to Burton's father who had been, until the day he died, a respected editor on Fleet Street. She was considered to be a commoner, living far and indecently above her station. I found her lovely though, and Charlotte's happy disposition and kind nature always made me wonder at why the family were up to that point, childless.

Henry had intimated to me that this was purely a matter of economics and that he expected, upon increasing his fortune to a sum he never disclosed to me, to raise a large family on that capital. In some ways, this seemed a sensible position to take, but I did wonder if he was, perhaps, lacking the ability to father a child rather than preparing his finances – after all, childbirth quite naturally followed marriage and, at thirty-six years old, Henry was not getting any younger.

This too, of course, was the subject of much speculation in the dining rooms and drawing rooms of Tyburnia. I could easily imagine that similar conversations were held about Margaret and I, so I never dwelt on the subject for long.

There was another aspect of Charlotte that society ladies found strange: she never spoke ruefully of her staff, nor would she treat them badly nor was she overly demanding. I personally, being one of few regular guests to the home of the Burtons could see that there was a direct correlation between the gentle nature of the lady of the house, and the order of the staff, their dedication and attentiveness.

Charlotte prided herself on being able to take

a girl from a workhouse and turn her into a servant worthy of the gentry. Only once had she relieved a servant of her position, when she caught the girl stealing silverware. Even then, Charlotte ensured that the girl left with enough money to get back to her family, or for lodgings for a couple of weeks. Such charity was unheard of. Charlotte had confided in Margaret of this affair – it was not for Henry's ears – and had said the act of stealing itself was an act of desperation, and the response to it was compassion not wrath.

On the night in question, while Henry and I took our gin and smoked cigars, laughing raucously at the drunks and whores around us, our wives enjoyed each other's company in the drawing room at the Burton home.

Someone screamed at the far end of the bar and several glasses shattered on the floor as Henry and I chatted about the difficulties of his industry and of Henry's suspicion that the British government were planning to outlaw British carriage of opium. He revealed that this would upset the balance of his business as the only way to wrangle tea from the Chinese was with silver, and the only way to wrangle that amount of silver was to carry opium from India, to China to satisfy the Chinaman's unquenchable thirst for that narcotic.

I turned to Henry with all curiosity, myself a man who had little contact with those from foreign shores. "Tell me Henry, does the Chinaman think like us?"

Henry took several thoughtful puffs on his cigar, but his train of thought was broken when we saw a flustered-looking fellow in a top hat and riding cloak pushing his way through the crowd at Charlie's.

The red-faced man approached us and I recognised him as Henry's coachman.

"Henry, Charlotte has asked if both of you would return to the house. A girl came to your door, bringing news of young Judith," the coachman announced.

Henry frowned and puffed on his cigar. "Judith? The servant girl?"

The situation was so out of the ordinary, neither Henry nor I thought to question it and we immediately climbed into the coach. I wondered on the way back to Henry's house, if the girl in question was not the servant girl who had been relieved of duty.

When we arrived at the Burton house, Charlotte was the image of concern. "Doctor Blessing, do you have a medical bag at all?" she asked.

"Yes," I replied. "I always carry a small kit with me. I left it here after dinner."

Judging by Charlotte's urgency and the pallor of the young girl who had brought the message, something was obviously gravely wrong with this Judith girl of whom, it would seem, Charlotte was clearly very fond.

"Doctor, would you be so kind as to accompany me? This girl is in terrible trouble, she isn't far away." Charlotte's eyes pleaded with me so, I could hardly deny her request.

Henry cleared his throat and grumbled, "Charlotte, this is highly improper. George, please excuse my wife's impertinence." Henry's gaze was fixed on Charlotte, his expression one of fury, his eyes flashing like rifles of rebuke.

"Not at all, my friend," I reassured him. "Not at all. One must play his part." I begged Margaret's pardon and took up my bag. Margaret too seemed disturbed by what she had heard and she urged me to be careful.

Henry accompanied me to the door. "My coach is yours, George. My man will bring you back here, to take both you and Margaret back to your home. Never fear."

"I thank you."

Henry opened the front door for me and patted my shoulder. "This is a great act of charity, George.

I shall recompense you for any supplies you should expend. Forgive my soft-headed wife's affectation for former employees. She worries about them so."

Charlotte appeared behind Henry with her shawl and bonnet on, and having, I noted, changed from her house shoes, to her walking boots, ready to take on the muck of the city. "Do not apologise for me, sir!" Charlotte huffed.

Henry grinned, amused at the occasional hardness of his wife.

Charlotte slipped her arm around the young wretch at the porch, who herself appeared to have need of a good doctor. "Come my pretty, tell me where we can find Judith. Oh but you are frozen, let us get you into the coach first, out of the weather and you can tell the doctor and I everything."

Along the coach ride, this waif recounted the tale of a working girl who had become pregnant and who now seemed to be miscarrying or suffering a very traumatic premature birth. The girl herself, Judith, had known of no other charitable enough to help her, and so had sent this girl to seek Charlotte.

This girl, the messenger, who I presume was employed similarly to Judith, was clearly in shock. I had no tonic available, carrying as I did only a very basic supply of emergency equipment. "My dear," I said, leaning closer to her to be heard over the clatter of hooves and roar of wheels on the cobbles below. "Here is my address. Make sure to call upon me in the morning and I will provide you with a tonic which will pick you right up, I'm quite sure of it."

"Thank you, doctor," she said quietly, taking the scrap of paper from my hand.

Charlotte smiled at me in approval. I must admit to feeling quite warmed by either the deed itself, or by Charlotte's approval. Perhaps being in the company of one so charitable inspired this movement in me.

I explained to Charlotte that strictly speaking, I

was a physician. I had delivered many children in my time, but given that there were complications expected, surgery might be necessary. The truth of the matter was that I had some experience in surgery – I recognised it as a highly-skilled discipline, unlike many of my contemporaries who saw it as a job for barbers. Indeed, they could not bring themselves to call even a highly skilled surgeon doctor, simply referring to them as mister. I hoped to God that my limited surgical skill would not be called upon, for the patient's sake more than my own.

We disembarked from the coach in Bermondsey and followed the messenger girl through an archway, through a narrow passage leading to a cluster of what are referred to as dosses, small single-room shacks paid for by the night with room enough for a bed and perhaps a small fireplace, and very little else.

I saw lamplight ahead where the passage opened into a small courtyard of about fifteen feet by fifteen feet. A murmur of voices told of a small crowd. I correctly guessed that the lamp belonged to a police constable.

A scream from one of the doss houses rose to a chilling crescendo. Scream does not really do the sound justice. This was like the howl of a wounded animal, lingering in the air.

I stepped into that courtyard and saw about a dozen people gathered, straining to see around a police constable with his arms outstretched, into a doorway behind him. Upon hearing that horrible sound within, the crowd's own noise increased in response. Someone screamed, "They are murdering the woman in there! They are murdering the woman in there!"

Charlotte called out, "I have a doctor here!"

The doorway to the doss opened fully. From where I approached, with the doss ahead and to my right, I could not see the scene within. Evidently some of the people gathered, could. A second policeman had emerged from the doss. He hurried past his fellow and ran towards my small party. His hands clamped over his mouth, he quickly darted around us. I heard him vomiting in the passage.

We pressed on and the policeman granted us entry to the small shack. The scene within, I shall carry to my grave.

A chubby midwife hunched over the bed – this woman in her late thirties, perhaps early forties – her skin as ashen as the messenger girl's. Her clothes were drenched in blood.

Judith, a thin girl in her late teens or early twenties, lay on the bed, in the position one would instruct her to assume in readiness for birth. Her belly was swollen with pregnancy, the bulge sitting low. She let out a low moan as an attack of convulsions wracked her body. With every wrench of her body, a dribble of blood pushed from her sex. The bedclothes were soaked.

All of this I had taken in, in seconds. The messenger, I noted, cowered in the corner behind the door, hands over her eyes.

"This will not do," I said, voice raised. I pointed to the midwife. "Step aside. We have no need for eighteen shilling and four pence charlatans here."

The midwife did not protest. Most unusual, I considered. She was obviously well aware that she was out of her depth. However, I felt that further admonishment was in order, that she might take that Bishop's Licence of hers and tear it up. "See the damage you have caused with your amateur tending. See the blood lost already. If I lose this girl and this infant, by God you will swing, lady!"

Charlotte's hand met my elbow. She nodded to Judith, whose eyes were barely visible through the black hair matted to her face.

"Indeed." I took off my coat. "Charlotte, would you be so kind as to bring me clean water and any clean cloths you can lay your hands on?" I turned my attention to the poor wretch shrinking further and further into the corner. "My dear, please help the good lady to fetch those things for me."

The girl did not move. I knelt by her as I rolled my sleeves up. "I promise to use every ounce of my skill to ensure she will come to no harm, child. You can better help Judith by ensuring the cleanliness of the articles around her."

Charlotte reached down and helped the girl to her feet. "Come, lovey." She turned to the midwife and gently urged her to the door. "You too, dear. You look like you need air too."

"Please close the door," I called over my shoulder.

I turned my full attention to Judith as I picked up my medical bag and approached the bed. "Hello, I am Doctor George Blessing. I am here to help you. Your friend tells me you have been in the state of pregnancy for approximately eight months, is that correct?"

The girl mumbled that this was so.

"Can the father be contacted?" I had to ask this. It was clear that if the child lived, which was highly unlikely, Judith would not be alive to raise it.

"No! No! No!"

I was startled by the sudden burst of energy. "Judith, please. Rest, rest. The next contractions will give you plenty of work. You will require all of your strength."

I set my pocket watch on the small table at the bedside, annoyed that I had not noted the time of that first fit I observed.

Charlotte returned with a washbowl of clean water and as much clean material as she could find. In this area, that amounted to very little.

I handed a small knife to Charlotte. "Please, cut that sheet down to handkerchief sized pieces and that other, to strips as long as you can, that I might use as bandages."

Within five minutes of setting the watch up, I estimated within eight minutes of the first fit, Judith was contorting and baying once more. More cries of murder from outside.

I washed my hands with coal tar soap, and with several small cloths I wiped away as much blood as I could, but more flowed. Charlotte held a candle close by. The blood obscured my vision so badly that I was unable to see the head of the child – which had to have been near, given how low the child sat. Then I noticed something odd. The bulge of the child began to shift upwards, drawing away from the birth canal.

Judith screamed, this was shrill and long. Tears poured from her eyes. She cried again and again.

Charlotte provided what soothing words she could muster through her own tears.

I inspected her again and could see no evidence of dilation. I dared not to say it at the time, but I could see that Judith's body was not preparing itself for birth. I wondered and became more convinced that this was not a premature delivery at all. Nor was it a miscarriage, the child was yet moving inside her.

"My stomach!" Judith yelled.

"Don't worry, lovey, it isn't your stomach," Charlotte said, scraping hair away from Judith's face. "You'll be fine. Just a few big pushes and it'll be all over."

Judith screamed again. I know this, but I did not hear it. By this I mean, I was immediately distracted by a different set of noises. There was a crawling, squelching sound, then by God a ripping sound and the noise of bones breaking.

Judith lost consciousness. Charlotte screamed. The messenger girl howled in sorrow and rushed to the bedside. The midwife looked on from the corner of the room in horror. A burly thug of a police constable burst through the door.

In her state of unconsciousness, Judith vomited

blood. I knew that she was still breathing because she inhaled some of the blood and began to cough and choke.

The stirrings in her abdomen became more pronounced, more severe. Beneath her tattered, bloody nightgown, angled bulges pushed outward.

"My God," I muttered, wiping the sweat from my forehead.

"What the hell's going on, Doctor?" the constable boomed.

"Doctor?" Charlotte implored. "Her mouth."

"Jesus!" the constable cried.

Judith's body trembled violently. Her life's fluids poured freely from both ends of her. The flow was slow. Her pulse was waning. I dismissed the messenger girl to sit by the midwife's side for a moment, "Leave me to my work, child. Judith is not alone. I shall continue to do my very best."

Of course, it was a lie. I knew that this woman could take no more and that the child within her would pass into death's icy clutches mere moments after the mother.

"Cut it out of her, man!" the constable shouted.

"Are you a surgeon, sir?" I yelled back at him.

"My apologies, Doctor. I, I've just never seen anything so..."

Judith's body arched up, her shoulders and feet bearing her weight. The scream rose with her back.

All around me was chaos, screams and shouts. A high-pitched squeak was heard, like the scream of some small animal. The crowd outside roared; the spectacle had attracted even more spectators for the mob.

"Constable, keep those people back!" I ordered.

The constable was grateful for my demand and he extricated himself from this horrific show with all haste.

Charlotte raced to the door and slammed it

shut, resting against it for a moment. The midwife sat transfixed and the little messenger girl huddled by her side, weeping into folded arms, rocking back and forth in her trauma.

It was then that I noticed, to my surprise that the child within Judith's womb maintained a surprising level of strength. From her cavity, that little fist burst forth, bringing with it such gore and offal that I am convinced this tiny hand had opened the gate to hell itself.

Judith collapsed back to the bed. That was the moment I glanced at my pocket watch, convinced that we had reached the time of death. I knew that there was no way this poor young woman could have any life left in her. She lay completely still. I held my fingers under her nose. No breath. I used my fingertips to pry open her eyelids and saw no reaction to the light. I checked her pulse. There was none. "Make a note of the time, Charlotte. At 12:36am on this the seventeenth of July 1856, I have pronounced Judith..."

"Judith Cloonan."

"... Judith Cloonan, dead."

I looked at those about me. Charlotte shoulders heaved with each of her sobs, stroking Judith's cheek over and cover again. The messenger girl remained in her corner, crying quietly into her knees. Charlotte soon turned her attention on the young girl, knowing it was too late to give Judith any comfort at all.

I happened to glance back at the unfortunate patient's cadaver and again noticed the tiniest of movements amidst the gore. A hand, which on closer inspection appeared more like an animal's claw, such was the growth and pointed nature of the fingernails. Although the mother was certainly quite dead, it seemed her offspring was alive. I picked up the small knife that I had given Charlotte to cut the material. In the other hand I took one of the rags and wiped the tiny limb before me. The hand thrashed about, very deliberately, it seemed, attempting to cause harm. My grip tightened on the small knife.

"Doctor… what are you doing?" Charlotte muttered with no lack of concern in her voice. Indeed I am sure she thought that I had completely taken leave of my senses, tampering with the dead body.

I ignored her, silently praying that all three of my female companions would remain in the corner of the room, my new discovery obscured from their view. I pressed the knife against the flesh of Judith's labia and made a small cut. This action promoted such excitement in the tiny limb before me, and the body to which it was connected, that I leapt back, startled. The sound of bones grinding met my ears. Then the sound of bones snapping. The hand withdrew, back into Judith's body, then thrust back into view, causing new bleeding and further damage. This was repeated several times and Judith's abdomen flexed and moved as though this child was pushing itself out of her body.

Judith's vaginal cavity began to tear, soon a deep rent reached up over her pelvis and almost to her navel. Her lower intestine became discernible, two tiny hands clutching that tubing.

Peering into that black mass of blood and waste, I saw teeth.

Hastily I scribbled a note on a scrap of paper in my bag and pulled the young girl out of the corner. "Go outside, go to the coachman. Send him back to his master's house. He is to travel directly to my home with Margaret, my wife. She is to give him the items on this list, all to be found in my study. He is to return to me without delay. Do you understand, girl?"

"Yes, sir," she sniffed.

The girl left, I followed her to the door and saw the policeman who had vomited earlier. His fellow was roughing up a man who had tried to break their blockade of the doss. "Call for more men. Get these people far away. I feel that this woman may have suffered some terrible disease, which may be highly contagious.

I have sent a messenger to bring some scientific equipment from my office. Until then, nobody is to enter this building, and nobody is to leave without my consent."

The constable nodded his understanding. He was soon blowing on his whistle to draw other nearby constables to the site. I had noticed about thirty people gathered outside and others in the passage.

All I could think of at that time, was those teeth. These were no child's teeth – these were crooked, pointed, even jagged. This had been no birth, this creature had eaten its way through Judith. It had bitten and clawed through her organs – it was not even in her womb, but among her intestines.

In the doss I sat at the end of the crimson pit of a bed and stared into the tear, my heart fluttering in my chest every time the creature stirred. There were occasional squeaks and a noise like a dog lapping water from a bowl. My mind raced with possibilities and very few of them conformed to conventional science.

It was in one of my more lucid moments, that I turned to the midwife. "I must apologise to you, madam. I spoke harshly of your skill. I am now of the opinion that you did very well to keep this poor woman alive for as long as you did."

She said nothing, she stared down at her brown stained hands.

"My threat to you was… unforgivable. Would you accept my apologies?"

She nodded.

I turned to Charlotte, who stared down at the unfortunate who had once been in her employ.

"There is nothing more you could have done for her, Charlotte. You tried to spare her the need to take the path of prostitution," I said as I moved over to her.

"If I hadn't sacked her, she wouldn't have ended up in this state."

"What else could you have done, Charlotte? You gave her more opportunities that most would have.

I for one, would have had no hesitation to put her onto the street for theft. You gave her money and a character, you still tried to improve the girl when she was beyond your employ. And she knew that you cared, for who was it she turned to?"

Charlotte nodded.

"You know I'm right, Charlotte. You must never blame yourself."

Having ensured that things were as right as they could be with the two ladies, I turned my attention back to that creature and I was struck with an idea. I reached into my medical bag and returned to that savage wound with a small bottle of chloroform.

"What are you doing, doctor?" Charlotte asked, quite disturbed as I withdrew the cork from the bottle.

I knew that I must lie to them, in order to secure the time to study my new discovery. "I must cleanse the wound. In truth, I have found evidence of cancerous growths which may have ruptured, presenting as pregnancy. A most rare occurrence, but one with which I have had some experience. This will be a gory business. You should both take some air." I then commenced to pour the fluid over the wound, letting it pool deeply in the curves of the woman's lifeless organs as Charlotte and the midwife took their leave.

As they opened the door, the burly constable peered into the doss. I nodded and waved at him to let the women pass. He closed the door in their wake, leaving me alone to my work.

I breathed through my handkerchief, stepped back and observed as the little beast struggled and tore at its gruesome nest, viciously at first, and then becoming ever more sluggish. Then it was still.

I probed with the knife once more, careful to cut at the organs and musculature around the clawed hands, without injuring the creature itself. Within minutes I was able to draw the being out of Judith's body.

An hour later, with the women still absent from

the doss, the coachman and messenger returned. They had brought Henry with them. Henry and the coachman entered the room after the constable obtained my permission to let them pass. Henry and coachman both pressed their gloved hands against their mouths as they took in the carnage.

"My God! George, what have you done to her?" Henry asked, eyes wide like a madman.

"I have done nothing, Henry! Nothing save attempt to keep her alive."

"She has been torn to pieces!" Henry cried.

"Did you bring the items I requested?"

The coachman brought in a case from outside. The young girl appeared at the doorway and gasped as the disgusting scene began to register with her. The coachman must have been a man of family, because in a moment he had scooped up the child and carried her from the room. He closed the door once more upon leaving.

I turned to the bed, where my coat lay across my monstrous discovery. "I would have only you, Henry, present for this."

"This, George, is highly irregular."

I nodded. "I would concur were that not such a horrible understatement."

"What do you mean?"

"Under my coat is a discovery, some form of primitive life or birth defect, which, if made common knowledge, would terrify the nation."

Henry looked puzzled.

"I guarantee it. This poor woman has carried in her womb, the offspring of some vile, base creature. This resulted in her most horrible death. This creature, it seems, feeds upon human flesh."

"A cannibal?"

I shook my head. "This is no human. This is an animal. And it is to be studied. It is to be secret."

"You must be mad, George. Why would you

want to keep such a thing?"

I picked up my coat to reveal the outstretched baby, lying alongside its mother.

"Oh George," Henry said, taking two steps back. "George, what have you found? How was it that thing came to be inside Judith?"

I smiled at my friend and said, "I recognise that you are a man without children, but do you really require a doctor to instruct you?" I moved to my box of equipment and removed a bell jar 20 inches tall. "Help me prepare this, Henry."

Soon, my operation was complete. I sat with Henry for a while in the doss, the jar safely covered and stowed in the carriage. "The party for the inquest should be here soon," Henry said. "What the hell will you tell them?"

"I will say that a very aggressive cancerous growth had taken hold, swelling so as to take on the appearance of a pregnancy. Having sought no medical attention for this unknown cancer, her organs and part of her skeleton were eaten away, resulting in this gruesome death."

Henry looked at me with supplicating eyes. "George, shouldn't the authorities know the truth?"

"Absolutely not, Henry. Not until I have discovered more about its origins. Now, can you keep this secret – even from Charlotte?"

Henry nodded his head slowly. "I can. I don't approve, however. If you put anyone else at risk in order to achieve fame and fortune, I shall be left with no alternative but to make known what has occurred here."

"Tell me, dear Henry, how could anyone else be at risk?"

Henry pointed to the door. "That thing has a father."

We sat in silence until the inquest party arrived. They looked over the body of the prostitute. Somebody muttered, "One less pinchbrick to worry about."

The whole affair was wrapped up very quickly, very neatly. Who would question the word of the attending physician?

They removed the body from the doss. The landlord complained about the mess.

The young girl who had alerted us in the first place stood staring at a striped skirt, which had belonged to Judith.

Charlotte said, "Go on, take it."

The girl did as she had been permitted, bundling the item under her arm.

I was horrified but tried to muster a tone of stern disapproval. "I presume you are taking it for Judith to be buried in?"

The girl looked up at Charlotte. Charlotte turned to me. "It belongs to her now."

"I won't hear a bit of it!" I boomed. "Put that back at once. Is it not enough that the poor wretch has lost her life? Not enough that her body is so destroyed? Now we must add to her indignity by sending her to the grave in a soiled and tatty nightgown, must we?"

Charlotte ushered the girl to the door. "Judith won't need it where she's going. This will get little Niamh a few pence down the Petticoat Lane rag fair. These are desperate times, Doctor. No reason she should have to go down the same line as Judith just to make sure she doesn't freeze to death."

Ashamed, I maintained my silence.

Charlotte touched my arm. "I know you have charity in you, Doctor. I know you understand."

Three.

"So you see, Father Haddon, though I may live to be one hundred, I feel I shall never sire a child of my own," I concluded my story. The priest had sat rapt for the duration and had taken not a single sip of his whisky.

"It is an... interesting tale, George. An interesting diversion to say the least." Father Haddon rose from his seat, more concerted now than he had been during the telling of the tale. "And let me guess," he said, pointing up at the bell jar containing the inverted lamb, "this would be the happy little fellow here." Haddon allowed himself a guilty chuckle.

"No Father," I said, leaving my chair, to walk across the study. I lit another gas jet to illuminate a corner of the room as yet shrouded in darkness. There in the yellow light, on a wooden stand of its own, was a tall bell jar, twenty inches tall, filled with a swampy liquid, through which was visible the creature which had eaten its own mother.

Father Haddon had followed me a few steps past the desk, drink in hand. He saw the frightful creature, curled into a ball, suspended in the fluid. Gangly limbs connected by a jagged spine and protruding ribs. There were no eyes in its head, just a translucent bluish white skin.

Haddon stumbled backwards, as though assaulted by the vision. He fell back against the desk, knocking my glass the floor. The high-pitched smash of glass caused a stirring within the jar, the limbs stretching and contracting as though the beast was waking up. "It lives! My God George, what have you done?"

Haddon squeezed his glass so tightly that it shattered in his palm, causing thick drops of blood to run freely down to the floor. His eyes were fixed on the creature, though, and we both observed the face pressed against the glass, two slits for nostrils flaring and closing like the gills of a fish.

"Surely not! George, surely it can't see me!"

"Of course not. She has no eyes," I assured him. "She can smell your blood."

"Even through the glass?" he gasped.

It was then that the translucent lips widened into a monstrous grin, needle teeth displayed in purple gums, then a second row, then a third row, each set pushing the last set forwards, the jaw peeling back into the neck and the forehead rippling and peeling backwards.

"Abomination!"

The teeth scraped and chattered against the glass and the creature thrashed its limbs around as though trying to topple its glass home.

"Come here," I said to the priest. He complied, numbed in terror. I drew a few drops of his blood into a pipette and took a small glass button out of the top of the jar, which opened a small aperture into which I dripped the blood.

Coppery clouds spun in the murk, and the creature tilted its head back, teeth gnashing, a long, thick, forked tongue flicking back and forth.

"Can we leave the room, George? I feel I have seen enough."

I smiled and turned the gas jet off, returning the jar to darkness. "Let me tend to that wound." I returned to my desk a picked a wadded bandage out of one of the drawers. Unfolding it on the table, I invited the priest over as I located my tweezers. "The boon of gaslight, father, enables me to find the glistening fragments of glass with relative ease. If you could bear to remain in the room a few minutes more."

"Of course. I mean, it's just a lot to process really, isn't it?"

I nodded. "It certainly was for me."

I proceeded to pick the glass out of Haddon's hand. He seemed to become more composed. "I'm sorry about the broken glasses, George. I hope Margaret will forgive me. I will of course make full recompense."

"Do not worry yourself with such trifles, Father. Accidents happen. Plus, you have fed my pet. That will sustain her for weeks."

"Weeks?"

"Yes."

"When you told me the story, you said that the woman died in 1856."

"Yes."

"Then you have kept this creature alive and in this state for three years?"

"Indeed," I confirmed. "By feeding her ever such a little, I ensure that she lives on, but grows hardly at all. I must admit, the thickness of the jar has increased over the years. She does seem to be getting stronger."

"She?" Father Haddon gasped.

"Yes, I have been able to determine the sex of the creature."

Father Haddon pondered this for a while. "You mentioned Henry Burton was a friend of yours."

"He was."

"Really?"

"Yes. We never really spoke again after that whole affair."

"Yet he was your employer, or business partner, was he not? It strikes me as strange that during this whole story you have mentioned nothing of the fact that they found the body of your former friend in the Thames last week."

I continued my work, managing to steady my hand against the shake that swelled up within it. "I was not aware. Though I am not surprised. He seemed unsteady a few years ago. The cut-throat nature of his shipping business… all of that."

Father Haddon nodded his agreement. "No, that wouldn't come as much surprise, perhaps. But perhaps what would, is the fact that his body appeared to have been bled dry."

I dropped the tweezers. I stared at the priest. He stared back intently. Then he smiled. A knowing smile.

The child whispered to me. She liked the taste of this one.

I darted to the corner of the room and kicked the stand, sprinting for the door as the glass shattered behind me. I slammed the door shut, fell against it with my head in my hands and listened to the terrible screams and piteous moans from within, wondering what Margaret would make of all this noise.

End of Part 1.

Part 2:

Dr Blessing's Rapture, Or, The Beast And The Bell-Jar

In which Dr Blessing is forced to face the end of his world.

One.

I have told you how my tale of sorrow began, but that was by no means the full story. The next part of my tale is a little more complicated than the first. More complicated because I had come to understand so much more about the child I had taken from Judith Cloonan's womb and a strange new branch of medical science had begun to develop in front of my eyes.

More complicated too, because that was when I became aware of other parties, who had developed an interest in my situation. Their stories I shall try to interweave with my own, from what information I have managed to gather over time. I shall convey this to you as best I can in the time allowed.

I swore an oath to do no harm, but that seems like a lifetime ago – like someone else's life entirely.

I had not dreamed all night, or had forgotten the dreams the instant I woke up - into real life, into the nightmare. I had slept on the chair in my study for God only knows how many hours. At my feet beneath my desk lay the crumpled handkerchief I had fastened over my mouth to protect me from the worst of the gas. It was evident that I had succumbed at some point and had staggered to my chair before collapsing.

I rose unsteadily to my feet and opened the heavy curtains to inspect the London sky on another black-grey morning. The damned soot! I sometimes wished that I could have risen on wings, above the muck, above the clouds, to escape this foul place. To escape this foul situation. To escape… No, not her. I could never leave *her*.

Turning on my heels I glanced around the room and I took in the scene. A dead priest lay on the floor, wrapped in a rug, dried blood spattered here and there on the wooden floor. Father Haddon. Poor man. A nice man, but his death had been entirely necessary.

I turned to my left to see thick chunks of broken glass and the stained wood where preserving fluids had soaked into the floor overnight. And there on the pedestal, in a larger bell-jar than before, safely surrounded by fresh fluid, there she was. My baby, the child I have since come to call Panacea.

Entirely satisfied by her feast, she slept in the fluid. Despite her feed being only hours before, she already showed signs that she was growing. Panacea's bones stretched her translucent, milky skin. The violence of her appetite seemed completely forgotten as she lay curled in her home, safe, secure and content.

I wondered how long I would be able to contain her.

Already powerful enough to overcome a man, her strength increasing with every full feed, I knew that my position as her guardian grew more tenuous every day.

I turned my attention back to the priest. He had to be disposed of, somehow. And then my mind poked through the remains of the previous night and found further questions, further anxieties. These relating, chiefly, to Father Haddon's revelation that he knew I had been with Henry Burton on the night he died, and that Burton's body was found to have been drained of blood when it was fished out of the river. I wondered, if Haddon thought that I was possibly the last person to see Burton alive, had he shared his theory with others? Had a suspicious third party given the information to him? Or had he simply seen us on the street and had taken a chance with his words?

Casting my mind back to that night, even if Haddon had merely seen us on the street, it was incriminating to some degree. The blazing row we had. Henry arguing, "You have become obsessed with that creature!"

I had protested, "She is fascinating, and does she not have the right to live?"

Burton had learned of my experiments with the mice and rats. "What is it you hope to prove? What benefit can this possibly hold for mankind? I told you this would be a secret only so long as others are not at risk – so long as this was not for your own reputation and fame. I see clearly your motive, George! Your hubris! You ought to be ashamed."

"Who could possibly be at risk? Who could be harmed?" I asked. "Is she not safely ensconced in my study at home?"

"Charlotte told me that something was wrong in the hospital the other day! You had something to hide – there was something in your private chambers that you did not want her to see," Henry had snorted. "I think you and I both know what that was."

"Preposterous," I had exclaimed.

"You have put my wife at risk! You swore to keep it locked away in your study! I insist that you destroy that… abomination this very night!"

That was when the idea had become so clear to me. I leaned on the wall, hands over my face. "You're right, you're right," I sobbed. "It's like she has some hold over me. I *must* break free. I must. You are right."

Henry had patted my back. "There, there, old boy. We shall put this right. The two of us. Let us go up to your study, tonight. *Now*. We shall dispose of that demon together."

"Your presence will make me twice the man, and equal to the task, Henry. For I alone am weak, too weak to free myself of this curse."

Poor Henry.

I remember Henry once telling me of a carnival he attended when he was a young man. At this carnival a band of gypsies had set up a sideshow. He told me that at the sideshow there was one attraction that had caught his attention. It was called the magic mirror, or the cursed mirror, or something. He said that those who entered the tent and gazed into the mirror were never the same again. Some said the mirror revealed the image of a demon, trapped in the glass. Some said the mirror showed them the future. Others said the mirror showed men the most horrible aspects of their nature and they emerged utterly insane, soon to commit horrific murders.

I told him that he was the insane one.

He told me it was quite true. He said that he looked into that glass and saw exactly what he was capable of, saw his future wealth and the deeds he would have to commit to achieve it. He said that it was on that very day that he ran away from home, away from the path his father had chosen for him and went to sea to engineer the destiny he had seen within the glass.

Of course, he returned. He returned with wealth that his well-to-do father had only dreamed of.

I learned to believe him, for I have looked into such a glass, and as I observed my reflection merge with the features of the sleeping creature within, I could see my true nature and could somehow see my destiny.

I snapped out of my daydream and back to the task at hand – how to get rid of the priest. I glanced at my pocket watch, it revealed the time to be a little before 6am. I realised then that the watch had stopped and that it was probably much later. I would be expected at the hospital, I would be missed.

A knock at the front door. The maid answered the door. I heard Niamh's voice, she had come looking for me. I heard Margaret's voice. Niamh had been invited into the house.

Footsteps on the stairs. I grabbed the key from the door, and slipped out onto the landing, deftly turning to lock the door behind me.

"Good morning, Doctor Blessing," Niamh called in her cheery tones.

"Good morning, Niamh," I said, returning her cheer. Though forced, I believe my cheer was convincing enough. The last thing I wanted was a day's work, what with the priest's drained corpse lying in the study. The study to which, of course, I held the only key.

How long before someone noticed the priest was missing? How long before they came looking for him? Presumably it was known that he was a frequent guest for dinner in my home. I began to wonder at my own gullibility, allowing the man so close merely because of his station.

"What brings you here, my dear?" I asked the girl.

Niamh's expression revealed she was focussed on my appearance more than my words. I did look a sight, too, with stains of preserving fluids on my crumpled white shirt, hair ruffled from distress. I am certain I still smelled of alcohol.

"There is a queue outside the hospital, Doctor. Doctor Collier was worried that you might be unwell."

I patted the child on the head. I had admired Niamh since meeting her three years before, when she was only eight. She was but a waif then, protected by ladies of the night – one of whom had borne the child who lived in my study. In some ways that night, when I had tended to the whore Judith Cloonan, I had gained two daughters.

For propriety I had paid for a room at a clean, tidy boarding house near the clinic, where Niamh could live in comfort hitherto she could only have imagined. Margaret had begged me to let Niamh live with us, a child for her to love and fuss over. But, I had argued against this. How could we select a waif off the street to raise as our own? With the assortment of barely trained servants we had taken on through Charlotte Burton's arrangements, we would, I argued, essentially create a situation where the servants would serve one who was in many ways, beneath even *them*.

I stayed firm to my point of view: the common street-urchin can only be introduced to so much comfort, before he or she becomes uncomfortable with the luxury itself. A degree of poverty is ingrained into their very being. I could not bear to cause social and psychological damage to this child.

This had caused a number of rows between us, and Margaret had laid down many ultimatums. Several times she had cried, "Either give me a child, or give me *that* child!" Often she pointed out that my interest, even my work, had always been to encourage social mobility. She argued that my involvement in Burton's hospital was an attempt to elevate the living standard of the sick and injured poor. She asked me with suspicion, why it was that I strove to improve the situation of the poor except when it involved directly making her happy.

She was, of course, quite right to be suspicious. What I referred to as "my point of view" was, in truth, nothing of the sort. I simply had to keep Niamh away from the baby in the bell-jar. Panacea had some sort of hold over my mind. Sometimes I felt that I was some sort of automaton and it was Panacea who steered me. Were I to be right, I could not expose Niamh to that; it was bad enough that Margaret and the maid were in the vortex with me. But I had to continue. What gifts I could bring to mankind from this remarkable creature…

In any event, the laudanum had controlled Margaret's fits of wilful temper quite well; it was her other fits which had become a concern to me. Over the course of the three years since I tended to Judith Cloonan, Margaret had taken to ever more frequent bouts of apoplexy. Again, a little laudanum seemed to do the trick, but it seemed a curious condition, with no obvious cause. She had not suffered a head trauma. She had no history of such violently altered states of consciousness. It puzzled me.

I returned my attention to Niamh. "Whatever

would I do without you, Niamh? I am in good health, however, and I simply became overly involved in some experiments of great medical import." I smiled at Margaret, who I could see at the bottom of the stairs.

Margaret joked, "Doctor Blessing became overly involved in a bottle of brandy with his friends, he should say!"

"Margaret! Niamh knows that I am a paragon of restraint and respectability. The excesses that tempt other men make no impression on me," I returned. I turned back to Niamh and asked, "Be a dear and bring your old doctor a dish of water, would you?"

Niamh rushed away with all enthusiasm as I climbed the stairs to the master bedroom where I oriented myself to time once more – it was almost half past ten. After carrying out a shortened toilet routine, I made my way to the dining room, where Margaret was smearing jam onto some warm, buttered bread for Niamh.

I was about to make a jovial reprimand for indulging her, but a stern look from Margaret deterred me. I could see that she really adored the girl, at least as much as I did myself.

Besides wishing I could change Niamh's situation, I was wishing many other things that morning. Wishes of flying and escaping jarred against wishes of permanence and family. Wishes of making a lovely family home smashed against more urgent wishes of finding a way to get rid of that dead body.

After a short breakfast, a hansom cab carried Niamh and I to Oxford Street, which was choked with cabs and carriages of all descriptions. We disembarked there, turned off Oxford Street and walked the length of Poland Street, to the hospital. I saw patient after patient until well after noon. Diseased whore. Septic knife wound. Diseased whore. Falling sickness. Miscarriage. Severed toe (nothing I could do but stitch and clean the wound). Sailor with syphilis. Breast cancer diagnosis.

Rheumatism. Diseased whore.

I worked, but felt like a ghost. Words came out of my mouth, but I felt like I was listening in on someone else's conversation.

I sent Niamh to fetch us each a pie from a nearby baker's shop and decided to break for an hour.

This seems like a good opportunity to tell you about the hospital itself. The death of Judith Cloonan made Charlotte Burton and I consider how better we could empower the poor. The result was that Henry Burton bought up some property on Poland Street and the Henry Burton Foundation Hospital for the Gratuitous Treatment of Accident and Disease was born.

The hospital was modest, with beds for fifty patients. Ten of these beds were for private, paying patients. The first building purchased by Henry had swiftly been adapted for our use and I had been able to treat a great many outpatients, but only ten inpatients at a time. Burton's own pocket had been enough to create the original hospital, to which all of his workers were subscribed automatically. He then began to extol the benefits of a hospital plan with other businesses in trade with him. "Fewer days missed owing to sickness," he had told them. "Less need to replace injured men," he promised.

Any businessman with an ounce of sense tried his best to emulate Henry Burton in any way that he could. And so it was not very long at all that dock workers, warehousemen, rail workers, builders, factory workers and anyone else you care to think of, began to pay one penny a week for a right to treatment at the hospital.

All the while, Henry had his men working on the neighbouring buildings in the terrace, which at the last he connected to the original building.

From then, the inpatient beds were moved out of my original building which thenceforth served only as an outpatient clinic, and where I retained my office and a laboratory at basement level. I served as General Physician In Charge – to govern the whole hospital. Most other hospitals were run by a board of governors, who had the power to refer or decline patients as they saw fit. Generally, those hospitals would refuse to treat terminally ill patients, whereas I would occasionally take them in for treatment.

The dying were of great interest to me as I began to develop my interest in pharmaceutical research, as well as perfecting my rudimentary surgical skills.

It would amaze you, or perhaps it would not, what a dying person will allow you to do to his or her body in the hope of defying death. It was the ideal setting for experimentation, grasping into the darkness to find cures where no other doctor had dared look before.

Also on my staff were: half a dozen nurses – all hard, impatient women; a physician, Dr Collier; a surgeon, Mr Boorman; and two training doctors, Dr King and Dr Flynn.

The success of the Henry Burton Foundation Hospital had generated much interest, and importantly, many willing patrons, who wished to help Henry with his next project. So it was that ground had been broken on a new hospital in Marylebone, built to a pavilion design, with various wings for different classes of condition. I had specified that two particular wings should be included: one to specialise in gynaecology; the other to investigate birth defects.

Charlotte Burton had thought this a marvellous idea, and had convinced Henry to do as I wished. Henry had seemed reluctant. I always suspected that he had fathomed my true intentions: to increase my likelihood of finding another creature like the one in the bell-jar. I had sugared the prospect for Charlotte, by planting the idea that women might be educated to the level of doctor in such a facility. She had run with this – I knew that she would not take no for an answer and that Henry would have been harangued into submission had he shown any hesitation.

So it was, then, that Henry had managed to create a successful hospital, and had laid the foundation (both metaphorically and actually) for a much greater establishment in what was now, following his untimely demise, to be known as the Henry Burton Memorial Hospital. Who knew how many people would ultimately owe their lives to Henry Burton's generosity?

The Bilbao Devil, it seemed, had become an angel.

Niamh returned with the pies, but an expression of worry was firmly fixed on her face when she entered my office.

"What is it, child?"

"A man is asking for you outside, Doctor. I do not know his face, but he has come with Mrs Burton's coach and driver."

I went outside to meet the man. He was a burly brute dressed in a brown woollen suit, with a brown derby perched on top of his large, square head. His manner was brusque and by the way he wore his too small hat at the front of his head (making him peer down his nose, with jaw slightly jutting and raised) I could tell he was either a police detective, or had been a constable at some time.

The brute handed over a black outlined envelope, and said nothing.

I opened the envelope and found the black-rimmed letter within. It was from Mrs Burton, surely enough. She requested my presence immediately.

"Niamh, fetch Dr Collier and ask him to man my station. Apologise to our patients for the delay and inform them that an emergency has presented itself."

Niamh moved to do as I asked as I climbed into the coach. The brute got in beside me, and said nothing on the twenty-minute ride to the Burton home.

Mrs Burton - Charlotte - received me in the parlour of her luxurious home. Henry had bought the small Kensington mansion two years ago. It seemed ostentatious at the time, without children to fill it and even more so now, without Henry.

"You may leave us, Charles," Charlotte said, smiling at her hired thug.

When Charles had left the room, I took my time to look around, noticing that, although Charlotte wore the black crape and mourning cap that befit her loss, the curtains were open, letting in light from the expansive gardens to the rear of the property.

"I must say, Charlotte, even in mourning you look… well."

Charlotte eyed me with a curious look. I immediately fumbled with my derby. I ceased the fidgeting almost immediately – had she noticed it? Did she think I was nervous about something? My God! Could she know that I was responsible?

No, of course not.

How could she?

I steadied my hands. Breathed. And steeled myself, prepared to issue forth lie after lie to this woman, or to Jesus Christ himself, should it be necessary.

"I will assume your remark was meant as a compliment, George."

"You assume correctly, Charlotte. I bear nothing but compliments for your person."

"And yet it took a letter edged in black to bring you here."

"Your grief, Charlotte. I was showing you respect by allowing you time to mourn, without the need for worry about the hospital. I knew that the last thing you would want would be the suffering of those wretches out there." I cleared my throat and chanced, "Or did I assume incorrectly?"

"Not incorrectly, no," she responded. "But you did make an assumption. Surely our acquaintance is strong enough for a more direct approach?"

I knelt before her chaise-long, desperate to repair any damage I had caused to my mask of innocence. "Charlotte, I do believe I am not representing myself very well. And let me tell you, it is simply because of my own personal grief. At being here, seeing you, here at home, without him. This feels like half the home it once was."

"Then I shall have to become accustomed to that division of homeliness."

My eyes flashed at the sheer coldness of the woman. This woman, who had at one time held my respect – such respect… a level I only reserve for certain men of achievement, had become a cold hard thing in her grief. I felt as though I was stood in front of a different woman entirely.

"Charlotte, is there anything I might prescribe you for your grief?"

Charlotte shook her head, and waved a dismissive hand to me. "I require only one thing from you, George."

"Yes, Charlotte?"

"The truth."

I gulped and blanched. The urge to turn the derby around in my hand was overwhelming. I fought the sensation back.

"The truth, dear Charlotte?"

The dam broke, Charlotte collapsed into a flood of tears. She reached forwards and placed her trembling hands around my neck, clasping them behind my head, drawing me close.

Most uncomfortable with this sudden improper proximity, I tried to stand and eased her hands away.

"My dear, Charlotte. My dear, dear Charlotte. Tell me what I must do."

"They say he leapt from the bridge, George, but I do not believe it for a minute. They say he must have taken his own life."

I seized the chance. "Well... he was under a lot of pressure..."

"Pressure? The business was thriving."

"The debt of the house, perhaps?" I glanced at the walls and ceiling.

"Bought outright. With cash. He could have bought three of these houses without stopping for breath."

"Quite." My mind cast about for anything I might use.

"I know you were not on the best of terms before the end, George. But did he ever say anything? Did he give any sign at all that he was suffering?"

I closed my eyes for a long moment. I wanted to conceal my search for a lie and make it appear as though I was plucking up the courage to tell the truth.

"There was one occasion, only a few weeks ago, around the time of his disappearance, actually, when I discovered him drunk. In his drunken state he was pleased to see me... and he and I temporarily set aside our differences. He confided that for all the money, for all his success, for all the ships and tea and silver and opium in the world, his only desire was to have the ability to sire a child. He said that without an heir, he felt like an incomplete man, less than a man."

Charlotte's head rocked back on her neck. She stared at me with eyes full of disbelief. "He said that? Truly?"

"He did. He was very bitter, and drunk enough that he wished to restore our friendship, but in truth we never did."

Charlotte sat in silence for a few moments. "George, I believe I will have the rest of the day to myself. This has all taken a terrible toll on me."

"I apologise for not attending Henry's funeral, Charlotte. Given the terms he and I were on by the end, I felt he would have wanted it that way."

"I completely understand, George. I received a

card from Margaret. It was most welcome."

I nodded and stepped back towards the door. "Then I shall be sure to convey that to her. We shall pay you a visit quite soon. Until then, should you need anything..." I was about to tell her to send her messenger, but I stopped myself. I thought: if that messenger was this Charles character, I would rather be of no use.

As I moved to the door, Charlotte asked, "What was it you and Henry quarrelled about, George? What was it that made you drift apart for these last two years?"

I stopped at the door, my fingers clenched around the doorknob. What could I tell her that would perhaps deter her asking again in the future? She could never know the truth - that Burton had grown scared of the creature I harboured. That he had feared for mankind should the creature escape.

"We argued over you, Charlotte. As you and I worked on the hospital together, Henry became terribly suspicious of my motives. He believed that I loved you and that I intended to leave Margaret to make you mine."

Charlotte raised her eyebrows at this. "Really? That is most unlike Henry. I always thought it had something to do with the night Judith Cloonan died."

My departure from the house was the very meaning of alacrity.

Two.

Charlotte turned as Charles entered the parlour once more. "He has gone, madam," he said, waiting by the door.

"I want you to follow him, Charles. Keep an eye on his movements, especially in the evenings."

Charles nodded. "Am I to assume your suspicions now match my own?"

Charlotte nodded almost imperceptibly. "George Blessing has changed, Charles. He was a good, caring, guileless man. Now he has made a liar of himself."

"At the very least, madam." Charles wanted to add murderer and madman to his account, but saved his remarks out of respect for the lady.

Charlotte's hands smoothed her dress over her midriff.

"Your state suits you, madam," Charles commented. "I'm sure Mr Burton would have agreed."

Charlotte smiled weakly at him. "Henry was ever so pleased when I told him. He always wondered what people thought of him, having no children for so long. He worried about it, George was right in that. So when I told him I was with child, he was ecstatic. There were occasions when I would catch him in melancholy moods. Those moods were mainly about the loss of his friendship with George, actually. And I used to tell him off. Used to tell him to get in the coach and visit silly George and all of us could have dinner together like we used to."

Charles straightened up at the door. "Something happened that night, madam. I am sure that Henry was not aware of the greater part of it. That doctor, I am certain he stole something away. I think it was a part of that whore girl."

Three.

Mary Brigham stepped off the train in King's Cross and was immediately thrust into the frantic scramble for survival that was life in the capital. A porter brought her luggage from the coach and, being an attractive, twenty-one year old lady, fresh-faced from years of Northumberland coastal air, she found no trouble in attracting a strapping young man on the platform, to haul her luggage through the masses and out into London proper.

Her assistant managed to hail a hansom cab and Mary thanked him as he heaved her travel chest and two smaller bags into the cab beside her. She slipped the man a shilling, which he accepted gratefully, with a doff of his tatty cap. The driver cracked his whip and the horses surged off along the street, heading for Tyburnia, where her mission would truly begin.

Mary looked over her containers of possessions and was amused at the thought that she had never travelled so laden before. The realisation that in these three items of luggage were all of her worldly possessions made her all at once feel both frugal, and frivolous. Who on earth travelled carrying all that they possessed? And on the other hand: who on earth possessed so little?

Looking out from the cab at the Londoners going about their daily business, she saw the well-heeled and the down-trodden. She wondered if those scruffy, ragged men huddled around small fires in the alleys and lanes owned more than she.

Yes, she thought, I am fortunate. For it had been her choice to choose the life De Omori offered. To own little, to attach oneself to little, was a comfort in itself. Who would wish to die at the hands of some blood-drinking monster, knowing that in doing so, they would destroy the lives and hearts of a family? Better to stay alone. Better to move quickly and freely. Today in London, last month in Paris, and after this business in London, who could say where she would be?

She thought about the Paris mission. She had still been a novice then, still assigned to shadow an experienced operative. Together they had tracked down a governess who, having succumbed to the way of the vampire, had eaten her way through six wealthy families in various towns and cities. She and Dr McEwan had caught the evil governess halfway through the seventh family.

"We can not save everyone," her instructor had told her, as she had sat there in the parlour that looked like a charnel house.

McEwan had led her from that place, returned her to the hotel. They bathed and changed clothes and met each other again in the lobby. They dined together; as they had done every night on every mission they had seen together since her academic training had ended.

They had walked the winding streets of Montmartre, and climbed to the summit of the *butte Montmartre*, where they watched the lights of the city. The beauty jarred against the horrors she had seen.

"Smile for me, my Mary," McEwan had said, touching her cheek. "My Black Mary."

Mary had shied away from him. "I wish you would refrain from calling me that, Owen."

"But I have always called you that," McEwan had said, frowning.

"And now so does everyone else."

He had christened her that on their first mission together, in Edinburgh, when during a seek and destroy mission in the slums, she had become separated from her tutor. She had found herself surrounded by blood-crazed vampires, a family of them. Mary had been trained well, and killed well. When she slaughtered the first two beasts with her blades, the remaining four had retreated into their nest. Mary burned that building to the ground without hesitation, to flush them out. It worked, and her blades twirled amid the smoke and flames and the chaos and the fleeing innocents.

When McEwan followed the flames to the source, he found Mary, caked in blood and soot. The dirt washed off. The name did not.

Their kiss in Montmartre had been brief. As far as Mary was concerned, regrettably so.

As the cab trundled along its way through the dense London traffic, her hands fell to one of the bags. She opened it and took out the letter. She had received it at De Omori's safe house in Newcastle. The words were practically burned into her brain, but she liked to see his handwriting. It made him seem closer.

My Dearest, Blackest Mary,

When we parted company in Paris, I received orders to return to Great Britain, to Northumberland, to The Island. It seems I am to become part of the faculty of that great academy.

For all the action of the field brings with it fresh challenges and excitement, I must admit to growing weary of the hunt at times. I have run out of new ways of destroying the damned and so simply repeat myself, no closer to the annihilation of that race of beings than I was the day I almost succumbed to the fang myself.

Snatched from the precipice of damnation, it seems there was something of the damned left abrading my soul. Not wishing to lose your confidence I hasten now to add that I am NOT a vampire, nor anything like it. I cannot decide if that dark day enhanced or destroyed my humanity, but one thing is certain, I have had the appearance of a twenty-five year old for a great, great many years.

So then it seems fitting that my decline in service coincides with your ascent into the great ranks of De Omori and its operatives. You see, dear Mary, I knew when that letter arrived, it signified not only my retraction from active duties, but also the termination of my role as your mentor. I have, of course mentored many other novices, but none with as much promise as you.

I knew then, that upon my return to Great Britain, your first mission would not be far away.

First of all, I wish you luck.

Second of all, I apologise unreservedly for my lack of propriety in Paris. Every ounce of my being strained against all that I had been trained to do, and trained not to do. Let us both agree that our intimacy, however brief, however forbidden, was simply a matter of professional concern masquerading as personal affection. My pride for you as my ward and my admiration for you as my colleague swelled within my chest until it burst forth and the desire to kiss you was overwhelming.

It was a terrible thing for me to do, distracting you with personal feelings, affections and desires. I would not forgive myself if I in any way caused your attention to waver from our glorious mission.

I grew soft with my age, Mary.

You remain young, and vital, and strong. You remain Black Mary.

And until I see you again, I remain

Your loyal friend

And proud mentor

Dr Owen McEwan

Mary slipped the correspondence back into her bag. In telling her how he ought not to feel, McEwan had told her exactly how he *did* feel, and how his feelings mirrored her own. Since receiving that letter, she had been locked in turmoil. She had felt like throwing all of her years of training away. She wanted to get on a boat and return to that island and tell that Dr McEwan exactly what she wanted from him.

How improper. But then, she wondered, had the hardness instilled in her by her training, trained her innermost secret self to be as brash as any soldier? She dressed in fine things and made a handsome salary, but she was no gentle lady. She was schooled in such proprieties as would enable effective infiltration into the inner circles of the upper crust, but she could handle beer and gin as well as any common navvy, that she might infiltrate the public houses, brothels and alleys in search of her prey.

When she was summoned for the mission, Mary had been grateful for it. Some action to take her mind off things. A De Omori informant, a priest named Father Haddon, had reported that a well-known shipping magnate named Henry Burton had been fished out of the Thames drained entirely of blood. That smacked of the very essence of *vampire*, of course, and arrangements had been made for Mary to take a train to London, and for her to meet with the priest shortly after arrival.

By reputation, Father Haddon was known to be a heavy drinker and fond of concealing that he was a priest – Mary could imagine what sinful activities he pursued. His information was generally considered to be good, despite his fondness for gin. He had made clear in his report that he and the deceased shared a mutual acquaintance in a doctor. Dr George Blessing was his name, and the priest reported that he had eaten at the doctor's home on many occasions, and that at some point the doctor and the shipping magnate had come to a disagreement.

Mary remembered a reference case from the library on The Island about a liveryman who was enslaved by a vampire and who, under the monster's spell, did kill and dismember over thirty Christians before he was stopped. The dismembered bodies had been kept in water troughs and the vampire had enjoyed slaking his thirst from these remains.

She wondered if some similar fate had not befallen Henry Burton, drained by a familiar, rather than by a vampire. Vampires themselves tended to be less discrete about the disposal of bodies. Someone had tried to conceal Burton's death – the behaviour of a familiar who had to maintain the pretence of a normal life, as a husband, a father, a liveryman, or even a doctor.

"The Seraphim, m'lady," the driver called as the cab drew to a halt outside the grand columned edifice of the Seraphim Hotel.

Mary paid him and he quickly assisted her with her possessions. Before very long at all, Mary was settled in her room, which was richly decorated with heavy burgundy curtains and carpeted with a huge rug, which stretched almost from wall to wall. Mary sat at the edge of the bed and stroked the clean, crisp bedding.

She resisted the urge to read the letter again.

Church bells penetrated the noise from the street; the sound told her it was three O' clock in the afternoon. Her meeting with the priest was not until seven in the evening.

She closed the curtains and unfastened her dress. She removed her corset, but there was little change in her figure. Her physique was impeccable. She observed her reflection in the mirror at the washstand and enjoyed the way her porcelain skin looked against her white undergarments.

She lay back on the bed an allowed her fingertips to run from her cheeks down over her small breasts, down her abdomen, to the bare skin at the tops of her thighs. When the pleasure of the tickling sensation subsided, she closed her eyes, emptied her mind and rolled her eyes upwards.

Breathing deeply, Mary found herself in a state of deep relaxation. Lying perfectly still, her blood pumped through her muscles, replenishing them, cleansing her of fatigue.

In this state of meditation, her unconscious mind took over and a hundred encounters were fought and won, a thousand blocks and strikes, feints and counters were performed. The fighting patterns were not only ingrained into her mind but into her muscles, which were at complete rest, soothed, calm, waiting in readiness as always, to do battle.

Four.

I returned to my home by hansom cab, entirely unable to stand the din of an omnibus in my present state of mind, which was to say, disturbed.

Upon entering the house, I was greeted by the maid of all work, a pleasant girl – vouched for by Charlotte of course. What was her name? Lily or Annie, or something like that. Whatever she was called, she immediately told me that she had prayed all night that I would find a cure for Mrs Blessing soon.

"Prayed, my dear girl?" I asked her.

"Oh, I heard you with her in your study. She must have had another of her turns. It sounded terrible!" Lily or Annie explained.

I almost jumped with fright when I understood it was the commotion of Father Haddon's demise she had heard. "Do not worry yourself at all. I strive for that cure with my every waking moment, now if you will excuse me…"

"Begging your pardon, Doctor," the maid added, her fingers reaching out for my coat sleeve in barely restrained desperation. "If you could spare the time, could I impose upon you for some advice?"

"Advice?"

"I have been suffering terrible headaches. And bleeds. My nose bleeds something chronic in the mornings. Some mornings I find I can barely lift my head and I am terrified that I will be dismissed-"

I interrupted the maid with a raised finger. "Of course, dear. I shall find some time to look you over, but first I should look in on Margaret."

"Of course, Doctor. Please pardon my impertinence. My grumbles are nothing compared to the sufferings of dear Mrs Blessing."

"Quite so. And you and I shall both do well to remember that fact, and I shall prioritise my attentions accordingly," I said, with such pomposity and guarded threat that I knew this poor maid would die before asking me for help again. I strode through to the parlour and there, lounged across the sofa, beautiful and pale, was Margaret. The empty glass vial on the table by her side was telling of*her* state of mind, which was, to say the very least, troubled.

"My dear," I exclaimed, hands raised before me. I reached down and kissed her lips with the lightest touch. Margaret was talking and all I could think was I need to get upstairs and damn your slurred speech, Margaret, damn your intoxication. I needed a distraction for her so that she would let me go. "You look positively exhausted, Margaret! Have you eaten?"

"You look dead tired yourself, George," she moaned. "Are you? Are you dead tired?"

"Am I dead, did you say? What sort of a question is that?" I cried.

"I asked if you were tired."

"I should say you've had quite enough of what was in that bottle!" I grabbed the empty vial and inspected it. A small paper label indicated the strength of the tincture was 20 per cent opium. I wondered at this; I was sure I had only been issuing Margaret with a 10 per cent tincture. My mind began to fog over; I fought to retain control.

"You know what was in that bottle, you gave it to me," she replied.

"Am I dead? Well, I never! I think I shall retire to my study! Lovely welcome, that was!" I huffed and stepped away to the parlour door with a spring in my step – my God, I practically danced with eagerness to get to my study. That body! The blood! A flourish of both excitement and terror struck me at the thought of hanging for the death of a priest. My God! Excitement? At the thought of swinging from a rope! I had to wonder: had I become some sort of damned deviant?

"What did you call me?" Margaret groaned, running her fingers over her face. "A deevy-what?"

"Deviant, Margaret. But not you! No, I did not say it about you." I grinned and rolled my eyes to the left as though I expected to see someone else there, another Dr George Blessing who was looser-tongued than I. "I did not mean you, my love. You are certainly no deviant... simply a slave to opiates."

"I did not ask if you were dead, earlier," she droned. "Or did not mean it, if that is what I said..."

I started to scour the dark corners of my mind. I thought of maniacs I had sent to the asylum at Oakbridge. Men whose personalities had split into different characters, with different motivations. Had some part of me turned this whole cursed affair into a protracted, elaborate suicide plot? I became conscious of my words, the perspiration, the clumsiness and fidgeting at Charlotte's house. Did some warped aspect of my being want to get caught? Was that my way to bring an end to this? Self-destruction? I steeled myself against such thoughts, filling my cheeks with air. Of course not!

"Of course not, dear! I must have misheard you is all. I shall be in my study, all the same." I hurried from the room and up the stairs, tripping over the third step, righting myself and continuing at pace.

Once safely ensconced in my study, I slammed the doors behind me and twisted the key in the lock. As a doctor, one should never be relieved at the sight of a dead body. I was, though. Thank God he was still there. Knowing I had the only key to the study was not enough anymore. I learned that there is no comfort to any man hiding a corpse, until it is well and truly beyond discovery. How I would manage that, I had no idea.

Panacea was in the corner, the cloth draped over her glass home. I stepped quietly to her side and peeled away the material, not wanting to shock her with the light. Having no eyes it was not the shock of the brightness that concerned me, but in my time with the child, I had found her to be most lethargic, almost sickly, in daylight.

"There, my pretty, there," I said to her.

She was aware of my affectionate tone, I am sure of it. She seemed to turn her head in the fluids in the manner of a timid virgin.

"I see you learn your feminine wiles early, my child!" I said to her, unable to suppress my smile. "You have your silly old Doctor wrapped around your finger, do you not?"

I pressed my fingers against the glass. She pressed the translucent skin of her bony cheek against her side of the glass.

I could almost hear her purring. How like a woman! To have me wrapped around her finger so.

She looked taller, the effects of last night's feast even more apparent than they had been in the morning. A swell of sadness burst in my chest. My baby was growing up. How many more bell-jars would hold her?

Her teeth scraped the glass and I realised that my hand had fallen away to my side, away from her. I smiled, and pressed my face to the glass, adoring her.

She watched me as I stepped over the priest and moved to the side table. I poured myself a large measure of whisky, moved over to my desk and slumped into the chair. I gazed over at her. One had to wonder how she saw the world. With no apparent eyes I wondered how she had any spatial awareness at all. And when she detected me, did she recognise me as a man, or did she determine only the blood coursing through my veins and arteries?

I suppose one does not look at a cow and see a dinner. More to the point, one does not look at one's own father and imagine him as any sort of meal.

I pondered the dead man on the floor. What could I do with him? Curiosity struck me. I got off my chair and crouched over Haddon, unfurling the rug to observe him fully. For the first time, the terror imprinted on the man's face registered with me. There was no way he had anticipated his death, no way that he could have recognised the drinks we had together were to be his last. He had fought in the gloom against a foe he did not understand. The struggle had been brief - the outcome, inevitable.

I reached into his jacket and searched his inner breast pockets. I found a small rosary, some slips related to the priest's gambling, and a scrap of paper. On the scrap of paper was written:

O' Grady's Coffee House, Bayswater Rd
Tuesday, 7 O' clock pm

With whom had the priest planned to meet? And to what end? I decided that perhaps a walk in the early evening air was in order after all.

A plan was forming. Perhaps answers would come if I could find out what this slip of paper meant. That was assuming that the slip referred to a current appointment, and not one in the past, or future. Had it been a future appointment, surely he would have noted a specific date. It was worth a chance. The lack of detail implied urgency, immediacy.

It was then that I noticed an envelope by the study door. It had obviously been slipped under there when I had been at work, and I had missed it when I entered. When I inspected the envelope, I found it addressed simply to *George*. The handwriting was Margaret's. At my desk, I slit the envelope with my silver opener and inspected the document within.

Margaret had obtained, with the assistance of Francis Flanders, adoption papers for Niamh. All that was required was my signature. It was then that my brain became foggy again, and before I knew anything at all, the document was shut away in my desk drawer.

I replaced the cover over the child and left the study, careful to lock up tight. In my pocket I carried a small vial of laudanum. The solution was 20 per cent opium. Before leaving, I looked into the parlour to see Margaret in a deep sleep. I placed the full vial on the table by her side, reached down to kiss her and took my leave.

Five.

Charles observed the scene from the bustling street. Standing in the murky light of the summer evening, he was able to see his mark in the coffee house gaslight with ease. He watched Blessing get up, leaving his beautiful companion sitting.

He tucked his hands into his pockets and squinted as the structure of the building shielded Blessing from view. Blessing was only gone for a brief moment, for suddenly the coffee house door burst open and the doctor was there, heading straight for him at pace.

Charles turned away and lowered his eyes, fumbling for some change to hand to a pauper. He rolled his eyes left and saw Blessing break into a run. This was of great interest to him. He looked to the right and could see the woman still sat there, comfortable, clearly expecting Blessing to return.

But why such a hasty exit? Why the break in composure? Charles had never even heard of, let alone seen, a doctor running anywhere or for anybody. But here was his dilemma: should he follow Blessing, or should he take an interest in the beautiful young woman Blessing had abandoned? He decided to stay and observe the woman. She had, after all, provoked such a reaction from the doctor.

Who was she? A lover? A relative? There had been the briefest of physical contacts between them during the time he had observed them, thus lover seemed unlikely. A relative, a sister perhaps, would surely show, or be shown, more affection. So who the hell was this young woman?

Six.

Primed for her mission, Mary watched from the corner of O' Grady's Coffee House, hoping to see the holy man enter. What information did this man have? How was it that he, a man of religion had come to serve De Omori, and furthermore, to align himself with a businessman like Burton, who had, it was rumoured, a dubious history.

Mary detested waiting, she preferred direct action. Waiting afforded her too much time to ponder. She tried to fit her questions and wonders into compartments in her mind, tried to subdue her curiosity. If I can not control my focus, then what use am I as an agent of De Omori?

Then it occurred to her. An agent of De Omori. A *very new* agent of De Omori. This was the excitement. The thrill of the hunt.

Around her, she could see the eyes of the men, leering, imagining her naked, sprawled out before them. She could hear their words, although they tried to hush them. Do normal women hear this? Do they see this? She could only wonder, as it was impossible for her to block it out. She had to hear and see these things, as they might save her life one day. The training was both her boon and her blight.

It was that training that set her apart from normal women – freed her from their daily routines and tribulations, allowed her adventure and excitement. But it also meant that the entire world was seen through the filter of a threat that most people could not acknowledge even existed.

She saw a man sat at a table, conversing freely with a friend, fumbling for money and counting it on the table. There were strangers all around him. That man considered himself free from a world where crime existed, let alone blood-drinking creatures of nightmare.

So while her training allowed her to operate in that world of nightmare, where others would instantly perish, she was deprived the comforts afforded a normal woman. The luxuries of hearth and home. Images of home immediately snapped into her mind's eye and she wrestled to suppress them, to return to the mission.

And then a newspaper twitched, as it had done so several times, and the man behind the paper checked his watch again. He was waiting for someone. He was waiting for her.

Seven.

Before very long at all I was standing in O' Grady's Coffee House, I ordered a cup of Burton's Imported Special Tea, paying tuppence for it, which included use of a much-thumbed copy of the *London Illustrated Times*, and took a seat. The paper was perfect cover as I sat with my back to the corner of an alcove. With all stealth, I commenced to look about the coffee house, in the hope that the person Haddon had arranged to meet, would reveal himself.

I glanced at my pocket watch to see the time was five before seven. I was early. I read the news from Paris. More missing persons attributed to the dastardly work of a murderous governess chased to her death by British investigators. I read on until ten minutes had passed and looked around again.

A great many patrons filled the coffee house, and so I reasoned that I should be on guard for anyone who seemed impatient, waiting for a man who would never turn up. I glanced at my watch.

It was then, all on a sudden, that a lady approached me at my table. "Father Haddon, I presume," she said, offering a kidskin glove.

I took the young woman's hand as I rose to my feet. She thought I was the priest! Could I deceive her?

"Yes," I replied, "and you would be?"

"Did they neglect to give you my name?"

I cleared my throat, and perhaps in doing so, cleared the last shred of decency and honesty in my body. "I am afraid they did. I was given simply a note with the where and when, but not the *who*. I must admit to expecting a man."

We took our seats and the lady set her drink on the table. I thought it highly improper that she carried a drink around the coffee shop in such a fine dress – all to approach a man. She introduced herself as Mary

Brigham.

"I must attest," she said, almost to allay my fears that she would approach just any man, "to being somewhat surprised myself. I was expecting to see a white collar. It was your furtive glances at the pocket watch that gave you away. You looked like a man due to meet someone."

Damn! I thought. She beat me at my own game. Of course, the thought was preposterous – spying was not my game. But perhaps, I deduced, it was *hers*.

"I am told that you have some information for me," she said, leaning forward slightly.

I did not react. At least, I think I did not react. I raised my cup to my lips. This seemed to make her impatient and she said, "I am told you have information about the death of the shipping magnate Henry Burton."

I reacted. My tea spurted from my lips into the cup. I placed the cup on the table. Mary raised her cup and drank. I suspect it was a move designed to suppress her amusement at my clumsiness.

I stuttered and fumbled for a handkerchief with which to wipe my lips.

Mary eyed me with a queer look. Her eyes sharpened as she reached for a handkerchief of her own. She handed the frilly square of material to me. I noticed the elaborate, crimson embroidery, which seemed to show the initials D.O.

"I thought you said your name was Mary," I said.

"I find it alarming that you would fail to recognise the emblem of your paymasters, Father Haddon," Mary said, her jaw firm, not a hint of amusement on her face.

"I… no, of course. I was not thinking. You must realise, Miss Brigham-"

"Mary."

"Indeed, *Mary*. You must realise that I am not accustomed to the company of beautiful young women."

Mary smiled, her eyes softening. "You are but a young man yourself, Father. Surely you are not so blinded with religious fervour, that beauty is wasted on you? One would assume that London is blessed with its share of beautiful women."

I flushed. She was clearly accustomed to such exchanges. I instantly regretted my course of action. Instantly wanted to leave. Instantly wanted to die.

"As a priest, I find that the beauty of all God's works blinding."

"But not the women," Mary stated this, it was not posed as a question.

"The beauty of *all* creatures."

"You see women as creatures?"

"I mean simply, my dear Mary, that we are all of us beasts on some level."

Mary leaned closer. I cleared my throat again. I wanted to mop at my brow with the handkerchief. By God she was beautiful.

"Surely our civilisation, our morality, our rationalisation separates us from the beasts?" she reasoned. "I mean, it would be unseemly to think that we could each of us simply follow any primal urge."

"Indeed. You quite have the better of me, Mary. I am a simple holy man and you pose some provocative ideas which render me quite incapable of further discourse."

"Then let us waste no more time. De Omori has sent me to follow up your claim that Henry Burton was killed in a particularly strange manner."

My eyes must have flashed and betrayed me then, I am sure of it. "Of course. Well, it is said that Mr Burton had no blood in his body. Which is impossible, of course."

Mary's eyes narrowed. "You know it to be possible, Father. That being, chiefly, our area of expertise."

"Yes, well, I simply mean... by conventional

means."

"It is conventional for the thousands of blood-fiends that nest in The Island."

"There are thousands of them?" I gasped.

"Of course there are."

"Where is this island?"

"You know the regulations, Father Haddon," Mary chided.

"I simply ask because… presumably with such unholy creatures around, one would never be beyond the need of a priest," I added, pleasantly.

Mary was clearly reaching the end of her patience and I was clearly seconds away from being discovered as a fraud. I knew I had to bring this to a close when she said, "The word of God would serve no purpose there. Provided a person can wield a sword and a revolver, then The Island has use for all men, thugs, priests… doctors."

That damned priest! Clearly some sort of informant to this organisation De Omori, he had not only connected me to Henry's death, but had given some of this information away already. He had known something all along. Had he been in Charlie's Gin Palace that fateful night when I was called away to deal with Judith? It was certainly the sort of establishment he had enjoyed. He might have pieced it all together long before I ever showed Panacea to him. Christ! He could have been concealed, could have even seen the baby as I escaped the doss with her – had he been spying on me for this organisation all along?

"If you would excuse me, the old Haddon family curse has struck and I fear I may die of shame if I do not relieve myself."

Mary huffed at my feigned urgency. I made it out of the coffee house and waited not even a moment. I broke into a run, pell-mell all the way back to my house.

Once through the front door of my house, there was not a moment's hesitation. I scooped up Margaret from the sofa and carried her up two flights of stairs, to the master bedroom. She murmured only a little and thought she was experiencing some vivid, opium-induced dream. I lay her gently on the bed and wrestled with the covers, tucking her in, fully clothed.

I grabbed an outdoor dress and cap of Margaret's and raced down to the study. Lily or Annie or whoever emerged from the servant's bedroom and asked if everything was all right. I turned back to her and called up the stairs, "Yes, all is well. Mrs Blessing is very unwell. I am ministering to her in the study, but fear she will have to be admitted to the hospital if she does not improve. Please stay in your room tonight and get your rest as I fear there will be much work for you in the morning."

The girl agreed and disappeared back into her room.

May God forgive me for what I did next. I can not describe how I came to the idea, nor how I managed the actual act itself. It is enough to say that I burned the priest's clothes, white collar and all, in the fire in the parlour. Once done, I hailed a cab, and when I carried Father Haddon over the threshold of my house, he was it was not only darkness that cloaked him. He was dressed as my Margaret.

Off to the hospital we went. I had the driver take me right up to the door. Down into my laboratory did I go with Father Haddon, to my secret place. Sweating profusely, I took out my surgical kit and looked to my various glass cases about the room. Before long, Father Haddon was in several of these cases, a hand here, a leg there, his head! My God! A feast for the creatures in the cases. How they devoured his face. How they devoured all of him!

When I had ceased vomiting, I managed to

steel myself long enough to inspect the progress of my creatures. The sound of tooth grinding bone will haunt me for the rest of my days.

Oh Jesus!

Jesus Christ!

Eight.

Charles watched as the woman drank her coffee with a serene look on her face. She reached the end of her drink, glanced at a small watch she held in her elegant little bag and rose to her feet.

This woman had expected Blessing to return, of that, Charles was sure, although she hid her anger, or disappointment well. She had not meant to disturb him, perhaps. A misunderstanding? A guilty conscience? She was preparing to leave the coffee house. Once more, a dilemma. He could gamble and make a direct attempt to discover the nature of their relationship, or he could follow by stealth and uncover more about the woman herself by studying her actions. If he was wrong then following her would mean a wasted opportunity to watch Blessing.

The woman emerged from the coffee house and glided along the street with an elegance that made Charles wonder if her shoes did not float above the city muck.

He decided to be somewhat direct. At the very least he might find something he could use as leverage to force Blessing to confess.

“Excuse me, Miss,” he found himself saying, having caught up to her.

The woman stopped and turned side-on to Charles. The posture was almost a defensive combat stance. “Yes?” she asked, eyeing him with suspicion.

“I saw the man you were with before. Dr George Blessing. I wondered if you knew where he might be headed. He appeared to be in a hurry. I don’t wish to seem impertinent,” Charles said, removing his derby and holding it to his chest. “You see, he looks after a friend of mine in Belgravia and he left with such haste… well, I have had a vision that my friend has taken a turn for the worst.”

The woman concealed her shock well – it had been apparent for only a moment. She replied, "I swear I would have no idea of his business. Now, if you'll forgive me, I had best be on my way."

With that the woman hurried away. Charles grinned to himself. Lover. Lover's tiff. She is shocked at having the affair discovered.

He certainly is a man of secrets, this Blessing. Adulterer. Murderer. Deviant.

Waiting had not proved entirely fruitless. Charles could dismiss the lover for now. His next move was to hurry to Blessing's home – to try to get back on his scent. Doubtless he would have scurried off home to his little wife, Charles reasoned, to make up some time with her and salve his guilty conscience.

Upon arriving at Blessing's terrace, Charles hung back. There was a commotion at Blessing's front door. What was this? Blessing was carrying his wife out to a hansom cab. She looked terribly unwell, lifeless. Had he revealed his affair to her? Had she fallen into some sort of swoon or stupor? Where was he taking her?

Assuming that same authority that had come to him with years in uniform Charles stepped onto the cobbled road and called a cab to stop for him. "Get out," he snarled at the terrified old man and woman huddled on the seat.

"You can't just do that, Guv!" the driver called.

Charles pointed a thick finger at the man. "Shut it, or I'll put a bullet up your big, fat nose. Now you two, get down now!"

The old couple complied and Charles climbed into the cab. "See that cab up there, driver? Follow it. Lose it and I swear you'll suffer!"

"I should take this whip to you, you ignorant bastard!" the driver yelled. He quickly lowered his voice and addressed the elderly couple once more, saying, "Sorry, m'lady. It's this dog, here!"

Charles gripped the roof of the cab and leaned forward, craning his bulging neck around so he could just see the driver's head. "I said move!" he growled.

The driver could see that Charles was not to be trifled with and did as he commanded.

It came as no surprise to Charles when he stopped the cab on Poland Street. Whatever was wrong with Mrs Blessing, the doctor had obviously wanted to deal with it in a hurry. The doctor had needed something from the hospital and had not the time to retrieve it and take it home. But to take his wife out in that state? This seemed more than just a fit of anxiety, her condition must have been gravely urgent.

Charles climbed from the cab, but grasped the reins that ran over the cab's roof. He tugged hard and dropped to the cobbles. The driver was snatched forward, the horse shied.

Charles was at the driver in an instant, grabbing him from his perch, down onto the street. He kicked the man's back and backside, knocking him prone. Charles picked up the whip and cracked it several times over the driver's back, causing the man to howl, more with fright at Charles' savagery, than pain as his thick pea coat protected him. Charles kicked the driver once more, leaving him sprawled out on the ground. Out of sheer spite, he whipped the horse, sending it off down the road at pace. Dropping the whip next to the driver, Charles said, "I don't believe you'll call me a dog again." And with that he left the scene, thinking it imprudent to enter the hospital and walk straight into the doctor and his wife.

The night had not revealed anything about the Burton matter, but much about the private affairs of the doctor. If anything, it was clear that, affair or no, he had enough concern for the wellbeing of his wife to race to the hospital with her. Was she normally a sickly woman, Charles wondered? Was it this condition that had made Blessing seek comfort from another woman?

No matter, he thought, I am on the right track. It is a matter of time before there would be enough material to blackmail the murderer into a confession.

Nine.

Once more in her room at the Seraphim, Mary could not believe it! A murder suspect right there in front of her. McEwan would be furious. She could hear him berating her now, "How did you not see it? The man was aroused by your attention – no moral disinterest, he was practically flirting!"

And even though Mary knew that McEwan would have delivered harsh words to her, she had the urge to write to him and tell him everything that had happened. Perhaps his rebuke would be tinged with jealousy, for Mary had to admit, there was something in her that was drawn to the doctor. Even though at the time, she had believed he was a priest.

Shame! Mary thought. I would seduce a priest. Even in her most private darkest thoughts she would never have considered it until the man was in front of her. But he is not a priest, therefore not unobtainable. A doctor. No. A murder suspect. A murder suspect and possibly a vampire. Therefore unobtainable.

Why would I think like this? Mary almost screamed at herself. She was once more reminded of the shameful part of her nature, unlocked by her training. His eyes, his innocent eyes! She could not stop thinking about him.

Innocent. He had not the cold eyes of the vampire. He had been flustered.

He had been flustered not because he was a priest faced with an attractive woman, he was flustered because the only reason he had to be there was that he knew Haddon was meeting someone. He had gone to find out whom.

The chance meeting on the street with that burly man had clinched it. Haddon was dead. Blessing had found a message, or had been told, that Haddon was meeting someone. He had been daring, or stupid, to pretend to be the priest.

But no, *I* had revealed my hand, she admitted to herself, I made it perfectly clear I didn't know the person I was meeting. How bold of him to follow that up immediately. She had known, when she said the word 'doctor' and he reacted, she had known, but the large man confirmed it. She had not wanted to believe. Not wanted to believe he was a killer. He was so… gentle. He seemed so decent.

She trembled to her core. The doubts set in again. I was trained, she thought, trained to see through people, to see through the façade of decency – right to the corruption in their hearts. But I couldn't see it in him.

Sleep did not come easily. Her mind was losing its rigidity, its discipline. Ever since Paris. That damned Dr McEwan, he has awakened something in me! And now this damned doctor. His eyes, his gentle, innocent eyes. And a new thought: I have to save him.

Mary woke to another filthy London morning. On the street, an argument had developed between a patterer and the doorman of the Seraphim.

"-away from here!" the doorman boomed.

"-just trying to make a living like anyone else!"

"-not that sort of place. No place for you out here! You stand wherever you want, but not outside that hotel. Not that one."

Mary observed herself in the washstand mirror once more. Her soft eyes. Her delicate features. She still looked like a teenager.

She closed her eyes and breathed in deeply. The mission. I must fathom this mystery before my training is destroyed. The mission.

She looked into the mirror once more, and Black Mary noted her own features, jaw set, cheeks taut beneath her hard eyes. She bathed and dressed and secreted her weapons.

A breakfast of soft-boiled eggs and toasted

bread with two cups of tea prepared her for the day.

She considered the facts as she looked out onto the bustling street. First, the priest suspected Dr Blessing. Second, Dr Blessing had discovered the priest's meeting. Third, Blessing now knew that the priest was an informant for an organisation charged with hunting creatures who had the capacity to drain a human of his blood. Fourth, Blessing had assumed the identity of Father Haddon. Fifth, disturbed by the conversation, Blessing had fled the coffee house. He did not fight, did not protest, he fled. Leading to sixth, Dr Blessing is afraid.

Mary suppressed the swell of pity. Reminding herself of McEwan's letter, she whispered, "Remain Black Mary."

Thinking back to what the bulky stranger had said on the street, Blessing allegedly tended to a man in Belgravia. It was probable then that his home or practice, if he operated out of a separate office, was in Belgravia. It seemed unlikely that a doctor would be separated from his private clientele by any great distance.

Mary waved the porter over and placed a shilling in his palm. "I am not feeling quite myself today. I have heard of a Dr George Blessing, who is very capable and who operates near here. Would you be so kind as to gain his address for me?"

"Certainly, madam. But I must say, there happens to be a doctor here in the hotel; he arrived last night," the porter offered helpfully.

"Thank you, but I have heard that this Blessing is a man of remarkable skill," Mary replied.

The porter bowed his head and backed away a couple of steps before hurrying off to the reception desk.

Before half an hour had passed, the porter had managed to obtain the home address of the doctor, and Mary was on her way.

The midmorning sun barely penetrated the foul black shroud over the capital, and Blessing's street appeared a grey, dull place to Mary. She mounted the steps to the Blessing household and rapped on the door.

The young maid answered the door, showing such courtesy as was due a woman of class.

"I apologise for arriving unannounced," Mary began. "I wonder if I might find Dr Blessing at home?"

"I am afraid not, m'lady. He must have set off for the hospital early this morning."

"The hospital?" Mary asked.

"Yes m'lady. He attends a hospital to see to the needs of poor folk."

This jarred distinctly with the image of a killer. Mary pressed on. "I wonder then, if I might impose two requests. The first, if I could speak to Mrs Blessing, even for only a few moments, it would do me the greatest good. The second, if while I speak to Mrs Blessing, you could write for me the address of this clinic; I feel that a portion of my recent inheritance might assist Doctor Blessing's quest to bring care to the poor."

The maid, knowing that the doctor would not wish to turn away a potential investor, immediately invited Mary into the reception. She wrote out the address of the clinic immediately, in a clear, competent hand. In the parlour, Mary was introduced to Mrs Blessing, who, the maid assured her, had been quite unwell of late.

What burden could weigh so heavily on the doctor's wife, I wonder? Mary thought to herself.

"Please, sit," Mrs Blessing offered.

Mary sat close to Mrs Blessing and glanced about the room. There on the wall, a painting of Mrs Blessing and her husband – certainly the man she had seen at the coffee house. "A lovely portrait," Mary commented.

"I thank you, Miss…"

"Brigham. But please, call me Mary."

"Only if you call me Margaret."

Mary instantly took a liking to Margaret, although her pallor and shallow breathing gave away almost immediately an addiction to laudanum. Mary noted the two small vials on the side table, one of which appeared to be empty. Would the doctor leave his wife with laudanum, or was it perhaps paregoric?

"I have to inform you, Mrs Blessing, I fear your husband has become involved in some sort of… trouble."

Margaret's eyes widened for a moment, but she quickly regained her composure. "Should I send for some tea?"

"No thank you. I fear I have not much time."

"It would be no trouble. I shall call for Lily."

Mary reached for Margaret's hand and applied an even, gentle, reassuring pressure. "Please, Margaret. George is in trouble."

Tears broke free and streamed down Margaret's cheeks. "I know. I know."

"There, there," Mary said, shifting over to the sofa, wrapping an arm around her. "It is not too late for me to help him. But you have to tell me as much as you know. It is difficult for me to explain to you how I know, and how I can help him, but you must trust me for now. I can understand him and can get him the help he needs."

"He has been carrying out experiments, on himself, I think. He locks himself in the hospital all day and his study all night. Sometimes I hear him screaming in the study. Sometimes he screams in his sleep. It all started… was it two years ago? Three? I have lost all… There was a woman, a girl. He tried to help her, but she died. I think she died horribly."

"Yes?" Mary pressed.

"And my husband was never the same after that. He threw himself into research. I think he desperately wanted to stop anyone else going through the same agony. But, somewhere along the way… I lost him. I lost my husband." Margaret sobbed and turned to look Mary in the eye. "Promise me," Margaret said, wringing her hands, "promise me, that you will bring my husband back to me. The old George. My silly old George."

Margaret fell back across the sofa and descended into tears once more.

His study, Mary thought. I have to get in there.

Mary left Margaret in the parlour and entered the reception. She could hear Lily in the kitchen. Mary glanced up the stairs and saw a double-door off to the right. She mounted the stairs and moved lightly so as not to draw attention to herself.

She crept across the landing, keeping her feet on the large rug to mute her footfalls. Her fingers found the door handles. A charge ran through her, she could feel that this was it. The answers were behind these doors.

She turned the handles.

Locked.

She heard a handle turning.

The front door.

Mary rushed to the top of the stairs and looked down.

The front door opened.

There he was.

Looking straight at her.

She smiled and immediately a spear of pain stabbed through her mind, causing her to stagger a step or two.

He turned and fled, taking full advantage of the distraction.

"Doctor Blessing, no! Wait! I only wish to talk to you!"

Mary raced out onto the street and saw him vanish into the anonymity of the crowded street. Behind her, the front door closed and she heard the locks click home. “Margaret! Please, I want to help him!” Mary pleaded. She knew it was useless, for Margaret loved her husband dearly and anyone who could frighten him from his own home was not welcome there.

She caught a glimpse of Margaret closing the parlour curtains, a vacant look on her face.

Mary had seen that look on faces before. The laudanum could have caused that look, but it appeared to Mary, that Margaret was what De Omori referred to as “in thrall”, a state of hypnosis brought about by vampires.

She moved out of sight of the Blessing household and pondered her next move as she walked. De Omori would want a progress report, but she had no evidence, and no plan of action. It was then that she noticed the headache had passed. It had been a fleeting, momentary shock, rather like an attack. Whatever was in the study was powerful enough to stop her in her tracks and if it held a person in thrall, then everyone in that house was at risk. A direct attack from her would result in avoidable deaths. De Omori would not be happy for her to proceed without a carefully considered plan if a supposedly respectable family hung in the balance.

What has that Doctor done? Mary wondered, glancing back at the house. What has he let loose?

Ten.

It had taken me hours of walking the streets of London, to work up the courage to return to the house. My only concern was Panacea's safety. I had walked my street several times and sneaked in through the back door, with one of my surgical blades at the ready.

I moved through the rooms of the ground floor with a candle to guide me. Everything was as expected. I noted that the front door was fully locked and bolted. I crept to the study and found the lock was fastened and secure. Upon entering I found everything as it should be.

Panacea woke to my presence. I stroked the glass case and left her alone, hoping that she would not punish me for my cowardice. It had been close. Mary had been feet away from her.

I lay next to Margaret, a wreck of a man. The shadows of the room seemed to form a great net, closing in on me, ready to drag me into the murky depths with Henry. The grind of tooth on Father Haddon's bones seemed to fill the silence and mark the seconds until I would be caught.

From her sanctuary in the study, the child poured ideas into my brain, tried to calm me, tried to harden me to the fear. She drew forth in me a courage I would not otherwise have known. The grip of anxiety around my heart was replaced by the feeling that something was trying to escape me, trying to rise through my ribcage, desperate to break loose.

A poisonous dream rolled through my brain, like mist. More than a dream – an idea! To leave, leave before the net dragged me down. But no, I thought, no. How can I leave her? My precious Margaret! I have caused her such harm; I have been such an absent husband and she deserves so much better.

I had never heard Panacea's voice. She could

speak no words, but by God how she could take my vocabulary and rearrange it in my head for me. She told me what to do. Should I fail to comply, or resist her, or displease her in any way, she had perfected a method to make me obey.

In her sleep, Margaret reached for me, as she had on so many other nights. She frequently dreamed that we had a child together. Sometimes the child was a baby, sometimes the child was Niamh, but whichever form the dream took, it often instilled in Margaret a... desire. For three years I had been making excuses, or had avoided sharing our marital bed altogether. "George give me a baby," she muttered.

I ignored Margaret's advances - but they had been noticed by another. My words became reassembled in my brain once more and a suggestion formed. I cried out, "No!"

Margaret woke with a start and caressed my face. "George, what is it? George you are sweating."

The pain that I experienced at that point is very difficult for me to describe to you. I once heard of a terrible suicide. A gambler, who could not face his family to tell them of his terrible losses, placed his head down on a railway track and allowed himself to be run over. In an instant, the wound would have been so traumatic as to kill him before any pain registered within the man. But what I want you to imagine is that it did not.

Imagine the moments as the wheel first struck the head. Imagine that the train is moving very slowly, and that the wheel mounted the head instead of crushing it instantly, and for a few seconds, the weight of the train is pressing down, cracking, crunching, bursting the skull and brain. Imagine then that the train keeps moving and the head, magically intact once more, is struck by the next wheel, and the next and the next. Imagine then that the gambler survived, stood up, and could remember the sensation of each impact and each agonising, excruciating second.

Panacea inflicted that pain on me until I staggered from my bed and out of the room. Moments later I had returned.

Margaret had settled in her normal sleeping position. Her hand reached for my side of the bed and she moaned, wondering where I was.

She shivered at the shuffling of the bedclothes and moaned – this moan had taken on a different tone to the last – she was aroused. “I knew you would change your mind,” she whispered.

Margaret arched her back as a ripple of pleasure rose through her.

Even in the dark I could see and feel the white, clawed hands working up Margaret’s thighs.

I held my breath in anticipation of what was to follow, but not content with this course of action, the creature wanted to enhance her pleasure with one final act. She made my hands reach for the candle and matches at the side table. I struck the match and as the flame took hold and the light grew in the room, I noticed Margaret’s attention shift to the source of the light.

Her face was carved in a moment of terror, to be frozen that way in my memory forever, when she realised that it was not I who was beneath the blankets.

She tore back the bedclothes and saw the white flesh reflecting the orange of the candle glow.

I dropped the candle and the flame spluttered out, not burning hot enough to withstand the fall. As Margaret took in the huge gasp of breath that preceded a scream, I was upon her. My whole weight crushed down on her, fingers clasped over her mouth, squeezing her head to my breast.

Then in went the teeth.

The sun was rising, casting light on a new route, a new plan. I peeled myself from the sheets and made ready for the day’s tribulations.

I left Margaret to lie there. I looked at her and for the briefest moment sickening pain rose through my stomach and my heart felt like it was falling. Almost immediately I was dragged out of guilt, incapable of remorse. I was reminded that this was right – this was the only course of action. Margaret's demise had been entirely necessary for our survival. She was holding us back...

A theory had taken hold in my mind. Haddon was connected to the mysterious woman, but if he also knew Charlotte and Henry, then he may have shared his information or suspicions with the widow. Was Charlotte aware of this woman's presence? With Haddon out of the way, was Charlotte the one who directed the woman to my house?

Before I knew it, I was striding through the reception at the Burton mansion, yelling at the top of my lungs for the lady of the house.

One of her lackeys emerged and said, "Ahhh, Doctor Blessing. How lovely to see you. Mrs Burton is on the terrace..."

I did not listen to the rest of his sentence, but raced through the cold marble-clad hall to the parlour and through the parlour to the large glass doors, which opened onto the terrace.

Charlotte lay across a chaise, enjoying what sun could penetrate the London soot. "George, you are the last person I expected to see."

"I do not doubt it."

"What do you think of the view?" Charlotte asked, waving a hand majestically over the landscaped gardens.

There, by the pond and fountain, stood the brute himself, with two accomplices: one larger even than him, and the other a skinny rake of a man.

"I do not care for it a bit," I responded.

Charlotte sat up and stared at me directly. "George, is something wrong?"

"Is something wrong, Charlotte? Is something wrong?"

"George?"

"First you send that beastly man out to seek me and now you send another of your agents to my house! My house! What game is this you play?" I could see that my raised voice had caught the attention of the trio by the fountain.

"Another agent?"

"That *woman*! Do you plan to destroy my marriage, too?" I cried. I had a nerve, considering I allowed the same creature to kill both Charlotte's husband and my wife.

"I must confess to being at a disadvantage, George, now I suggest you just-"

I raised a warning finger. "No. Allow me to make a suggestion. Keep that man, those men, and *that woman* away from me, and away from my house. Fail to heed me in this, and I swear, Charlotte, I will not be responsible for my actions."

"You dare? You dare to threaten me?"

I continued, enjoying the strange feeling that pulsed through me. I felt like someone else was saying the words and I was sat back, as at the theatre, enjoying the whole scene. "Do not raise your voice at me Charlotte. It does no good to get excited in your… fragile condition."

"You know?"

"I am a doctor, Charlotte. And one of no small degree of talent. The faint tinge of vomit in the air. Your swollen breasts. Charlotte, your cheeks are flushed and I feel you have seldom looked more beautiful."

I could see that I had shocked Charlotte and thrown her mind off-balance. "George, you confuse me."

Excited and emboldened I leaned forward, down on one knee and grasped her hands in mine. "That night, with Judith Cloonan, you struck me as a remarkable woman. Oh, I love my Margaret, but you have this other quality to you. A worldliness, yes, experience. There were times, while we created the hospital together, Charlotte, I felt I would have taken you, right there, over my writing table. Henry, Margaret, everyone be damned!"

Charlotte was breathless now, and I felt the strands connecting the spiritual *me* to my corporeal form breaking one by one, like the moorings of a dirigible, snapping away unexpectedly, uncontrollably. Only a few tethers held me back – soon I would ascend.

"George, how can you say these things?" she asked, with a modesty I had rarely observed in her before.

"Mrs Burton, is everything all right?" Charles called, revealing that he had covered most of the ground between the fountain and the terrace.

"Yes Charles," Charlotte assured him, waving Charles and the other men away. "I need some privacy."

The men skulked away, along the lower terrace until they were obscured by tall box-hedges.

"George, this is highly improper."

I kissed her swollen lips and squeezed my hands against her hips, then grasped impertinently at her breasts. The gamut of emotions played out on her face, for all to see. Charlotte's guilt for her dead husband's memory was visible yet her response to my kisses, her probing tongue, revealed that she was enjoying this moment. Her pain as my hands treated her tender breasts roughly, juxtaposed against the thrill of the idea that the hands belonged to her dead husband's friend. Her abandon as her thighs opened, her greedy kisses, despite her friendship with my wife. She *did* want me – perhaps she had all along!

I stepped away, leaving her flushed and sweating. "That is quite enough," I muttered.

"What? George, what are you doing?" Charlotte

asked, confused and desperate.

"Also, you should know," I stated, straightening my clothes, "that our partnership is disbanded. The hospital can burn for all I care. Remember what I said: leave my father alone."

"Your father?" She looked puzzled.

"I said, leave me alone."

And with that, I left, no longer making it up as I went along, but moving in accordance with a plan. The next part of the plan: Niamh.

I arrived at Niamh's lodging an hour later and found her sewing a hole up in one of her socks. "Leave that, darling child. I shall buy you all the fine clothes you could possibly want, if you would do something for me."

"Anything, doctor."

"Here is some money. Go to the rag market and bring your dear old doctor a full set of clothes."

The poor child looked confused and said, "But Doctor, you can afford those nice clothes, ones that just you have worn."

"Yes, and that is the point, my dear. Now, do your best. Take this note of my measurements. I am sure you will find me something suitable. And remember this: your dear old doctor likes to stay warm when outdoors."

"Should I get me a pair of socks, too, doctor?"

"No, child. Not from the rag market. Did I not say you would have all the fine things?"

"You did," she replied.

I pulled her in close, embraced her for a long moment and kissed the top of her head. "And I meant it. No more rag markets for you. Now, do as I asked and bring the clothes to my house."

Eleven.

Charlotte's coach was as comfortable a transport as any Charles had been privileged enough to ride in. He had followed the doctor's hired carriage from the Burton home, to the streets near the clinic. Charles was surprised when they turned left off Oxford Street and did not head right, for Poland Street, and the clinic – where the hell was Blessing going?

The coachman drew the carriage to a halt and spoke into the tube that enabled his voice to carry clearly into the coach itself, and informed Charles that Blessing had entered a building. Charles climbed down to the street and the coachman pointed out the boarding house into which Blessing had gone.

The mistress. This had to be where she lived.

Charles looked about the place. The woman he had seen at the Coffee House with Blessing looked too classy to live in a boarding house on Wells Street. Was this yet another woman?

Charles could have spat on the ground with temper. This murderous, deceitful monster had attempted to take advantage of Charlotte – oh, Charlotte may have dismissed him, but Charles had one duty, and that was to protect her. He had watched that beast's hands all over Charlotte's breasts, his mouth crushing her lips. At the time, his hand had gripped the revolver. He would have intervened had he not seen Charlotte's thighs part shamefully. She had allowed herself to be seduced. She wanted that doctor to take her.

Observation was the key. Surely the answer would present itself soon enough, but Charles was growing impatient. The matter at hand was that of Henry Burton's sudden and mysterious death, not the affairs of a depraved doctor. That the doctor was guilty was not for debate, so far as Charles was concerned

- guilty of Henry's murder, and guilty of the butchery done to that prostitute. In a normal investigation, Charles would want to get to know as much as possible about the man to ensure he could build up a picture of his movements and lifestyle – but Charles knew enough.

That night, that fateful night, when Judith Cloonan died, Charles had stood in uniform with his lantern, holding the crowd back, so moved by the woman's piteous, animal howls, that he had had to suppress the urge to take his truncheon over the doctor's head in the vain hopes that the woman could be saved.

He had seen the doctor and Henry Burton steal something away, in one of those glass containers used for pickling organs and deformed babies. Doctors! Charles thought, ruefully. Butchers, every one. What had the doctor discovered that he had allowed that woman to die a horrible, agonising death? What secret had Burton concealed that had driven the doctor to kill him those years later?

It was then that the doctor emerged from the boarding house, with a small girl who looked about ten or eleven years old. A daughter? Blessing himself looked only to be in his late twenties, so he would have sired this child particularly young. What a shameful secret, what a burden to carry, through the years of studying his art.

Would a woman carrying the child of a man wealthy enough to practice medicine allow herself and her child to live in such meagre circumstances? Unlikely. Blessing's father would have been shamed into parting with such monies as would buy silence and raise the fallen woman's status.

Charles concluded: the child is not Blessing's.

Therefore what is the link?

The child is another lover? Charles tensed his whole body and felt his suit strain at the seams as his chest and shoulders expanded. That. Damned. Beast!

The doctor and the child parted company. Blessing headed back along the road towards where Charles stood, but across the road. Charles stole back to the coach and climbed in. "Wait here for me. I'll follow him on foot, driver."

"Aye, sir," came the reply.

Blessing was absolutely oblivious to Charles' presence as he weaved his way down Wells Street, across the bustling Oxford Street and down Poland Street to the clinic. Blessing had stopped only once along the way, to buy some matches from a scruffy street-pedlar.

Charles looked at the ragged crowd of people outside the clinic, appealing to the doctor, imploring him to heal them or a child, or a sick friend. The doctor stopped and addressed them.

It certainly jarred against the image of a murderous madman, the knowledge that this man had helped to form a hospital with the sole aim of healing the downtrodden. Charles could feel almost admiration swelling in his breast, tempering the hatred that had thus far rendered him incapable of objectivity.

Charles seemed to be in a trance, staring at the ground, wondering: have I got this right? The charitable visage masks a monster? Or is he a monster at all? Does he hurt people? And if he does, does he help more people than he hurts? Does he only hurt people to achieve a greater good?

He could see the benefit to the many at the sacrifice of the few. He could understand it easily; it was the principle upon which almost all religion was based. But when one considers the individual, he thought, does it make it right? Individual people used as matchsticks, expended to light a fire to warm the many. And, if he continued on his own present course of action, what would happen to the many? What would become of the poor, tatty wretches who appealed to the doctor if the doctor was in gaol, or dead?

A dizzying sensation of pressure came down on Charles' skull and he turned to move away, glancing back at the clinic only enough to notice that the doctor was gone, probably inside. He staggered across Oxford Street, sickened by his own anger and obsession. How can I bear him such ill-will, when the widow Burton saw fit to allow him to paw her so? If we were all so convinced that he had killed Henry Burton, then why would she behave that way? The doubts collected and spiralled. His exhaustion became apparent. Indeed he had barely slept over the last weeks, since offering his services to Mrs Burton. He had been certain that in assisting the widow, he would untangle the mystery that had taken over his life. The same mystery that had consumed him, and poured drink down his neck and eventually taken away his uniform.

He climbed into the coach and instructed the coachman to take him back to Kensington. The coachman turned the carriage expertly and made for Oxford Street once more. They both noticed that a panic had broken out on the street. People were running past them, back for Poland Street.

"There's something wrong, sir," the coachman called through the tube.

Charles had already detected it, for the smell of smoke had already reached his nostrils. Shouts of "Fire!" reached him from the street.

"There's a fire, sir! The hospital is on fire!" the driver called.

"My God! Take me there!" Charles ordered.

Poland Street was blocked by the crowd and almost inaccessible from Oxford Street. "I can go no further!" the driver called.

Charles climbed down from the coach and pushed his way through the mob, barely recognising that anyone stood in his path. True enough, the receiving clinic of the hospital was ablaze, and the fire threatened to spread to the hospital proper. Charles could see invalids being dragged from the doors of the main hospital. Glass shattered and flames licked from the ground floor windows, reaching up for the floor above. "Jesus Christ!" Charles cried. "The doctor is in there!"

His own outburst had surprised him. His fatigue lifted. If Blessing was a killer then he had to be brought to justice. If he was innocent of the crimes he suspected, or if he had the potential to do more good than harm, then he had to be saved.

Charles raced into the burning building.

Twelve.

Mary took an omnibus to Oxford Street, where she disembarked and nodded to the man who had kindly given up his interior seat for her. The man had braved the elements on the roof so that she had not had to.

She had decided to stay away from the house, not wishing to jeopardise the safety of the doctor's household unless she absolutely had to. The hospital was a better place to set an ambush, or at the very least, to speak to some of Dr Blessing's contemporaries and try to piece together more information about the man.

Oxford Street was abuzz and she was glad to turn off to Poland Street, where she could see the hospital, and the unfortunates gathering outside, waiting for their chance to seek the doctor's counsel, hoping for a cure, or admission to the hospital proper. Mary slipped unnoticed down the narrow alley between the hospital and the neighbouring tenement building. She continued round to the rear of the hospital, which was littered with the waste of that building and adjacent dwellings.

A rear door to the building was set within the wall. Mary tried the handle and found it locked. From her bag she produced her invaluable lock-picking kit. The lock was not exotic and was very easily picked. Mary entered the building and closed the door behind her.

The sun was fighting its way through the soot and smoke of London, but with the windows shuttered, the receiving section of the hospital was still in darkness. She considered lighting one of the oil lamps hanging from the walls at various intervals. She decided against this course of action as with the growing crowd outside, it was clear that the clinic was due to open soon. She might reveal her presence immediately, costing her precious time in which she would otherwise make her escape.

She walked through the waiting area, which was well maintained considering the filthy state of some of the patients, if those assembled outside were anything to go by. She struck a match and inspected the sign on a door. It was the doctor's office. She shook out the match and investigated further.

The doctor's office was as she expected, with desk, side tables, bookshelves and chairs. She moved to the door at the side of the room, tried the handle and found it locked. Once more, the lock was easily picked and Mary found herself standing at the top of a long staircase, leading down to another floor.

Grasping the handrail she made her way down the steps. The basement was shrouded in deep darkness and she struck another match, hoping to find an oil lamp. She was surprised to find that gas jets had been installed in the basement. She wondered, why here and not the ground floor of the building?

She lit the nearest jet and moved to the next, then to a third, creating sufficient incandescence to survey the scene. The room was large, probably a third of the size of the entire floor above.

The walls were covered in white tile, which aided the illumination, washing the room in bright light. In the centre of the floor was an operating table, which was adjustable, and which was perforated with many holes and scored with gutters. Beneath the table, hoses ran from beneath each hole and bound together by a metal strap. The hoses ran into a large glass container.

Nearby, a surgeon's kit was arranged on a trolley and in the corner of the room was a washstand. The mixed smells of coal tar and formaldehyde made breathing through the nose unpleasant. Another door led from this operating room. Mary found this unlocked and moved straight through, unhindered.

She lit the nearest gas jet and found a room that appeared to be a study, with another door at the far end of the room. The study contained a great number of medical books and journals, besides the many already seen upstairs in the doctor's office. Another desk sat covered in notes and sketches. In one corner of the room was a table with a wooden maze built upon it, large enough for small animals to run. Here and there about the maze were dark brown stains.

Mary noted a pipe projecting from the wall, with a valve at the end. She took this to be the control for the gas jets and realised that she was partially correct, when she saw the large containers of chloroform beneath it. That was it! He could fill a room with the gas, subduing the creature.

Excited by her discovery, she moved to the door and grabbed the oil lamp hung there from a nail. Clearly the doctor used this to light his way when the gas was off and the sedative was pumped through the pipes. She lit the lamp and opened the next door. There she found herself in a narrow corridor, lined with heavy doors, each with a glass viewing port installed. It reminded her of a prison, or lunatic asylum.

The lamplight was mostly reflected by the glass and it took time for her eyes to adjust to the gloom beyond. More glass within, and something moving beyond that. A squirming, swirling mass of eyes and teeth. Tiny creatures swarmed over each other, gathering in the corners of the glass tanks closest to her, as though they knew she was there and were desperate to break through, to find a way out to her.

She moved to the next door. She held up the light.

Something moved in the darkness, the light shimmered against white flesh and teeth. Mary heard a scream and realised it was her own voice filling her ears.

Something banged against the other side of

the door, a hard, steady pounding. She heard the bang against the outside of the door, saw stars and felt the dizzying pain before she recognised that her head had been struck from behind and that she had hit the door herself. She fell to the ground, dropping the lamp. She heard the lamp shatter and then she was out cold.

She had not been unconscious for long. The fire from the broken oil lamp had only just reached her dress. Mary patted the flames out and staggered to her feet.

Immediately the heat registered against her skin. The arid air burned her lungs and forced her to blink rapidly, as the moisture was instantly robbed from her eyes.

Whirling, she took in the scene. First, the cell doors were open. Glancing in the two cells closest to her, she found them empty. Glass cases had been shattered and whatever had been stored within had escaped. Escape from the flames had been the priority rather than feeding, as she checked herself over and could find no evidence of bites.

Second, the sound of fire roaring and crackling told her that whoever had attacked her, had decided to destroy the building. She did not need years of De Omori training to determine the identity of that *some-one*.

In a moment she was back in the small study. The desk had been upset and drawers emptied out over the floor. The bookshelves had been toppled, their contents scattered and doused in oil lighting. Leaves of paper and journals curled in the heat just as the flames took hold, destroying the information forever. Mary stayed low, as the smoke billowed overhead in a streaming cloud that pushed into to the operating room.

Blinded with tears, Mary grasped whatever sheets of paper she could reach, patting flames out against her body and moving to another page or book, extinguishing the flames again.

In less than a minute, the room was an inferno. Mary took her last deep breath and burst into the operating room, breaking into a sprint across the burning pools of liquid. Soot and ash swirled in the air as currents from the fire twisted upwards, grasping for the open air of the London streets. Mary's muscles burned, her lungs feeling like they too were on fire. She swatted at her burning dress, as the flames licked at her flesh. Burning oil splashed up her legs with each footstep.

A barrel of oil rolled and bashed its way down the stairs, oil sloshing out in every direction. Mary ducked back into the operating room as the barrel sailed past her and the flames burst forth once more, invigorated by this sudden feast of fuel.

Mary's trembling hands reached the railing as she ascended.

The flames howled around her.

Her dress was burning again.

She could smell that her hair was burning.

She let out her last breath as the doctor's office came into view.

More fire.

An inferno.

She tried to breath, it hurt.

She inhaled fire.

She coughed.

Smoke raced around her like spectral hands trying to overcome her.

She gulped the smoke in.

Coughed smoke out.

Vision gone.

Blinded.

Coughing.

Knees on the burning rug.

Hands burning on the burning rug.

Face burning on the…

"Doctor?" a man's voice.

A voice in the smoke.

"Oh, God! I have you, madam. I have you."

Small animals screaming in the flames, burning but not quite consumed.

Hands around her forearms.

"Ah!" a hiss of pain. "Cut my fingers."

He found her secret blades.

Animals screaming, frenzied.

"What in God's name?"

She was floating, out of the flames, he was beating her as she floated. The heat subsided but her flesh still burned.

Fresh air! She gulped fresh air and coughed and coughed and vomited black in the muck of the alley behind the clinic. Tears streaked down her face.

The big man she had seen outside the coffee shop was stamping on something and rubbing his hand.

"What was that?" Mary asked.

"A bloody mouse bit me! And what the hell is in your dress? Something cut my hand!" the big man shouted, moving over to her.

Mary staggered to her feet.

The man's teeth were bared, he was angry. He would take the blades out.

Mary beat him to it. Her fingertips found the small circular buttons at her wrists and, spreading her arms apart, drew two short, flexible blades, each with one razor-sharp edge. The buttons she had grasped led on to a thin handle, wide enough only for her fists, followed immediately by the deadly little blades. Mary slashed out, using the flat of a blade to deliver a stinging slap to the side of her saviour's face.

Her muscles twitched and pulsed, striving for the memory, the shapes, the way to fight, hoping that she could deter the man from stepping closer. Hoping she would not have to fight him at all.

"I only wanted to help you, madam!" he gasped. "Wait a minute! I know you! The doctor's whore!"

Mary's face contorted, confused. How did he know about McEwan? "You know of De Omori?" she asked.

"De what?" the man barked. "Listen! Is the doctor still in there?" the big man boomed.

Mary waved the blades at the big man. "Stay away. You can't understand this! This matter is beyond you."

He stepped forward, still rubbing the bite on his hand, which had further opened the incision caused by the concealed blade. "I wanted to help you! I wanted to help!"

"Step no further!"

Hand outstretched, the man ignored her warning. Mary struck with precision, blinding speed, and solid force. She caught the man's jaw with the handle of one of the weapons, sending him spinning to the floor.

Secreting her blades once more, she dragged the big man around onto Poland Street proper, not wishing for him to die if the fire spread to the alley. He had saved her life, after all. She staggered off Poland Street, onto Oxford Street, slapping the hands away and ignoring the offers of help and cries of horror.

She had to get to the Seraphim, only there could she compose herself and read the stolen documents she had stuffed inside her dress. Mary hoped she had managed to steal enough to make sense of this whole affair.

Thirteen.

Niamh had carried out my instructions to the letter. She had returned in the early afternoon, with her mission accomplished. Spread out before me were the items needed to become a navvy, an artist, a wandering musician, anything I so desired.

The power swelled in my breast as I raked the razor over the strop, again and again. One last look in the mirror.

I sensed my enemies aligning, the demise of Doctor George Blessing near at hand! Goodbye George. Silly old George. Silly old George was not so silly. He could not be trapped in the body and life of Doctor Blessing! I was warping into something else entirely, with new ideas and new strategies. Nothing was impossible. The machinery of my brain drove on, fuelled by I knew not what, but I knew that I would stop at nothing to secure my safety, and the safety of Panacea.

I spread the lather across my face and already saw a new man looking back at me.

Charlotte had suspected me and had involved a man whose instinct alone had implicated me in the crime of which I was entirely guilty – the destruction of my friend! I was still unclear on whether Charlotte knew of the strange woman from the coffee house – she had been so adamant that she knew nothing of her.

The razor cleaved its way through my moustache.

The woman agent was nothing more to worry about, whether Charlotte had guided her or not. She had perished in the flames. I do hope that D.O. will not miss her! I thought.

I raised the scissors and tilted my head in the mirror, taking my time, savouring the metamorphosis.

D.O. That symbol. I had seen it somewhere

before. I turned my attention to my stacks of books, journals and magazines. Running a finger from spine to spine, from my scientific texts, to my arcane, spiritual books... nothing. And there, on my desk, in the exact spot I had left it so audaciously hoping that Father Haddon would be shocked by it – right in that spot, lay 'The Anatomy of the Blood-Fiend'.

Grasping the book in both hands, I inspected the spine and cover, and there, embossed behind the name of the author, Doctor Samuel Brown III, was the very same symbol shown on Mary's handkerchief. "She knew!" I bellowed.

That woman had nothing to do with Charlotte, after all! Perhaps she could have helped me, could have instructed me, and guided me in my research and care for the child. She had said there was an island for these creatures – presumably the very place this Doctor Brown had carried out his research.

Dizzy with the discovery, I dropped the book back on the table and spun back to the washstand. I grasped the scissors once more and cut away, frantically, recklessly.

I had caused the deaths of a great many people, but now, included in that number, an agent from an organisation charged with the protection of mortal man from supernatural enemies – creatures of the night – beasts – monsters! I had become their enemy, a monster!

My lies had compounded and under pressure, they had ruptured. I had contradicted myself; I had lied or told half-truths, unaware of facts that would show me instantly to be a liar. I had remarked on Henry's inability to sire a child, when it had become clear to me in hindsight that he had, before his death, impregnated his wife.

In pretending to be Father Haddon, I had revealed knowledge of his clandestine meeting with Mary – placing myself quite obviously to the suspicious mind, as the last person to see him before his disappearance. Mary and that brute knew where I lived, knew my work and almost everything about me.

Hair gathered at my feet in great tufts as I continued to destroy my own image.

My instinct had been correct. It was time to leave London. Those great swells of energy that had gathered in my breast and altered my normal patterns of behaviour – great leaps of instinct and motivation had pushed me, driven me to this point. Certainly there had been mistakes along the way, but perhaps my sudden charges into this battle had made my pursuers hold back and take stock. Perhaps they had mistaken my naivety as a dangerous, malevolent courage. My instinct, then, I reasoned, had bought me time.

But had it been my instinct at all?

I dropped the scissors to the floor and spread lather across my shorn head. I grasped the razor once more and entered the next phase of my transformation.

In the mirror I could see him looking back at me, a soulless thing trapped within the glass. But the glass was about to break. Every scrape of the razor's edge brought this new creation closer to liberty.

My mind churned with suspicion and paranoia: they are coming. They had to be. If my instinct told me to leave now, then there had to be a reason, I thought.

I raised the towel and patted my scalp dry. I turned to the bell-jar, and considered her. Despite her lack of eyeballs, I knew that she could see me as I tore at my clothes. I knew that she marvelled at the spectacle of my reconfiguration as I pulled on the tatty garments assembled by Niamh. I could feel her approval; it warmed me and soothed me. Her approval kept my mind from straying to the lifeless body of my wife and her terrible death.

In a moment of unfettered, almost animal freedom, I growled a deep, throaty rumble. The noise sent ripples of excitement up my spine. This was it now! My soul was wrenched from my body, ascending, ascending – that body crumbling to ash in a moment, discarded… expended.

My hessian sack was prepared, the other, smaller jars already within.

Gently I cradled my child in her glass chamber and placed her in the sack, which I tied about me tightly, slung from left shoulder to right hip.

And then came the sound. The knock at the door.

Excitement and pride burst forth in a moment and I roared, an ungodly howl – my voice, mingled with the screech of a beast - not caring who heard! Let the world know it! I am here! A new animal! I live! The hunt is truly on!

Fourteen.

Charles beat heavily on the door to the Blessing home with his bandaged hand. His impatience caused him to beat again before it was proper to do so. He glanced at the two men accompanying him.

Both of his accomplices wore brown woollen suits, topped with derby hats similar to his. The first man, to his left, wore a gruff grey beard and had dark eyes set into his head, close to his crooked nose. His shirt caused the skin of his neck to roll and overhang slightly, so tight was the garment against his bulk. He had the appearance of a bear, giving him his nickname, The Bear.

The other man, to Charles' right, was more slightly built, but a good four inches taller than Charles. He wore a finely trimmed and waxed moustache under his long nose, the nose ravaged red with excessive alcohol consumption. He was known as Wet Freddy, for all his drinking, but only behind his back. Face-to-face, he was known simply as Freddy.

The trio created a menacing sight to the maid of all work who opened the door. Her enquiry into their business was cut short when from upstairs a roar issued, startling her. Charles froze for a moment then suddenly surged forwards, shoving the door inward and Lily to the floor.

Charles started for the stairs and Freddy began to search the ground floor, heading for the kitchen, pantry and copper.

"I know you are here, Blessing!" Charles boomed.

Lily picked herself up and drew in a breath ready to release a scream.

"Stay quiet, pretty!" The Bear growled, raising a thick finger to his lips, inches away from Lily's cheek. She winced at his rancid breath.

"What is it you want?" she whimpered, backing away into the parlour.

The Bear turned, hurrying to the stairs upon hearing Charles battering against a door on the first floor.

"Open this door, coward!" Charles yelled, red-faced as he recoiled and charged the door again. Charles turned to The Bear. "Mrs Burton said she thought if he had anything to hide, it would be in the study, through these doors."

The Bear arrived at the study door. He and Charles concerted their efforts, ramming the door with all their momentum. The lock burst and the doors slammed inward. Both men staggered into the room, but only Charles managed to stay on his feet. The Bear lost his footing and hit the floor.

Charles raced to the billowing curtains and the open window. He peered down into the backyard, where he saw Freddy looking in one of the outhouses.

"Freddy! Any sign in the yard?"

Freddy looked up at Charles, his jaw fell slack and he raised an arm, extending a finger, pointing at the roof. "He is above, Charles!"

Charles leaned out of the window, arching his back and clutching his hat. He caught a fleeting glimpse of a trousered leg, which promptly disappeared out of view, onto the roof.

Freddy became distracted by movement in the kitchen. "Oi! You in there!"

"Who is it?" Charles called.

"A girl. Doing a runner."

"After her, Freddy!" Charles ordered. He began to climb out of the window.

Freddy raced through the house, back to the front door. There the maid Lily was waiting, having emerged from the parlour once more to see if she could make out what was happening in the study.

In his haste, Freddy failed to notice her outstretched foot, over which he tripped and careened out of the door, falling at full pace over the steps and down to the front street.

During the fall, Freddy lost his hat. His forehead smacked the pavement, opening a bloody split above his eyes. Dazed, he saw the running waif leap up onto a passing cab. She spoke to the driver, who glanced back at Freddy and cracked his whip at the horse, which broke into a trot, the driver yelling a warning to pedestrians at the end of the street.

Freddy cursed loudly and attracted many glances of remonstration from passers-by. He stood and turned back to the house to see the door slam shut and heard the locks engage from within.

Charles clung to the window frame with his thick fingers. The Bear grasped Charles' forearms for added support, until he could take his own weight for the climb.

"That drain shan't bear your weight, Charlie," The Bear cautioned.

"He got up it, I can do it!" Charles snapped.

The Bear shook his head, "Get Freddy up there. The doctor's just a skinny little slip of a man. You will fall, you will!"

Charles ignored his accomplice and grasped the drainpipe. He scuffed his boots along the wall and began the climb. The pipe rattled and trembled in its couplings all the way up to the roof and all the way down to the ground.

As he ascended, Charles saw a man, staying low and picking his way across the rooftops of the terrace, two sacks tied around his shoulders. He looked nothing like the doctor. This man had not a hair on his head, no moustache, and wore shabby work clothes. For a moment he was fooled, but the fugitive glanced back at him and Charles could see the resemblance. His years as a constable had taught him to try to see a man through his facial hair, as when he commits a crime, it is the first thing he will change.

He was making good use of his head start, was the doctor. Charles wanted to call out to him, order him to stop or return, but his breath burned in his lungs, his arms ached from the effort and the pipe seemed ready to collapse, such was the noise it made.

"He has to come down, Charles!" The Bear called from the window, below.

Two feet below the rain gutter, one of the long bolts holding the coupling in place began to work loose. Charles saw it. He pressed on, hand over hand, teeth gritted, spittle frothing from his lips with each breath.

The bolt fell loose. On the other side of the coupling, the other bolt was almost completely free.

Charles braced himself, changed his plan and began to descend with all haste. That he would fall was inevitable, but he wanted to be as close to the yard as he could be when it happened.

The rain gutter groaned. The first coupling fell free.

"Christ!" Charles roared.

The second coupling began to judder, this only a foot above Charles. He squeezed the drainpipe with all his might and looked down. The coupling strained, the bolts scraping away from the stone. Charles passed the study window, where The Bear observed his movements. He had not dared reach out to The Bear, or the window frame as he passed for fear that the shifting weight would have instantly sent him to the ground.

Another groan and the coupling broke free. The pipe buckled, tearing free of the roofline gutter. Two segments of pipe parted beneath Charles' feet and he tilted away from the wall. He fell only a few feet, onto the roof of the coalhouse. The collision winded him and he rolled over, knocking the segments of broken pipe aside.

To his left he saw a man peering from the rooftops, four or five houses away.

"You look like you need a doctor!" Blessing goaded from the roof.

Charles wheezed and got to his feet. In a moment, he scrambled over the wall dividing Blessing's yard from that of his neighbour. He stood on the neighbour's coalhouse roof and drew his revolver.

"What the hell are you doing?" The Bear yelled.

Charles ignored him and watched as Blessing picked his way down the furthest drainpipe.

The first shot cracked out, the report reverberating violently in the enclosed yards of the terrace. Brick dust burst from the wall above Blessing's head.

Charles took aim again, one eye squeezed shut, one eye wide open. He could see the panic in Blessing's movement, sliding and scraping down the wall. The second shot roared out and again missed.

Charles breathed deeply; in a moment, Blessing would be obscured by the yard wall. Charles knew that he could take the time to make the shot, but if he missed, Blessing could make good his escape. If he abandoned the idea of firing again, he might be able to race around the yards with enough time to catch his man.

He fired. This time he heard the doctor yelp. The doctor fell a few feet and vanished behind the brick walls. A cacophony of glass striking glass met Charles' ears. He put away his revolver and dropped from the coalhouse roof.

Blessing's neighbours peered at him from the windows. Charles wanted to tell them what a deviant had lived among them, endangering their lives with his secrets, but what could he tell until the secret was brought fully to light? He made his way from the yard with all haste and wanted to sprint along the lane to the end of the terrace, but his legs would not bear him quickly enough.

By the end of the terrace, he limped and

wheezed. He could see a trail of blood and another fluid leading to the end of the lane, around the corner and out onto the open street where he was obscured in the hustle and bustle.

Blessing had escaped, but without his home, there were only a few places it seemed likely he would go. Only a few people it seemed he could trust. Charles collected himself and returned to The Bear, Freddy and the housemaid.

Fifteen.

Mary had carried herself with dignity through the reception of the Seraphim Hotel, covered with soot and reeking of smoke though she was. She cleaned up in her room and changed her clothes, restoring her respectability once more. Her cleansing had been rushed, though, as the documents she had taken from the clinic demanded her attention.

From one of the journals, Mary caught a description of a young creature – a creature not known to most people, but only too familiar to her. The journal entry was dated almost three years ago. She wondered what size the creature was presently, if it was indeed alive.

Reading through the weeks and months she found evidence of the doctor's interactions with the creature and various measurements. It seemed that the creature was not feeding freely and as such had remained only very small. Some entries held more interest for her than others. She read:

"Now sedate, and fastened securely to the table, she managed to struggle and evade my scalpel. Her evasion was so precise one could be convinced that this is evidence of some higher brain function, even beyond consciousness. It would appear to be a form of precognition. Since observing this behaviour, and since returning her to her jar, I have had time to wonder, and to grow concerned. How long will it be before she takes precautionary action against the chloroform gas I employ to subdue her? Thus far it is the only method I have of bringing her to heel."

Mary realised that she had been correct in her theory about the gas mechanism in the laboratory.

She returned to the journal and fell upon another entry of interest:

"I managed to extract some of the clear secretion from her fangs. When introduced to the bread, water and milk, ingestion of this fluid shows no immediate effect on the mice. The bacteria in her mouth must be tolerable to the mice, unless it is sterile. Time may be a factor. I shall continue to observe."

Another entry:

"The observation jar has shown some growth of mould, indicating that the secretion is not sterile. I can assume that either the bacteria lies dormant, or is susceptible to the digestive processes of the mice."

Mary read on:

"It appears the secretion simply requires a driver. Injecting the fluid into one of the mice revealed horrible consequences. The infected mouse almost immediately attacked his fellows with intense aggression, which continued into some cannibalistic feeding frenzy. The infected mouse seemed to draw forth the blood of his fellows from the wounds he inflicted…"

"… the mouse has not eaten for two weeks, yet appears vital…"

"… allowing the mouse to feed on another of its fellows appears to have had a direct effect on muscle mass, speed and intelligence…"

"… the infected mice appear to work in harmony to slake their bloody thirst…"

"… the newborn mice have taken on the traits of the infected father, feeding on their mother from

within. Their distorted features, lack of eyes and tail give them an appearance similar to miniature versions of my child..."

Mary raised a hand to her forehead and considered what she was reading. The experiments that Blessing had carried out in a clinic on mice were a microcosm of years of bloodfiend research on The Island. On The Island it had been much more difficult to gain useful samples, as the capture and harness of a live bloodfiend is no easy task. Blessing took his samples at his leisure and worked on rodents at his will, with many offspring in each generation, and a short gestation period.

She reached the end of the first journal's entries and scoured the second.

"... almost impossible to crush underfoot. The gas works well at rendering the creatures unconscious, though, and from there it is a simple matter..."

"... not as difficult to dissect a living infected mouse as it was to take samples from her. I have discovered in one of the dead newborns a deviation in the alignment of the teeth and what appears to be an additional gland or lobe on the brain, by comparison with the father and another, uninfected specimen..."

"... The cholera-infected blood from the Bermondsey whore has not had the slightest effect on the mice, the rats or the dog. She is hungry again. She won't let me sleep. This blood will be safe for her..."

"... She is displeased with my efforts. She sees the dog as an abomination of her kind, a mockery. I wither under the weight of her disapproval. Although a fascinating aspect of my research, the dog will have to be destroyed. I must admit, the thought of unleash-

ing the terrier in Lambeth or Bermondsey, has some appeal…"

"… With the dog gone, I have returned to her favour. She has allowed me to retain the body of the dog in another vessel, away from her. I pray she understands the importance of my work…"

"… hungry again. Under the pretence of finding a cure for her cancer, I managed to bring the maid back to the clinic. She took some convincing as my certainty at the fatal nature of her growth before had caused her to abandon all hope. She was resigned to her certain death. But why should one creature not benefit from the death of another? Otherwise, all would die and no good would come from any of it. Her belief in my blend of Redskin medicines has restored hope for her. It made my heart sink to see the maid's unwarranted optimism…"

"… it made my heart soar to see my child, my little Panacea, feed so greedily on the maid. Oh, she thrives again!…"

Mary slammed the book down and bundled the journals and papers away into one of her bags. That poor man, she thought. His proximity to that fiend has quite warped his mind. He had even named the beast.

She opened the trunk, which sat against the wall by the door and drew from it a garter belt upon which was attached a small pistol and three throwing knives. She fastened this to her left thigh. Two short, flexible swords, each just shorter than the length of her forearm slid home into folds in the sleeves of her dress. She grabbed her bag, which among the items one would expect to find on a woman, also contained certain tools to assist her in her work.

So armed she struck out to return to the Blessing home, hoping to free the poor doctor of his slavery – and to prevent any further deaths. Her mind was set. Blessing had caused the death of Henry Burton, and was likely behind the disappearance of Father Haddon.

It was unclear to Mary if Blessing had acted under his own volition, but the doctor's change from medical man to obsessed slave confirmed that the creature exerted some psychical control over his faculties – exactly as she had suspected when in his house the previous day.

No matter how many unknown factors remained, one thing was clear: the baby in the bell-jar must die!

Sixteen.

"You have done brilliantly, Niamh... Whatever would I do without you?" I said, between gritted teeth as I slumped on the floor of the cab.

"You are hurt, doctor," she gasped, pointing at the wound on my right shoulder.

"It is but a graze, my dear. I will be quite well, I assure you," I said, beginning to gather my faculties as the cab roared along the busy afternoon streets of Tyburnia.

Niamh ran her fingertips through some fluid on the floor of the cab and inspected it. She glanced at the sacks I carried and nodded at one of them.

My heart raced. No! Don't let her be harmed in any way. Say it is the jar of the rat, say it is the shrunken head. Anything but her!

My fingers peeled away the sack to find her one-third exposed above the level of the fluid, which seeped from a deep crack in the glass of her jar.

"Those men wanted to kill you, didn't they, doctor?" Niamh asked.

"I do not know, child," I replied.

"They wanted to kill you, and it was for her. She makes you do things, horrible things and I know it!"

"Niamh! Hold your tongue!" I barked.

Niamh lunged for the jar, her fingers slipped on the wet glass as I tore at her hands. "This would never have happened if that thing was dead!" she cried. "It has made you cruel!"

She kept struggling for the jar, clawing at my hands. I twisted away, and felt the burning wound on my shoulder open up further. Blood ran freely down my right arm.

"Leave her alone!" I boomed, shoving Niamh back into the seat, with enough force to frighten her. I raised my hand, ready to strike her, should she attack my child again.

"You have changed, Doctor Blessing, sir," Niamh sniffed.

I knocked on the roof of the cab and felt our momentum slow.

"You will need a bigger jar soon," Niamh said, staring at the cracked jar.

"You are quite correct; she is growing rather rapidly, is she not?" I said, tilting the bell-jar slightly, considering Niamh's observation.

The cab stopped and Niamh stood, pointing an accusing finger at me.

"No! For the other monster! For you!"

And with that, Niamh leapt from the cab and ran pell-mell among the other pedestrians. I slumped back to the floor. "On, driver," I called.

Quite exhausted from the afternoon's exertions, and my wound, I felt I could sleep. I secured the child in the jar upright and open on the floor and I lay across the seat. For a moment I caught sight of my reflection in the cracked glass. Soulful eyes – a kind, caring, doctor's eyes looked back at me. Savage movement beyond the glass snapped me out of my reverie.

I did not care for the way the child thrashed in the murky fluid and sniffed at the surface of the glass, clawing in my direction. I did not care for it a bit.

Seventeen.

Charles stood before Lily. The Bear stood by the door, making sure the maid could not escape. Freddy was wandering about the house looking for clues to where the doctor might have escaped.

Charles struck Lily with the back of his hand, holding back at first, not wishing to knock her insensible, and merely seeking to set the tone of the interview. Lily collapsed onto the chair and stared up at him with hatred in her eyes.

"Where has the doctor gone, pretty?" Charles growled.

Lily sat in silence, defiant.

Charles grabbed her by the hair and pulled her to her feet in a moment. His face was inches away from her cheek and as he spoke, flecks of spittle sprayed onto her face. "Where has that murdering bastard gone?"

Lily spat in Charles' face.

Charles released her hair and delivered a solid punch to the woman's midriff.

"Jesus Christ, Charles," The Bear groaned.

Lily yelped in pain as she doubled over and dropped to the floor.

"I have all day, my lovely," Charles warned. "The longer you take to tell, the further away he goes. That means I have to be absolutely sure you send me in the right direction, do I not?"

Charles leered down at the maid. She was a very attractive woman. He certainly knew how to pick them, did the doctor. He crouched beside her. "I will never understand why he had to look elsewhere for whores, with you stopping under his roof," Charles sneered.

"You lie! He loves Margaret! He has no other!" Lily cried.

"I lie, do I?" Charles licked his lips. "I bet he has barely touched her in months, has he? I bet you would hear them at it... if they was at it at all."

Lily blinked rapidly.

"I knew it. She has not had a man between those thighs of hers for long enough, has she? Perhaps if you told me where *she* is, I could help her." Charles felt warmth in his trousers, spreading, surging, growing. "How could he have the energy, anyway? What with seeing to Mrs Burton, that other young whore he tried to burn in his clinic. And I am not sure I *do* believe he would miss out on you, though-"

"What are you-?"

Charles grabbed Lily roughly. "Shut up! And that child he has been at an' all! Yes, yes! He has been quite a busy chap has your old doctor. Not been looking after the wife, though, has he?"

Charles let his bandaged hand glide up Lily's calf, higher, higher. She squirmed and kicked, clawing at him. She could see that she was being attacked by a madman; there was something in his eyes... something detached, something inhuman.

He pinned her to the floor, his bulk pushing her thighs apart.

Lily screamed, feeling his thick fingers around her arms, forcing her back to the ground. An arm now braced across her chest, his free hand tore at her dress and undergarments.

The Bear gulped, unsure what he should do.

Freddy appeared at the door. "Charlie! Jesus Christ, Charlie! Fasten your trahsers ap! You need to see this."

Freddy shoved a young girl into the room.

"Niamh!" Lily gasped.

"Lily!" Niamh cried, racing to Lily's side.

"Caught her in the kitchen, messing on with the stove, she was," Freddy declared.

The Bear looked relieved, as Charles' lust

seemed to be broken as he got to his feet, towering over Lily and Niamh, his face contorted in confusion.

"What were you doing in there, eh?" Charles barked.

Niamh shrugged. "Nothing, I swear to it!" she said.

"You leave her alone!" Lily shrieked, holding Niamh's head tightly to her breast, wishing she could spirit the child away.

"Shut it, you!" Charles leaned forward and shouted in Lily's face. "And do not fool yourself that I have finished with you, yet!"

"Yes you have," The Bear muttered.

"What was that, old chum?" Charles asked, teeth gritted, rotating his head to loosen the muscles in his neck and shoulders.

"I said, yes you bloody have! I didn't come out here wiv you to watch you try and rape girls! What the bloody hell is wrong wiv you?"

Freddy eyed Charles with disgust. "Charlie? What you thinkin', eh?"

Charles scratched at his bandaged hand and breathed heavily, his shoulders rising and falling, ready to burst out of his suit.

"You gone bloody mad, or what?" Freddy cried.

"Mad? I shall show you mad!" Charles said, rushing at Freddy.

Lily shrieked and held Niamh ever closer, wondering what fate would befall them at the hands of these bickering men.

The Bear grabbed Charles before he could reach Freddy and twisted, throwing him towards the fireplace.

Freddy drew a small club from inside his jacket. "Charlie, let us discuss this, eh?"

Charles reached into his jacket and pulled his revolver. "Like that, is it, Freddy?"

The Bear raised his hands and began to inch

closer to Charles. "Come on, old friend. This won't do us any good… Come on, now." The Bear was about six feet away from Charles. The revolver was still pointed at Freddy, who had backed away towards the door.

"Charlie, please, put that away," Freddy pleaded. "We are still friends. We need only make a plan. I mean, where is his wife? She hasn't noticed all this hammering on in her house. She must be out. Maybe she has gone to meet him. Maybe she has no idea he has even gone. She could be home any moment, with answers. Who knows? But we should find out."

"You know the Peelers hadn't the stomach for all that violence, Charles. They shan't take kindly to it any more now that you've left them… Let us put the bad buggers in jail, not join, them, eh?" The Bear said, keeping his voice as soft and calm as he could. He was four feet away and inching closer all the time.

The room was filled with the sound of breaking glass, as two cylindrical objects smashed through the windows and rolled across the floor, spewing a noxious fume as they went. It was at that second, when the glass shattered, that Charles discharged his revolver. The Bear had twisted to see the exploding windows, and the bullet glanced across his back, tearing his clothes and flesh, causing him to cry out in pain at the searing heat.

Charles was moving for the door, his left lapel and hand clamped over his mouth. He recognised the smell - chloroform.

Eighteen.

Upon arrival at the Blessing house, Mary leapt from the carriage and started up the steps to the house. Immediately as she reached the front door, she heard cries and shouting from within. She tried the handle, gently, not wanting to give away her presence. As she expected, the door was locked. She wondered if using her pick would draw unwanted attention from outside the house, or within.

She heard men shouting within. A woman pleading desperately. Mary knew there was not a moment to lose. She slipped off her shoes, dropped her bag and decided to investigate the rear of the terrace, hoping to gain access through the kitchen. Hitching up her skirts, she broke into a run, unimpeded by the awkward heels of her shoes, flitting from pavement to cobbled street to avoid passers-by who stared at her in disgust.

Wheeling round the corner at full tilt, she almost collided with a barrow-boy, but nimbly sprang onto his cart and vaulted over his shoulder, landing on the pavement with no loss of pace. She turned onto the lane behind the house and maintained her pace. She deduced the correct gate and was soon in the yard, then kitchen of the Blessing house. The men had evidently not anticipated an intruder from the less civilised side of the building.

Able to hear more clearly on this side of the front door, Mary made out more commotion in the parlour and the voice of a young girl. Were the men squabbling?

Mary turned her attention to the kitchen. She recalled from the notes that the doctor had used chloroform to subdue the beast. He had rigged up a mechanism to feed the vapour through the illuminating gas pipes at his laboratory – perhaps he had done the same in his own house. She reasoned then that the containers of chloroform would be kept near the oven and gas workings, rather than hidden in the study as the study was where the creature was concealed. It took her moments to discover, in the back of the lower part of the pantry, several large tin containers. She removed two and was soon hurtling down the lane, a container under each arm, fingers pinching her bunched skirts.

Outside the Blessing house, she threw all caution and care to the wind. She could hear the muttered scorn of the gentlefolk on the street, but this was not the time to consider her appearance and behaviour – this was the time to act!

She drew one of her daggers from her sleeves and deftly punched a hole into each tin, which she promptly drew up, one in each hand, and hurled at the parlour window.

The shattering glass caused a stir on the street; cries of "Vandal!" went up. Those who stepped forward to detain her thought better of it, when they saw Mary pick up her blade once more.

As she took to the steps she picked at her hair clips with her free hand, and collected four metal pins, which had each been secreted within the hollowed ends of the clips. Two of the pins were coated with curare, and their tips had been dipped in wax, to create a small section safe for Mary to touch. It was this wax portion she placed firmly between her lips. The remaining two pins had each a gutta-percha bladder at the end, which she placed between her lips. Within these hollow pins was her specially balanced blend of strychnine, chloral hydrate and sodium nitroprusside, dissolved in ethylene glycol.

She kicked her shoes and bag to one side, drew her second blade and readied herself as the lock turned and the front door opened.

The door opened and she recognised the man

from the clinic and coffee house immediately. Her punch was solid and stung his nose. Still clutching both blades, she jabbed his eyes with two extended fingers, slapped his left ear with the side of a blade and barged him aside.

His own momentum carried him staggering to the side. She knew that she had only seconds before he would recover and meet her in combat.

The second man, taller, thinner, he was prepared for her. Freddy grabbed her hair and yanked her close to him.

Big mistake, Mary thought. Her lips drew near to his neck. He shivered as her warm breath tickled his skin. She kissed his dirty flesh, but his pleasure was fleeting as the bite of the pins shocked him. A quick click of Mary's teeth ensured that the tiny bladders discharged their toxin and she stepped back. She thumped the handles of both blades against the side of his head as he yanked at the pins.

The man had managed to draw the poisoned darts from his skin, but it was too late. Mary knew that his blood pressure was already dropping, his limbs becoming unresponsive and nausea building in an unstoppable wave.

She turned towards the street and slashed with both blades, narrowly missing the first man's midriff.

"Fancy us meeting again like this," Mary said, cheerily.

In the reception, the second thug vomited violently and collapsed into a heap.

"He better not be dead, missy!" Charles boomed, levelling his revolver.

With a flick of her wrist, a blade streaked out at Charles, catching his upper arm as it twirled along its arc. The moment's distraction was enough to put Charles off his aim. The revolver barked to life, a bullet tore loose, past Mary, into the thigh of the poisoned Freddy, who lay prone on the floor, bubbles of vomit dribbling from his lips. The shock and pain of the bullet wound failed to register with the man, so deep was his sedation.

Mary twirled, turning her back to Charles momentarily as she reversed her grip on her remaining blade. This she thrust behind her, low, finding Charles' thigh. The blade bit deeply and Mary twisted away again, opening up a savage wound.

Charles dropped the revolver and clutched at his wound. As Mary darted for the parlour, she felt Charles's hands grabbing at her dress, his strength and her momentum pulling in opposite directions, tearing the material from around her waist.

In an instant, Mary slashed the material, abandoning the garment to prevent further entanglement. Those who had gathered on the street gasped in disgust as Mary returned to the stumbling Charles and, her stockings, garter belt, hidden weapons and undergarments fully exposed, she delivered a kick to his jaw with such force that he was snapped into unconsciousness. To a further gasp of horror, and she knew, gasps of feigned horror by some of the men who wished to hide their delight, Mary bent over to scoop up the discarded revolver and left Charles where he lay.

She was inside once more. The largest of the men, The Bear, leaned in the parlour doorway, gasping for air, tears streaming down his face, almost overcome by the chloroform. Between breaths, he cried for Freddy to get up. His eyes fell on the half-dressed woman before him.

Before he could say a word she drew back the hammer on the revolver and fired a round into his foot, sending him howling to the floor.

Mary took a deep breath and plunged into the room. Niamh lay unconscious with Lily, in the middle of the floor. Mary dragged them as close to the door as she could.

The Bear cried and howled, clutching his shattered, bloody foot. Mary pointed the tip of her blade inches from his face. "Gather yourself, and leave!"

"My bloody foot! I need a doctor!"

"A doctor lives here, but I shall assume you have chased him away. Now get out and leave these people alone!"

She heaved Freddy out onto the front step and locked the door, once she had gathered her bag, shoes and the discarded blade from the steps. She pulled Niamh and Lily out of the parlour, clear of the vapour, which was fully discharged from the tins, and which was dissipating in the draught from the broken windows.

Mary detached her garter belt arsenal and concealed it in her bag. From that bag she produced a vial of pungent smelling salts, which, once waved under the noses of the two unconscious, newly rescued maidens, effected an almost immediate recovery.

"I feel that I owe you a debt I can never repay," Lily gushed, taking in her tattered saviour. "Follow me upstairs, please! I am worried that the lady of the house has fallen to some harm. They said she was out, but I have not seen her all day – I took her to be in bed. She has been terribly unwell lately."

Mary thanked her and followed the maid. "Those men have made quite the mess, have they not?" she said, nodding to the battered study door.

"Indeed. Thank goodness George escaped when he did."

"I wonder why he felt he should escape, and abandon you, and his wife?" Mary asked.

Lily led Mary into the master bedroom. The door was closed and locked. "Thank God they did not make it this far," Lily muttered. "There must be a key somewhere."

Mary produced her pick and within seconds had released the lock. Lily opened the door and let out a sharp gasp, her legs buckling. She almost slipped back into unconsciousness again.

Mary saw immediately the drained body of Margaret Blessing and turned instinctively to grasp the child, steering her away from the bedroom. “You should not see this, child.”

“What is it?” Niamh cried, muffled by Mary’s embrace. “What is it? What has happened?”

“Something terrible.”

“Is Mrs Blessing all right?”

“No, child. She is not all right at all.”

Nineteen.

Panacea was unwell. Our flight had upset her. I could hear the vixen screams in my brain as she supplicated for some drops of tenderness, some care. Bracing my legs and holding the fractured bell-jar on my lap, I twisted the glass lid free. Reaching into the lukewarm fluid, my fingers slid over her skin.

Her slits of nostrils sniffed at me. Oh, this is it, I thought! She means to drain me! I cradled her as one would an infant, keeping her head away from my injured shoulder. Holding her to my breast with one arm, I placed the jar on the floor of the cab. My fingers slid up her spine and across her ribcage. I leaned back and inspected her. She was weak.

I could not let her just die! Killed by some animal!

I offered her my wounded shoulder and braced myself. This is it, George! You had a good run, but you connived and slew to keep this creature alive and now she slays you! Any fear for my own safety was swiftly overcome by the urge to protect her.

Her lips peeled back and I felt the icy tongue scrape across my flesh. She knew the taste of this blood; she had sampled small amounts before. I had teased her with it, these three years, giving her just enough to survive. I noticed a small, bleeding wound on her head, no doubt caused by the same impact that cracked the jar.

Her lips formed a seal over my skin, and the needle teeth bit in, dozens of them at once, clamping down – then further in, working their way deeper.

"There, there, girl," I said, rocking her back and forth, cradling her tighter and tighter as the wound began to throb. "Shhhhhhh," I soothed.

Somewhere in my brain I heard the sound returning to me, "Shhhhhhh."

I looked down at my child and felt the needles withdraw, my wound numbed. Her saliva formed pink webs as her mouth disengaged. She rubbed her head into my shoulder, pressing her own blood against mine as she nestled into me.

Her control – her discipline... Astounding. To be so weakened but to show such restraint... I wondered if even I was capable of such composure any more. I felt immediately both proud of my daughter and ashamed that my own self-control had declined beneath the level of a mere child. I wondered if the gas was necessary any more, to bring her under control.

Miraculously, the numbness of my wound was replaced by a warm throbbing and I could see the blood coagulating in the cut even as I watched.

"You truly are remarkable, my darling," I whispered and clutched her to my chest, sharing my warmth with her. We rested together on our journey. The roads of London had been slow, choked with travellers. On three occasions I had been forced to hide the child and change transport. Drivers were fearful of longer trips, in case the passenger refused to pay. The hiding and waiting had slowed matters somewhat.

The sun was all but set and the chill of the night bit into us, exposed as we were in the last hansom cab. I wrapped her in my tatty jacket and huddled down with her. "Soon, we will be there, my dear," I whispered to her. "We are almost safe."

Twenty.

"What do I need you useless bastards for, eh?" Charles boomed at The Bear. He glanced at his hands, which were soaked in a mixture of bloods - his own, The Bear's and Freddy's. The tattered bandage on his hand was stained bright red.

The Bear narrowed his eyes at Charles and continued limping along the pavement, dragging Freddy's unconscious frame. "Never mind that, give us a hand with Freddy, eh?"

Charles sucked his fingers one by one then yelled, "A woman! All of us beaten by a woman."

The Bear lowered Freddy to the ground and straightened up. "Listen, Charles," he growled, "I'm not carrying on with this. That was no normal woman. Lord only knows what unholy business you've got me into, but that woman beat three of us in less than a minute."

"I know that!" Charles snapped, before running his tongue over his palms in two quick, unconscious movements.

"Well, look at Freddy. What help is he going to be now, eh?" The Bear asked, tapping a foot against Freddy's rump. "Well, you can forget about me following you. You're on your own now."

"Is that it, then?" Charles asked, squaring up to his old friend.

"How common," a woman remarked to her husband as they passed, having observed the blood leaking from each of the men, and the gruesome trail they had left in their wake.

"Shhh, dear. Let them go about their business in peace," her husband chided, knowing that either one of these men alone looked strong enough to pick him up and throw him away like a doll.

"That's it, Charles. Without your gun you should think twice about laying hands on me. I would not enjoy it, but my word on it, I would dash your brains out on the pavement and take my chances."

Charles felt the ache in his back from the fall and the burning sensation in his hand, beneath the bandage. His jaw hurt like hell, his leg was leaking blood, but his forehead was no longer bleeding freely. He was surprised at how quickly the wound had scabbed over. Nevertheless, he had to consider, was his collection of injuries worse than The Bear's shattered and bleeding foot? It certainly seemed to be hindering him very little, even though, when Charles glanced at The Bear's burst right boot, he guessed that at least one toe had been severed.

"All right, then, Mister Bear. Have it your way. You and that drunken pig can bleed to death here on the street for all I care." Charles stormed off in the opposite direction, pressing a hand against his slashed thigh, hoping to find a doctor before he blacked out.

He managed to hail a cab, eventually, as several drivers refused to pick him up in his injured state. The driver knew of a doctor nearby and drove Charles to his house. The same house he had raided less than an hour earlier. "Find another! Another!"

The driver managed to locate a doctor's surgery only a few minutes away. Charles limped into the building and through the reception, past two sickly children with their mother, and a young man in the butcher's apron with a crimson towel wrapped around his bloody fingers.

Nobody protested as Charles barged into the consulting room. Something about him gave off an air that he was not to be trifled with.

The doctor cried out in alarm, "You may not simply barge into my office, sir! I am with a patient, and have other patients waiting!"

A terrified young woman was huddling away in the corner of the room, hoping that this madman would not harm her.

"You'll tend to me, doctor!" Charles demanded, cuffing the man across the jaw. "You'll tend to my leg now!"

The doctor rubbed at his jaw and looked at the woman in the corner with a look of apology in his beady eyes. "All right then. All right!"

The doctor had doused Charles' open leg wound with a liberal amount of Lugol's iodine, disinfecting the cut. With cotton swabs he cleaned the area, spreading a reddish-brown stain around Charles' thigh.

Charles had braced himself for agonising, stinging pain when the iodine was introduced to his wound, but he was surprised to feel very little pain at all. His bitten hand itched, however, to a maddening degree. He clawed at the bandage while the doctor stitched up the leg wound.

As the practitioner plied his trade, and Charles scratched at the small, scabbed puncture marks in his hand, he wondered at Blessing's flight. Where had he left to hide?

Surely he would not be so bold as to return to the Burton household? No, surely not, Charles thought. Not when he knows I would almost certainly catch him there. Charles reached into his jacket pocket and produced a small notebook. He leafed through the pages. Friends, friends, friends… Father Haddon, vanished. The accountant, Francis Flanders and the crooked art dealer Edward Summerscale. An address was written on the small page – Flanders' domicile was known to him, but Summerscale lived God knows where. Mrs Burton had lost track of his movements over the years.

"Hurry, Doctor! Hurry about your business and I shall be sure to set about mine!" Charles urged the older man. He thought about his two 'friends': damn those cowards, those drunk cowards! I shall end this the way I started it! Alone – for it seems Blessing has but two friends in this world who may be able to help him and though I know the whereabouts of only one, it is with him I will find Blessing, or find the location of the other, and from either I will certainly find my man!

Francis Flanders, the accountant who handled all of Mrs Burton's financial affairs, was a mutual acquaintance of her late husband, and Blessing. Indeed, he believed that Flanders and Blessing had eaten together two nights hence.

Once more Charles found himself in a cab as the sun began its descent into the choking muck of the city. He hoped to catch Flanders at his office. Flanders was known to be a fastidious timekeeper and would not leave his desk until after five O' clock.

Charles bounded up the steps off the street and burst into the office. The gloom of the dusty office was permeated only by a few candles scattered here and there. Four men were hunched over their books, but quickly turned to face him, wondering at the sudden draught caused by his entry.

"Where can I find Francis Flanders?" Charles barked.

The oldest of the four men squinted, trying to make out if he recognised Charles. "And you are?"

"Never mind who I am, you silly old bugger! Where is he?"

One of the younger accountants rose to his feet. This man's tight-fitting suit belied a sound physical condition and the promise of a good struggle. "A bit strong, don't you think?" he said, determination in both his voice and his eyes.

"Tell me where he is and I will leave you in peace."

"He has gone to meet a very important client. Now if you don't mind," the young accountant said, issuing a dismissive wave, flicking two fingers towards the door.

Charles pounced and grabbed the same two fingers, twisting, turning the young man's hand and arm over, pinning him to his desk. The other men cried out in protest as books and papers were upset. “Tell me where he is, whelp!”

“Mrs Burton! The clinic! The fire!”

“Fire? I’ll give you a fire!” Charles exerted more force and heard the fingers snap. He pushed the young man over onto his desk, howling in agony and clutching his broken fingers. Charles knocked a candle over onto a rough stack of papers and watched as the leaves curled and blackened, bursting into flames. “There’s a fire for you. Bastards!”

He was on the street again, yelling at the driver, “Poland Street, now!”

Twenty-one.

Having ushered Lily away to the study with Niamh, it had taken Mary mere moments to inspect Margaret Blessing's corpse. Margaret's wide eyes spoke of her terror and reddish purple marks around her jaw and upper lip told of a restraint over her mouth as she was murdered. This explained to Mary why Margaret's mouth was closed and not wide open mid-scream.

She had been drained. Of course, it was almost impossible for a body to be *completely* drained; that was just an expression. It was possible and likely, however, that the creature had drawn up to nine pints of blood from her victim. *Its victim,* Mary corrected her thoughts. No good thinking like Dr Blessing, she thought, the creature is a *thing* and an evil thing at that.

Mary noted that Margaret was in her nightgown, and the puncture wounds on her inner thigh made her shudder as she realised that the creature had possibly been hiding in the bed, or had manipulated the doctor into releasing it under the covers. A horrible way for anybody to die, Mary considered, but one she was only too familiar with.

Being, by De Omori standards, *drained* and there not having been left with sufficient quantity of the vehicle with which to carry the venom around her body, Mary knew that Margaret was truly dead. There was no indication that Margaret had consumed blood following her bite anyway, so on the strength of both of these factors, Mary knew that driving a stake into Margaret's chest, or to sever her head was both pointless and an indignity too far for this poor woman.

The only consolation Mary could think of was that shortly after the initial shock of the attack, the creature would probably have drawn a pint from her. Soon after this, Margaret would have lost consciousness, rendering her completely vulnerable to the creature.

The bite pattern showed that the creature had taken several holds of her, showing desperation or frenzy. This had been a hungry animal. Mary had no doubt that death had taken Margaret very swiftly.

Mary joined the others in the study and gestured to the heap of clothing on the floor. "He is on the move. He is moving fast and light. He means not to be caught and those thugs who attacked you, well, they mean to catch him."

"Or worse," Lily added ominously. "I can tell you he has two friends. An accountant here in London, Mr Flanders, Francis Flanders and another man called Mr Summerscale. I think he is called Edward Summerscale but I am unsure where he lives."

Niamh knelt by the clothes and clutched them close to her face, stroking her cheek with the sleeve of the discarded white shirt. "You are right. He is going to see Mr Summerscale. I know he is heading out to Richmond Upon Thames. He said so," Niamh sobbed.

Lily rested a hand on the child's head and stroked her hair. "Then you have saved Miss Brigham some time and trouble, then. Haven't you?"

"He made me swear not to tell!" Niamh cried.

Mary bent to Niamh and joined Lily in soothing tone and placating hands. "Don't worry a bit. I'll have him safe and sound before you know it. This has all been a terrible misunderstanding."

"But Mrs Blessing is..."

"I know, child. I know. And that is why it is all the more important that I find Dr Blessing," Mary reasoned.

"It wasn't him! It was that... thing he takes care of. It has poisoned his mind! It tells him to do things."

Lily cooed and soothed Niamh, or tried to, and looked at Mary with a half-puzzled, half-apologetic look on her face.

"I know the thing you speak of, child," Mary stated, looking the child in the eyes. Her tone had changed; she spoke to Niamh as an equal, assuring her that she was believed.

"What is this you speak of?" Lily cried. "A *thing*? What thing?"

"It would be difficult for me to explain to you in such a short span of time – I must away to bring this matter to a close as soon as possible. Suffice it to say that within this very house, feet away from you, a dark, nightmarish creature has hidden. It has controlled the good doctor, I suspect his wife, and has possibly had a hold on your own mind."

"Impossible!" Lily protested.

"I realise that it must sound so," Mary said, picking up the book Blessing had been reading. "When I am gone, see if this book would convince you otherwise."

Lily was barely literate. Mrs Blessing had been teaching her to read, but her progress had been slow. She chose not to share this with Mary and Niamh, remaining silent even though she could not for a moment imagine what they were saying to be true.

Mary took the seat usually occupied by Blessing at his desk. She searched the desk drawers and found a small address book. Flicking through the pages, she quickly found a Richmond address for Summerscale.

Mary stood once more and motioned for Lily to join her on the landing. She spoke in hushed tones and informed her, "I can only hope that Mrs Burton's man will go for the closest option to home, and track Mr Flanders. I have to collect some items from my hotel room and I will fly to Richmond. I promise you, I will do my utmost to reach Dr Blessing first, and to try to save him. This child needs him, he is the closest to a father she has… and now with no mother…"

"I will keep her with me, Miss Brigham, I swear it. I shall try to find a way to prevent her from going back to the streets."

"Before I leave I have a request. It would seem rather… indelicate."

Before very long Mary was once more striding across the lobby of the Seraphim, wearing a blue dress formerly worn by Margaret Blessing. Margaret had been a slight woman and the fit was close to Mary's size. Taking the dress had seemed improper, but it had been the only apparent solution – Mary could not have travelled in her own tattered dress.

Before leaving, Mary was sure to give Lily instructions to inform the police only after another hour, to give her a head start. She said to avoid the subject of Blessing's flight to Richmond, and to give no details of her involvement at all. Mary had no time to give a detailed cover story, and no time to involve her masters at De Omori who might have smoothed things over with the authorities. Mary could not afford to become embroiled in such matters.

"Excuse me, Miss," came a voice from by the reception desk.

Mary turned to see the porter who had previously produced Blessing's address for her. "Ah, yes?" Mary hid her impatience as best she could.

"Were you able to find the doctor earlier?" the porter asked.

"Oh yes, thank you. Your directions were perfect. Allow me to find you something for your trouble…" she trailed off as she searched her bag for a penny or two.

"Oh, ma'am, no trouble at all. I was just thinking, what with seeing you there, like, if you hadn't found Doctor Blessing, the other doctor is here. Doctor McEwan."

Upon the sound of the name, Mary turned to find standing next to her, her mentor, her ally, her love. "You!" she gasped.

"Mary. We need to talk."

"I haven't much time," Mary urged.

"Your room?" McEwan offered.

"All right," Mary sighed, despairing at the delay.

Once in the safety of her room, Mary took out her largest case, opened it on the bed and selected a few weapons and other items of use, placing them in her bag.

"Preparing for war, Mary?" McEwan asked.

"Something like that. What are you doing here, Owen, anyway?" she asked, curtly.

"I had my doubts that this case would be straightforward. I read the notes you left here in your room. It would seem that my doubts had foundation. This doctor has been carrying out unsanctioned experiments with *the blood*."

"He has stumbled onto knowledge it took De Omori decades – *centuries* – to discover!" Mary snapped.

"Mary, you seem to be distressed. Whatever is it?" McEwan reached out for her. She recoiled.

"Shall we leave that to Paris? And memory. If even that."

McEwan stepped back, his eyes betraying his shock. "I am sorry, Mary. It was not my intention to… confuse matters."

"You know the rules. We are not meant to be together. They *know*. That is why they want *you* on The Island. And that is why they want *me* here."

"Dead, Mary? Is that what you think they want? *That* is why they sent me here, to watch over you from afar. But something unforeseen has occurred, do you not see? This laboratory – the laboratory where this Doctor Blessing has been experimenting – the place that you discovered, do you know that infected rats and all sorts have been streaming out of the place all afternoon? The bites and wounds inflicted, if not checked properly, could cause a vampiric incident the likes of which has never been seen! Imagine: London, tearing itself apart!"

"I have *my* mission. You have yours," Mary said, snapping the fastener closed on her bag.

"They are the same mission, Mary," McEwan reasoned. "Limiting the damage of this mad doctor."

"He is not mad! He is a victim, Owen. A pawn! That creature has him enthralled. I must – I *must* save him," Mary urged. "I have no time to lose. There is another man, a true madman, who is chasing him. If he gets to Blessing first, then he will kill him."

McEwan pinched the bridge of his nose and sighed, exasperated. "You have to listen to me. This is more important. We must prevent this epidemic."

"Is that an order?" Mary snarled, her eyes blazing, defiant.

"No. I can't order you, Mary. My Black Mary."

"Don't call me that."

"Mary, I beg you. Do not go alone. I fear some harm will come to you. I think you might die. Help me to manage the situation here in London first, and then we shall see if we can help this doctor."

"Have you heard nothing I have said, Owen? He will be dead. And the crime of it is that the creature will probably survive, to enthral another. And what then? The trail will go cold until God knows how many more innocents will die. I will have none of it. I will fight for every last one."

"Except everyone in London," McEwan snapped.

"That is *your* mission. If you need help, then send De Omori a message to request it. Get them off their bloody arses on that island and down here. In fact, why don't they contact Parliament to declare an emergency?"

McEwan walked to the window, shaking his head, his hands pressed against his face. "Oh, why do they not simply put up a sign reading: De Omori, vampire hunters, this way!"

"You can't stop me from saving him. I have to go now. You should not have come for me. You should have gone to The Island."

"I came for you anyway! I came for them! I came for me!" McEwan said, turning on his heels to face her. "I came here because I love you and the thought of never seeing you again frightens me more than anything I have ever faced."

The words stung her bitterly, and she longed to throw down her bag and run to his arms, but Mary grasped the door handle instead. "Then be careful," she said, "I shall return to help you as soon as I can."

With that, Mary left her room and left the Seraphim. She decided to take her chance with a coach and horses for the journey, rather than take a hansom cab to the train station and then possibly wait hours for the next train. With the sunset upon her, her coach fought through the crowded roads until she reached the outskirts of London, after which the roads became quieter, and the team of horses were able to thunder freely along the road.

Twenty-two.

I was awoken from my slumber by the driver, who had brought the cab to a halt. "Richmond Green," he announced.

As my eyes adjusted to the darkness of the late evening, I could feel Panacea's icy flesh under my coat. I jostled her a little and felt a slight movement in response as well as a grinding disapproval sent directly into my brain. My blood had sustained her thus far, but I could feel her hunger. She needed to feed fully in order to restore her strength. I leapt from the cab, abandoning my remaining jars of curiosities and ran pell-mell into the darkness of the green.

The driver gave chase, both of us sliding on the damp grass. I stuck out my elbows and sprang forward, with back arched, my child safely fastened in the hollow of my body as I lay prone.

"You thieving bastard! I should have known the look of you, you were no good!" the driver spat, kicking my backside. "Having me drive you all the way out here and you about to do me out of a fare? Thieving bastard!"

"Wait, stop, listen to me," I protested, feigning to wretch and convulse as if suddenly overcome by nausea or apoplexy, "listen to me! I am not a well man! I am not trying to rob you!"

The driver crouched beside me and muttered, "What in Christ's name is wrong with you?"

I glanced ahead and could see nobody in the gloom. I took my chance and rolled onto my back. The man's eyes grew suddenly wide as I opened my coat and allowed him to see the child.

She was ready for him, and sprang forwards as the driver drew breath to scream. As soon as her weight shifted from me, I tackled him to the grass and pressed my hands down over his mouth not a moment too soon, stifling his scream into a horrible, muffled moan. I pressed my weight down on his head and curled my legs and body around him as he kicked and clawed.

His struggles intensified suddenly and I knew that he could feel those icy teeth biting into him. He writhed from side to side, his fingers clawing at my face. I could taste the muck on his fingers as I bit them. His head was coming away from me as he tried to turn his body over, but I twisted with him, rendering his escape impossible. He gasped a lungful of air and I chuckled as I removed a hand from his face and struck his throat, once, twice, thrice. His tongue made a curious clicking sound.

In my mind I was transported to the bed, pinning Margaret down, seeing the look of betrayal in her eyes. My grip on the driver began to slip.

Panacea must have sensed my wavering motivation. Immediately, my skull felt as thought it was shrinking. Margaret was forced out of my brain. Panacea needed more, I could sense it. Her will played through my mind like a pianist's fingers. She wanted greater commitment, needed purer devotion. I had killed for her. I had killed with her... She wanted me to kill *like* her.

"You there!" I heard from the footpath nearby. There, a couple had been walking across the green. Our fight had alarmed them.

"Help! He is murdering me!" I cried.

The man raced towards me as I felt the driver's struggles subside. I knew she could manage him from here.

"What the Devil?" the man gasped, his eyes falling immediately on the small white creature attached to the driver's neck.

I rolled and smacked my elbow against his knee, hard. He yelped and staggered back as I got to my feet and threw my weight into him. Sprawled on the ground and in shock, I was on him immediately, landing a right jab on his jaw. I heard teeth *clack* together violently. I brought both of my fists down on his nose and eyes, twice, three times, four!

Oh, to fight like this! To fight for survival, for the protection of my child! I had never before experienced anything like it. I trod over him as I chased his woman, bursting into speed I had never exhibited before. I tore her dress as I dragged her to the ground. I cuffed her jaw and she stopped screaming. I beat her head against a tree until she was unconscious. My eyes did not recognise her as an attractive, delicate woman, I saw her as the enemy. She could bring about the end of Panacea!

When I dragged my victim back to the child, she had already abandoned the driver and was feeding on the stroller. A part of me knew that I should stop her, that she was growing too rapidly, both in stature and in her psychical ability. I knew that I had already lost control. I could hear her contented sucking and purring. She sent ripples of pleasure throughout my mind and I served her the woman. Oh, to watch her feed! To see her thrive!

What is this you have awakened in me, daughter? I pondered, my chest heaving with exertion and anticipation as the needles sank into that equine neck. This stranger's legs, her exquisite legs, twitched as the life was drawn from her.

Crouching on the grass I reached out and touched her ankle. Her calf. Her thigh. Dare I press on, I thought to myself.

I crawled over her body, my face inches away from my child's torso. The child worked from the throat, down to the breast and bit down once more, drinking deeply. I licked my lips and before I knew it, my mouth was at the savaged neck, tongue lapping this stranger's vital fluid. The metallic taste of blood filled my mouth. I had no desire to *drink* it, I wanted to *experi-*

ence it! Taste what she tastes, feel what she feels. I sucked and sucked and gulped until the woman's life fluid was no longer spurting into my mouth. I knew that she was dead. I drank another gulp to see what that was like – drinking the blood of a *dead* woman.

Our hungers sated, I sat upright and cradled the child once more. I laughed and wept all at once. My head shook from side to side and then nodded, next moment my head rolled forwards and then aside drunkenly. My tongue hung loose one moment, then squeezed behind my clenched teeth the next.

I knew one thing: By God, my body does not know what to do!

And there we sat, on the green in Richmond Upon Thames, for God knows how many minutes, until it was clear to both of us that we had to move on, lest we be caught here.

Panacea twisted in my arms, her mouth open, reaching for my jaw. Her tongue snaked outward, sliding across my flesh, lapping at the core that had accumulated on my face. Like a cat at a bowl of milk, she worked her tongue over me, cleaning my face in case I was encountered by another as we made progress.

Clever Panacea, I thought, stroking her back as she worked.

I dragged the bodies as close to the cab as I dared, then took down my sack of curios. After wrapping the child in the sack and leaving her hidden in shrubbery beneath a tree, I loaded the bodies onto the cab and drove to the riverside. Three corpses, bloodless, thrown into the river. I could see Burton, Haddon and Margaret in the murk too, staring back at me with unnatural, pure-white eyes.

How many more would join them? How many more innocents would lose their lives? I could not pretend to care. At that moment, I thought, as I stared into the black water, lots more. I do so hope it is lots more.

Twenty-three.

Charles leapt from the cab, never stopping to pay the driver as he pushed and jostled his way along through the crowd. The Poland Street Hospital was a husk. The London Fire Engine Establishment had taken over in force, with one horse-drawn and three man-pulled engines at the scene. Ash and soot snowed down on the street and the hundreds of people gathered there. London's foul air was particularly gloomy over Poland Street as the cloud of smoke hanging over the street blotted out the orange sunset, casting those gathered in an artificial twilight.

Charles could see that the buildings that neighboured the hospital had been burning for some time. The firemen had taken to dampening the adjoining buildings along the street to try to prevent any further spread, as the buildings already burning were clearly beyond salvation. He could see that their technique was effective, the flames had nowhere else to go and the ordeal was almost over.

At the end of the street he could see Charlotte Burton crying and shaking her head in disbelief. A well-dressed, academic-looking man who he immediately took to be Francis Flanders, offered solace and held Charlotte, trying to soothe her with his words as a severe-looking man in full fireman uniform offered words of consolation.

As Charles drew near he heard Flanders say, "Thank you for your kind words, Firemaster Braidwood. As you can see, Mrs Burton's grief is so great that I doubt she will make sense of this until much later."

"A grand and noble enterprise has gone to waste," Braidwood said. He added, "However such instances can be expected with some of the undesirable characters that this establishment attracted."

"Poor George," Charlotte sniffled.

"Poor George!" Charles boomed, startling the small gathering. "Poor George! It was your Poor George who struck the match!"

"Who is this... man? Do you know him?" Braidwood asked.

"I do, he is an associate of mine," Charlotte responded.

Charles turned to the Firemaster and snarled, "Had you not better tend to that fire? Sooner you get it put out, the sooner you can get yourself to that accountant's office that went up in smoke."

"What?" Flanders cried as Firemaster Braidwood left them, disgusted at this newcomer's blood-caked attire, and shocked that either Mr Flanders or Mrs Burton would be associated with him.

"Yes, Mr Flanders. Terrible accident. One of your lads done himself a mischief and lit the place up," Charles enjoyed the look of terror on the other man's face, even though he knew the four men in the office would have easily stifled the flames without the need of more than a jug of water. At least, if they had acted quickly enough, he reasoned.

"Who is this man, Charlotte?" Flanders asked, horrified by the bloodstained thug before him.

"Charles, you are being highly improper. Particularly when you are paid to represent me and my interests," Charlotte reproached him, managing to control her sobs. "From what I gather you have left a trail of destruction in your wake this day and have harried people I know and love under the guise of duty to me."

"Mrs Burton, now you must listen," Charles began. "I have uncovered a monstrous conspiracy involving your Doctor Blessing."

"I will hear no more of it, Charles! I just want everything back as it was! The hospital, poor, terrified George-"

Charles interrupted, "And Henry! Back from the dead, eh?"

Charlotte moaned in pain at the sudden attack of Charles' spiteful tongue.

"This is terribly inappropriate, sir!" Flanders protested, turning his shoulder, trying to shield Charlotte from this ruffian.

"Inappropriate? I have discovered a murderer! Henry Burton's murderer. I am close to bringing him to justice, you buffoon! And since I can see that you have been otherwise occupied, I can assume that you do not harbour him."

"What is this madman talking about, Charlotte?" Flanders groaned, trying to usher her away.

Charles struck out with the hand covered in tattered bandage. He felt hot blood throbbing through his head and a rage burning within him, sudden, uncontrollable. His blow struck Flanders on the back of the neck, knocking him against Charlotte's profile. She staggered and Flanders managed to help her maintain her balance.

Flanders turned to face Charles, rearing up to his full height, which was only three inches shorter than Charles, but his frame was slight. Equally apparent to Charles was Flanders' lack of fighting ability.

The accountant lashed out with an open hand, delivering a stinging slap to Charles' nose.

Charles responded with a blow to Flanders' midriff, before rolling his shoulders, stepping in and hitting him with a left in the same spot. The first blow doubled the accountant over; the second knocked him to the floor. He kicked Flanders savagely as Charlotte protested and clawed at him.

"Stop this madness, Charles! You are dismissed! You have overstepped the boundaries of decency, you disgrace!" she cried, mortified as the nearby crowd of onlookers turned their attention from the fire and started to watch them.

Charles crouched down, ignoring Charlotte, and grabbed Flanders by his hair. "I want you to tell me where that crook is, the art dealer."

"Who, Edward?" Flanders sobbed, trying to catch his breath.

"Yes. Edward Summerscale. I want to know where he lives."

Flanders hesitated until Charles raised a fist to strike him again. "All right!" Flanders cried. "All right! Just leave us and go about your business. He holds a house in Richmond Upon Thames near the end of King Street. He should be easy to find."

"He had better be," Charles snarled, pressing his nose into Flanders' face. "Or I shall be back for you."

Twenty-four.

Looking back at London with eyes half-closed, the haze of filth that rose from the city could easily look like smoke, Mary thought. The whole city on fire. It would not be the first time, she thought.

Her temper had subsided on her ride out of the city and she was able to think more clearly. It did not take one of the telepathy teachers at the school to suggest that the lust she felt for Doctor Blessing was a simple matter of displacement and distraction of her feelings and frustrations for Owen. Both doctors, both of them attractive, but there was something that set them apart.

Blessing was normal.

Doctor McEwan had killed for De Omori, had killed to order.

Blessing had killed because he was a victim, under the spell of one of the most deadly creatures alive. He was innocent. Innocent and normal.

So which was safer for her?

To live with a normal man, one had to be normal, surely?

And, being something other than normal she was destined to live an abnormal life. With abnormal people. Mary pondered this as the team of horses pressed on along the road at pace. She liked the word unconventional. Abnormal sounded like she should be encased in glass and placed in a museum, or prodded at by doctors.

She allowed herself a chuckle. When she was not thinking about killing creatures of the night, all she did seem to think about was being prodded at by at least two doctors she knew.

Mary sighed and thought, remember your training. Put everything back in its compartment. She knew that everything she had said to Lily and Niamh was a lie. Not with regard to saving Doctor Blessing, but she had no intention of delivering him home. If she could have that man to herself, she would. And she would finally be free of the spell Owen had over her. He could go back to The Island. He could go and teach new students. Or he could die trying to save London from his imaginary outbreak of vampires.

Mary allowed herself a rest with her eyes closed and tried to silence her thoughts. Breathing deeply, purging her mind, she found balance. She desired them both, for different reasons. Blessing was a gentle kind of man she could get to grow old with. Owen was a mysterious kind of man she would have to grow old in front of.

"Almost there, Miss," the driver called.

Black Mary opened her eyes to see the lights of Richmond along the road ahead.

Twenty-five.

After collecting the child, who lay shivering in the night air, and my collection of jars from the damp, chilly grass of Richmond Green, I made my way to the southern tip of the park. I looked about me to get my bearings and could see the lights and hear the throng of patrons of the Cricketers public house. Henry, Edward and I had taken a good drink there not long after it was rebuilt. The original building had burned down in the 1840s. Were it not for the presence of the child, I might have taken a beer or gin there again.

I cut down Paved Court and onto King Street, where Edward rented a house. He was not difficult to find, and it was evident that he was home, or at least, someone was in his home. I can not imagine for a minute that Edward was liked or respected by his neighbours. Fortunately a closed shop took up the property to his left, but a well-to-do family clearly lived in the large house to his right.

Singing and piano music rang out into the night and couples courted on the steps immediately outside his front door. I watched with disgust as a woman leaned against the pilaster of the entrance as her suitor vigorously rubbed her sex beneath her hitched skirts. Her hand was equally vigorous, occupied as it was, in his trousers. The house sounded full and I feared that the child safely ensconced within my coat would not remain hidden for very long.

I had no option but to proceed as planned and pushed past the couple and into the reception of Edward Summerscale's home. Panacea squirmed against my body, unaccustomed as she was to such noise, so many voices and, I would have wagered, so many scents.

Here two women were kissing and caressing, there two men, here another couple groping feverishly, there a woman with her tongue protruding from her lips, for it to be licked by two doting men. I thought for a moment I had walked through a door into an orgy in the time of the emperor Caligula!

The revellers seemed not to notice the stranger in their midst as I followed the sound of the piano into the parlour.

A squeak issued forth from my coat. Although I heard it, I knew that others nearby had not.

"Edward!" I called, seeing my old friend stood by the piano, patting another man on the back as he played.

Another squeak, louder, more despairing. Two revellers looked at me and frowned.

"Edward!" I called, pushing my way through the tangle of well-dressed socialites and shabbily dressed artists.

A prolonged squeak and a shorter echo sounded. Others in the room detected the noise and traced it back to me as easily as they would have located a shattered window. I ignored them, knowing the child to be in distress. I pressed her closer to my body, willing her to close her auditory canals. I hunched over slightly and rocked gently as I stepped further into the room. "Excuse me... excuse me there," I said, stepping over the legs of those leaning against the walls and furniture.

A low squeal rose and rose. I could feel the webbed fingers and curved claws writhing against my flesh. "Edward!" I cried.

The squeal increased in volume until it could be heard over the piano. The player stopped. All eyes were on me. There was a horrifying moment of silence, achingly long, accusingly empty.

"What was that noise?" people gasped, finally free of their shock. They shook their heads, both in dismay and in an attempt to shake off the disturbance the sound had caused them.

I saw a man dab at his bleeding nose with a handkerchief.

Edward was looking straight at me, but had no idea who I was. His blank eyes regarded me a stranger. “George! My God!” Edward boomed, finally recognising me without my customary attire, moustache and hair. He approached me, arms raised in welcome. He embraced me, but paused when he noted that I clutched my body tightly, not returning his gesture. “Is something wrong, old friend?” he whispered.

“I need to talk to you… in private.”

“All right, go straight up the stairs, to the second floor. I shall join you in a moment,” Edward said, keeping his voice low as the twenty or so others in the room began to chatter among themselves. Edward turned to address his guests with arms spread wide, and announced, “This is George, a new discovery of mine from Soho! He has decided to join us for the party. He needs to freshen up from his tiresome ride, however. We will return presently! Benjamin, the music, if you will! Something we can sing to!”

I was out of the room before Edward had finished his announcement and as per his instructions, had pushed up the stairs, onwards past more drunken, lust-filled revellers. How clever he was, upon noticing my condition, to assume that something grave was at hand, and to introduce me as George, without surname or title.

Edward caught up to me at the top of the stairs, unlocked his bedroom and ushered me in. He lit an oil lamp on his dresser and set it on a small desk. He offered me the seat at his desk, and I was grateful for it. I maintained my support of the child and rocked her. Away from the clamour of the party, she had settled somewhat. Again in my head I could hear her reflecting my soothing tone from earlier, “Shhhhhhh. Shhhhhhh.”

Edward’s face was caught somewhere between pleasure and concern as he said, “George, I wish I had known you were coming."

"I'm sorry. I should have sent word in advance."

"No," he said, patting my shoulder, which was now thankfully completely healed. His fingers found the tear in the material and he glanced at it, puzzled. "Not at all, George. I simply mean that I could have prepared something for your arrival. This is just a gathering of a few friends. You are more than welcome to it."

I chuckled at the idea that Edward considered this to be a gathering of a few friends. He strove to integrate his poor artists into high society, hoping to find wealthy patrons for them. He maintained that the artist, musician and actor were underprivileged and a society who sought their wares often treated the artists themselves with scorn. Why that meant they all had to get drunk at his house and commence to fornicate all over the place was beyond my grasp, but then I remembered who this was before me. And why I had come to see him.

"I am in terrible trouble, Edward," I sobbed.

"I did assume that, what with your drastic change in appearance. What sort of trouble?" he asked, without a pause or waver in his voice.

"I am a wanted man. At least I think I am," I replied.

"Wanted? By whom? Surely not the constabulary?"

I shrugged. "This man. This bloody man, Charles someone-or-other. He has hounded me these past two days."

"But I ate with you just the other night," Edward said. "Why did you say nothing to me then?"

"It was next morning that it all became clear to me. And there is a woman who seems to know something about me..." I trailed off trying to make sense of it all and what I could tell Edward.

"George, forgive me, but this is difficult for me to understand." Edward stroked his moustache and grasped my shoulder, squeezing me in encouragement. "Now look, you are talking to me. Eddie. You can tell me anything."

"The widow Burton… she has sent someone after me."

"Charlotte? But why would she do that?"

"She blames me for Henry's death," I said, looking my friend in the eye. "She thinks I killed him and dumped him in the river."

"Ridiculous! You are a doctor, not some bloodsucking vampire savage." Edward shook his head in disbelief. "I have a mind to visit her in her ridiculous house and put her straight. Jumped up little maid of all work!"

I stared at the floor, my eyes tracing the pattern of a Turkish rug that took up the centre of the room.

"Of course, I am sure all of this has to do with whatever that is under your coat."

My eyes immediately met Edward's and I took in a sudden gasp of air.

"Open your coat. I might as well see whatever it was that made the noise down there. I will see it sooner or later; you may as well not look so shocked. There must be some reason you came to me so suddenly."

He was right. I came to Edward, because I knew two things about him. One, he is a murderer. And two, he knows how to get away with murder.

I peeled open the coat and watched as Edward covered his mouth, never taking his eyes of the child.

"Some sort of deformed baby?" he muttered, as if to himself.

"No. I am certain she was meant to be born this way. I think this is her at the height of perfection."

"So bony. Her skin looks as though her ribs will tear through any moment," he said, his fingers reaching forwards, closer to her.

"I must warn you, do not touch her. Not yet. I am not sure how much she listens to me."

Edward looked puzzled. "What do you mean? Does she scratch, or bite or something?"

"Yes, she bites. She most certainly bites," I responded. "She is tired and afraid and I have no idea what to do for the best. These three years I have kept her half-starved in a bell-jar. She has become accustomed to that environment, but her hunger... her *thirst* has exceeded my will."

"Your will?" Edward asked, crouching closer to the cowering child.

"She talks to me, Edward. She can tell me things."

"She speaks?" he gasped.

"Not exactly. But we understand each other. She can do something. It is akin to that noise you heard, but my mind seems to divine her meaning now."

"Telepathy," Edwards said. "I have heard of such things, but dismissed it as fancy."

I steeled my jaw and cradled the child, pressing my cheek against the white flesh of her head. "This is no fancy, Edward."

"What does she eat? Is there something I can get her?" Edward asked.

"No, she has fed sufficiently for tonight."

"And she eats?"

"*Drinks*, actually. She drinks... well, she drinks blood."

Edward sniggered and raised his hands to his forehead, pushing back his hair so that his fringe stood on end. "Oh dear. Poor old Henry."

"What?"

"So this is what happened. It all becomes clear. Henry knew about this creature, disapproved and so you killed him. Fed him to it... *her*. And off he went into the river."

I raised my eyebrows.

"I am correct!" Edward turned on his heels and danced away from me, laughing.

The child stirred. She could detect my uncertainty. I had immediately become uncertain of Edward. Was he really actually amused by this? Or was he horrified and about to bring about my downfall?

"The Bilbao Devil got his just desserts in the end," Edward announced.

"Shhh, Edward!" I hissed.

Edward's mouth widened into a grimace momentarily, by way of an apology. He approached once more. "You are without a doubt, George, the most interesting of all the men I know."

"So… what I need to know is… can you help me to escape?"

"Help you? George… I want to come with you! This could be the greatest adventure I have ever known!"

"Are you mad, Edward? I am a hunted man. God's wounds, that brute, Charles, or that damned woman could be here already. I need to disappear. I need to be able to escape into… into nothing. Thin air. I need to be where nobody can find us!"

Edward smiled and shook his head. "No, George. That is not what you need at all. For if nobody can find you… how will she survive?"

He was right. I knew he was right. And she knew what I knew. Her purr of agreement touched our minds like silk.

The child was asleep before long, stretched across a hastily prepared collection of cushions and blankets Edward had arranged on the floor of his room. Safely ensconced in her warm furnishings, she resembled a desert princess of Persia.

So fatigued was she, that I noticed my thoughts, though conflicted, were my own. Her hold on me had slipped.

"You had better make use of my bedroom tonight, George," Edward had insisted as we stole from the room and locked the door.

I was ready for the gin Edward thrust into my hand. I savoured the bitterness as it washed away the lingering flavour of the woman's blood. In my disguise as a navvy I did not look too dissimilar to the artists who fraternised with the wealthy and well-to-do guests also present. Edward introduced me as George Branding, a Soho artist he had known for years. Summerscale cruised through the murky waters of criminality with astounding ease, propelled as he was, by a steady stream of lies.

In moments where we had the time to steal a conversation in secret, Edward revealed that he had already conceived of a plan to spirit me away. There was a travelling carnival nearby. The master of this carnival, a man he referred to only as Smokey, was a good, loyal friend of his. I was under the impression that they had conducted some illicit business together. Indeed, Edward intimated that Smokey was a man who was good at making things, or people vanish.

The carnival, he said, roved around the countryside, never to a scheduled route. They travelled at night, he told me. Only Smokey knew where they would go. Ideal for me, he said. Ideal because he was certain that Smokey was going to head North, it being unlikely that he would remain in the South for very much longer, lest he be caught for one thing or another. Smokey knew secret places, he told me. Places a man could lose the past and start over. Ideal for us both, and the child, he said.

Before I knew it, I had partaken of several gins and had sung along to songs so lewd that they would have made the Devil blush. It reminded me of the good old days with Burton, down in Charlie's Gin Palace. A flutter of regret swept through my innards. I clung to my insight like a buoyant plank in a shipwreck.

One moment I felt I could kill everyone here assembled and feed them to my little Panacea. The next I felt as though I should mount the stairs with a knife drawn and destroy the creature as it slept.

One moment I thought of Burton's smiling face in the music halls and gin parlours. The next I saw his snarling lips, his fiery eyes and his accusing finger, pointed into my chest, his voice booming, "Murderer!"

"Shhh, George," Edward said, wheeling me away from the piano. "Christ! These people have no idea what I've done," he muttered.

"I meant someone else," I whimpered.

Edward kept his tone hushed, hoping that the other guests had not heard my apparent outburst over the music, as he said, "I know, I know. Listen. Perhaps I should tell you about Alexander, but not tonight. I am sure you realise, however, that an artist's work is more valuable when he is dead. Well Pond… he was producing nothing. Supposed to be a great! One of The Greats! Oh, that was Alexander. He had to go. He was costing me money. And that woman of his!"

"Woman?"

"Remember Dominique from the other night?" Edward asked, his eyes beaming with excitement.

"Yes, where is she?" I asked, realising that I had not seen her since arriving.

"She and I have a little arrangement. She is posing tonight."

"Oh!" I exclaimed, and raised my eyebrows somewhat saucily. "A nude, I do hope."

"Not that kind of posing, my old friend," Edward said, guiding me through the scullery to the long, narrow garden to the rear of his property. "Her artist lover is having dinner with his parents tonight and… well, what can I say? If I were to point you towards the garden gate…" he trailed off, gesturing with his glass, one finger outstretched.

There, in the darkness, I could see two figures locked in frenzied intercourse. I heard the voices and could just discern that the figure bent over had no breasts, and when they altered their footing, I saw the male genitalia.

With the interest of a doctor, concerned with matters of the human body I watched as they contorted and twisted to kiss and each man touched the others face, stroking so gently, the movements and sentiment seemed so to contrast with the savage pumping at the lower portions of their bodies.

"Tell me, Edward," I said, pausing to gulp at my drink, "does the sodomite think like us?"

Edward paused and stroked his chin, giving his answer much consideration.

Before he could answer, I received a tap on my shoulder. I turned and reeled in shock, as there before me stood Margaret. No! It was another woman, wearing one of Margaret's dresses.

The woman. And almost immediately I felt desire stirring within me that I had not directed at poor Margaret for a long time.

Twenty-six.

Charles arrived at Richmond Green. He lambasted the driver. "Do I look like I want a bloody picnic?"

"If you have no address, sir, the green is central."

Charles paid the man and immediately made for a group of well-dressed young men walking towards him. Charles had never been to Richmond before, and hoped to God that Edward Summerscale was well-known.

"You there," he commanded, walking straight into the group of half a dozen men. He grabbed the man who looked least inebriated and shook him roughly, barking, "Summerscale! Edward Summerscale. Where can I find him?"

"You a detective or something?" the man asked.

"A shabby detective, if he is," another added.

"Never mind what I bloody am!" Charles grasped the first man's jacket lapels and practically lifted him off his feet.

"Get your hands off him!" one of the others protested.

Charles pushed the first man into another and turned, slamming his forearm against the jaw of the man who had raised his voice. He turned again immediately, assuming the man now behind him, to be the next to strike. He was right. A bottle was racing towards him. With his other forearm, Charles redirected the bottle blow harmlessly and followed across his body with a right cross that opened up both of his attacker's nostrils in an explosion of blood.

As he pulled back his right arm, he continued, smashing his right elbow into the face of another man, extending his arm to deliver a back-hand to his cheek with a *crack* sound. Charles grabbed hair and clashed two heads together like symbols, but with a dull *thud* not the metallic crash.

With each blow, he imagined Blessing's face opening up. It was Blessing's jaw broken, it was Blessing's teeth skittering across the ground like dice, it was Blessing's stringy saliva-blood, it was Blessing's hair clumped between his fingers, it was Blessing screaming for him to stop kicking, it was Blessing saying, "You've killed him! You've killed him!"

"What?" Charles muttered, trying to focus on the battered and bloody men scattered around him. A noisy public house nearby was emptying out, and the evacuating patrons were showing an interest in the scene.

"David! Wake up!" one of the men shook his fallen friend and tried to rouse him. The man's head lolled to the side, bubbles of blood bursting at the corner of his mouth.

"He is breathing," Charles said. "He is breathing, the blood bubbles are his breath. Now tell me where this whoreson Summerscale lives."

One of the dazed men, terrified of what damage Charles would do next, pointed back up to the Green. "Turn left and carry on through Paved Court. His house is usually easy to find."

"What the hell does that mean?"

"If you hear the noise of a party at any point along the way, you have found your man."

"Oi! What happened here!" another group of men, five this time, slightly older-looking than the first group, joined Charles and his victims. "Is he dead?"

Charles drew in a deep breath, feeling his muscles and chest expand. "None of your business. Keep to yourself!"

The leader of the new group of five men pulled a knife from his coat pocket. "This knife says it is my business now," he said, shifting his balance into a stance ready to slash out in a wide arc.

"Careful, I think he may be a copper!" one of the

first men cautioned.

"I could care less than a monkey's arsehole what he is. He is a dead man!"

The man charged. Charles was ready. He raised his left hand above his brow and stepped to the right. As the knife drew closer, Charles slammed his left hand down, fist balled, like a hammer, striking his attacker's forearm, pushing his momentum down. The attacker was off-balance. Charles twisted and swung his right fist into the back of the man's neck, staggering him.

He charged his whole weight into the man, knocking him sprawling, punching his ribs viciously as he pushed him against the wall.

Charles took the knife away from him as though he was seizing a toy from a naughty child. He glanced back at the other men who had gathered. "You all want to be third, then?" he spat, knowing they could see he had the muscle to support his arrogance. "Now, where should this knife go?"

"Spare me!" the man begged.

Charles bent the little finger of the man's left hand back, twisting it slowly and then suddenly snapped it back. He enjoyed the crack sound and the ensuing screams as he worked quickly with the knife. "You shan't miss this one, eh? This can be my little souvenir from Richmond!"

The man bayed and wept while all the other men who had not already felt Charles' wrath ran into the night, hoping to keep all of their fingers.

Charles hurried away up the street and observed his newly acquired blade. Not as good as his revolver, but it would do. He was handy with all sorts of weapons. Following the young man's directions, he saw a house in which a party was clearly in full-swing. He correctly assumed this to be Summerscale's place.

There seemed to be a houseful, would Blessing notice if he walked straight in through the front door?

People seemed to be wandering in and out, chasing and kissing, drinking on the steps in front of the door. He decided to take a look around before making his move. Blessing had already escaped once. He could not allow him to do it again.

On his way to the rear of the property, Charles was overcome by a sudden urge. He removed the finger from his pocket and placed it behind his teeth, sucking upon it deeply.

Twenty-seven.

Mary grasped Blessing by his shoulder and hand. "Care to dance, Doctor?" she asked, leading him, turning him away from Edward.

"What the hell are you doing here?" he asked, still in shock. "And what the hell are you doing in Margaret's dress?"

"You can not simply run away, Doctor Blessing. You have to face up to this. I can help you." Mary kept turning him, holding him closer and tighter, her breasts pushing into his chest. Without his moustache and hair, and without his usual attire, he looked like a different man entirely. Rougher, stronger. Part of her found him more appealing this way. She was glad that those eyes could never change. Those beautiful eyes.

"Are you going to answer me?" he asked, shaking her, fixing his feet in position, ending the dance immediately.

"I found her – your wife. I saw what happened to her. Lily and Niamh are quite safe, however. The men who chased you threatened them. One of them is still after you. He could be outside for all I know."

What does it matter to you what he does? You both want me dead!"

Mary stepped back from him and looked in his eyes, pressing her palms against his chest, which seemed more muscular to the touch than she had imagined it would be. "Dead? I don't want you dead, Doctor. In fact I very much want you to live."

"But?" he asked, raising his eye brows, assuming there would be a caveat.

"But that *thing* must be destroyed. And if not destroyed, then contained and taken to a safe place."

"This Island you spoke of?"

Mary nodded.

"And just where is this mysterious island of

yours?" Blessing asked, almost managing to smile.

"If I told you, then there would be no mystery."

Blessing allowed himself a snort of amusement. "What a strange profession you have chosen!" Blessing exclaimed. "You are a most adaptable human being, in my opinion!"

"What has brought you here?" Mary asked.

Blessing glanced at Summerscale, who cleared his throat, a warning. He was listening in.

Mary gripped Blessing's drink and finished it in one draught. "Why do we not get another drink and discuss our matters in private?"

"Why not join us in the party proper?" Edward asked, quickly stepping to Blessing's side. He looked Mary up and down. "I can only imagine you have a voice as beautiful as your figure, my lady. Will you join me at the piano?"

"I will not," Mary snapped, striding away, leading Blessing by the hand.

Mary and Blessing sipped their glasses of gin and stole away to a corner of the drawing room. Mary had seen parties like this before, in many different cities. They did not excite her. They did not disgust her. They were simply background. The bare flesh, the tinge of opium in the air, it was all just data, registered and stored. She knew how to defeat every person in the room if they all turned out to be hostile. That meant spotting the weaknesses and vulnerabilities of twenty-three people.

It had taken her less than a minute. The man with the limp – his right knee the problem, the glass, the opium pipe that could be smacked to the back of the throat, then removed and used to poke out an eye, or swing as a stick at the next attacker, the embers this action would kick up would provide a distraction… the ways she could hurt people were endless.

"There is something very familiar about you, Miss Brigham," Blessing said. "You frighten me. There is something that tells me you will hurt me, or worse, but when I look at you sometimes I see something else."

"Do you see the truth? That I wish you *no* harm?" Mary asked, raising her glass.

Blessing shook his head slowly. "That is not it. You know what you want. You are in control of any situation you find yourself in, are you not?"

"Not true. I could not *make* you give up the creature. Although I can guess that she is in this building. I can assume that you have hidden her as far away from the party as possible. The attic perhaps?"

Blessing shrugged. "If I told you, then there would be no mystery."

"And I believe you to be quite yourself, right at this moment. But it is not my controlling nature you should fear. It is the creature's. I believe she has made you do things, terrible things. I can help you to overcome her power. I can help you regain your normal life again."

Blessing inched closer to Mary, his eyes locked on hers. "Who says I want that normal life again?"

"You crave something different?" Mary asked, the glass once more at her lips, her tongue flicking out to catch a drop of gin at the edge of the glass.

"Something more."

"Adventure?"

"You could say that."

Mary smiled and raised a suggestive eyebrow. "Sometimes adventure is no substitute for home comforts. The warmth of a bed, for instance."

"Like an adventure, I suppose it all depends on who you share it with. And you may call me George, if it pleases you."

Their lips were an inch apart, eyes locked.

"George it is, if you will call me Mary."

The voices in the room seemed to quiet down, to silence. But there was another sound replacing it.

Was it music? The strain of a drawn-out violin note?

No. A scream. An animal scream.

Blessing was on his feet, his glass smashed off the floor, he was out the door and racing up the stairs.

Mary was a moment behind.

Twenty-eight.

I was at the top of the stairs and I could see the bedroom door was open. Panic filled every inch of me, a cold, liquid sensation that momentarily turned my muscles into a sluggish gelatinous mass. A moment later and my heart was pumping hot, vicious blood around my whole being, driving me into the room – damn the danger! Damn the consequences! My child!

She screamed again, that shrill, migraine-inducing whistle as I reached the bedroom door. Charles was there, drenched in blood – the child's? His knife drawn, his posture defensive, his movements hesitant, his eyes fixed on something beyond the bed and the nest of cushions.

The child had backed away into the corner of the room; she was crouched like a dog, her nostrils flaring. She was trying to locate me, terrified.

I stepped into the room and Charles saw me in the periphery of his vision, he turned and slashed the knife through the air, nowhere near me, but warning me to stay back.

The child pounced then, bounding across the room, jaws thrusting open and forwards. Her needle-sharp teeth bit into Charles' leg. He screamed and slashed with the knife, slicing her back open.

Another scream brought me to my knees. She was in my arms. I could hear the power of her suggestion, "Shhhhhh, shhhhhh." She knew that her screams had caused me pain and she was trying to sooth me! Remarkable!

I turned and staggered onto the landing, where Mary stood with a revolver drawn. "Put her down!" Mary ordered, levelling the revolver at my head.

"Mary! Please! She is an innocent. We can not simply destroy her for her very nature," I protested.

"*She* is a monster! *She* has no nature! She has

only thirst, a lust for death!"

"And you? You would kill, under the guise of duty!"

From over my shoulder, I heard, "So, we meet again. And that, by the way, is *my* gun!"

I leapt aside, still clutching the child. My other jars were lost to me, left as they were beyond the woman and the brute. This was my only chance to escape with the child.

The stairs had filled with revellers who had ventured to see what the commotion was and no doubt to find the source of the horrifying shrieks that had once again seared their skulls.

The report of the revolver sent a shock through everybody, some of them leapt back and stumbled with fright. I ducked as I rounded the staircase barging my way through the tangled bodies.

I was at the ground floor, next to the front door. Edward stood waiting for me. "My God," he gasped. "She is wounded."

"She will be fine!" I assured him, still moving for the door.

Another gunshot roared on the top floor, they were still fighting. The guests screamed. Scuffling and cries issued from the staircase. Whoever had won the fight sounded like they were stumbling over the tangle of limbs on the stairs.

"George! Back door!" Edward called, grabbing my sleeve. Another gunshot sounded and the front door cracked, spitting splinters into the air.

I raced through the kitchen and out into the garden. By the open gate I saw a tangle of bloody bodies, the two men I had observed earlier, they had been slashed wildly with a knife, gutted in fact. Their organs spilled out onto the path and I almost lost my footing as I picked my way through the gore.

I darted from the garden onto a road I later discovered was aptly named Retreat Road. I recognised the area as I reached Water Lane – I was close to where I had disposed of the bodies earlier. I hoped the horse and cab was still nearby – would someone have taken them, or would the horse have bolted?

I rounded onto the Riverside and could see the horse had gone, taken by some opportunist who had no need for, or could not quickly conceal, the cab, which stood redundant near where I had left it.

I peered into the darkness and left and right along the tar black Thames, hoping there would be a small boat with which I could make my escape. The luck of the damned! The pier was on the other side of the river. There was no way we could both make it. I knew that the current would doubtless drag me away even without the burden of the child, so together we stood no chance.

"Stop!" Mary commanded. I turned, slowly, still cradling my wounded Panacea.

"Mary. You will have to kill me."

"I can not do that, George. I have no desire to kill you. Enough innocents have died for that monster!"

"This monster?" I boomed, stepping forwards. "Did you see what I saw in the garden? The havoc wrought by that *man*, capable of full and conscious thought!"

"The creature in your arms, George, I have seen it before. I have seen many like them. I have hunted them, not for sport, but because of the things they are capable of. They hunt in packs. They communicate with their thoughts, making it impossible to tell what they plan, and when they will strike. They descend upon towns like a pack of wolves and destroy every soul they find."

I gazed at the wounded child, unable to believe the woman's words. "No! She has lived with me all her life. She is able to defy her nature! She can control her urges."

Mary lowered the gun and was immediately

pressed against me, our bodies surrounding the child. A family. Our kisses were hard, frenzied. I freed a hand from the creature and slid my fingers through her hair, wanting her, willing her to stay locked with me.

She broke the embrace and stepped back, her eyes, blazing before, demure now. "No creature can control its urges. Not completely. Not even us."

She raised the gun, but I struck her hand, knocking her off her aim. I charged in low and in one movement planted the child on the cold stone of the riverside walk and lunged forwards, tackling Mary to the ground. He heard the child scamper away to cover. I pressed my weight down onto her, grasping for her hands as she clawed at my face and gripped the revolver, desperate to prevent me from taking it.

A moment before we had been lovers, born to be together. Presently we were mortal enemies, locked in a struggle that only one of us could walk away from. I sacrificed my hold on her arms and snatched the revolver from her, immediately smacking her head with it, opening an ugly red crack at the upper right corner of her brow. I raised the grip of the revolver again. The pain of the first blow had registered with Mary. Her eyes were wide in shock and the terror that this was it. This was the end of her. She could scarcely believe that I could be quick enough, strong enough and deadly enough to defeat her. I brought my arm down again and delivered a sickening blow to the same spot on her brow, opening the wound further.

"George, please," she gasped. "I wanted to save you."

I felt a cold, sticky wetness, seeping through my shirt and quickly dipped my fingers low to see if I was injured. I was not. But Mary was. Her dark dress was drenched in blood, a tear across her abdomen. Charles had cut her badly in their struggle – she had taken this injury for me.

Fingers, iron hard, grasped me around my

neck, yanking my head backwards. I gurgled a scream as Charles' voice came. I silently prayed the child would not reveal herself.

"First you, then her!" he hissed, arcing the blade across to the left side of my throat. I abandoned the revolver and brought my left forearm up between the blade and my neck, and pushed. His strength was immense, the blade inched closer, closer. I felt the icy touch of the metal as it sliced into my skin.

Charles screamed.

The child screamed.

Mary screamed.

I screamed.

Each of us fell away. Charles slashed with the blade, trying to cut the creature biting his shoulder, his legs, his fingers, his face. The child moved lightning fast, scampering about him, tearing at him with teeth and claws.

Her shrieking stopped, my head cleared. I grabbed the revolver again, looked over Mary who lay absolutely still and turned to see the child and Charles in time to see the eruption of water as the brute fell into the Thames. The child perched at the edge of the walk. If she had eyes, one could say that she was looking down to make sure he drowned.

After a moment, Panacea limped to my side. Her back bled profusely and her limbs were bruised. It clearly pained her to walk.

When I returned to Edward's house, it was empty. His tenuous social web did not do too well with fear, it seemed. The child slept once more, but uneasily. She was not at all accustomed to sleeping outside the confines of her bell-jar and it was clear that exhaustion was all that had allowed her any concession this night.

Mary lay asleep in the guest room. I had tended to her wounds as best I could. There seemed to be nothing wrong that clean dressings and a good rest could not fix. Inspecting her bag I found no clue as to her organisation or the whereabouts of the island she had mentioned. I did find vials of poison and small daggers that looked as though they could be held between the fingers when boxing to deliver horrific damage. After playing with the grip of the daggers I discovered a small compartment inside, just the right size to house a vial of poison. I could see in the tip of the dagger a tiny aperture.

She really was a killer.

Yet she had not killed me.

"You are sure that I can not join you, George?" Edward asked, taking my attention away from the bag and that damned woman.

"Perfectly sure. Your letter of recommendation to Mr Smokey will be enough. She prefers me to have no close friends or family. I fear your presence would only cause you to be harmed."

Edward thrust a scrap of paper into my pocket. "Here, these are the directions to Smokey's camp. He will be there tomorrow and gone at night. Do not miss him. I shall try to delay this woman as long as I can." Edward sighed, his disappointment undisguised. "I would have helped, you know. We could have had a great adventure together!"

I am sure we would have, but the problem with Edward is, he is so easily bored. Hiding a secret like the child would not be made easier by fraternising with a creature of Summerscale's personality and with his appetites.

"Perhaps, when I have found a resolution to my present circumstances, I will find it possible to return. Who knows."

"Until then, keep moving, old boy."

"Do not forget the letters for Flanders and Charlotte, my friend?" I reminded him, momentarily arrested by a nagging doubt that Edward was the right man with whom to entrust matters of a financial nature.

"Late tomorrow, or first thing the next day, depending upon my success at delaying this spectacular woman. And I shall look in on Niamh regularly, have no fear."

I collected my jars and slung the sack about me, from shoulder to shoulder and did the same with a makeshift sling fashioned from a torn curtain, with both ends pinned together to form a loop. Into this sling I gently placed the child and opened the material about her, to cradle her and keep her warm.

And with that, we set off into the night once more.

Twenty-nine.

Charles clambered out of the Thames and rolled onto his back on the grassy bank. The act of drawing himself out of the water had taken a quarter of an hour, once he had floated to a suitable point of egress. Waterlogged as he was, and with so much blood shed and energy expended over the course of the day, the effort required to move was immense.

His chest heaved and jets of mist rose from his mouth with each long, slow breath as he tried to return his breathing and pulse to a normal level.

The bites burned and he wondered if that *thing* might have rabies. He wondered if *he* might now have rabies.

His exhaustion overcame him and his vision clouded over. Through the icy cold he managed to sleep on the riverbank for an hour.

Once awake, he rose up on his stiff legs and began the journey back to the West, back to Richmond Upon Thames. Back to Edward Summerscale's house.

He knew that Blessing would be long gone, the creature with him. But it was a matter of time before he would track the doctor. Summerscale would give him information eventually. Charles had nothing to return to, no reason to head back to London, no reason to stop hunting his quarry.

He thrust his hands into his pockets and found a small cylinder in one of them. He picked it out and recognised it even in the darkness as the finger he had severed in one of his fights that night.

There are so many ways to get information from Summerscale, he mused. The severed finger made him think of ten ways immediately.

He threw the finger into the Thames and continued his relentless march.

Thirty.

Her head throbbed. Immediately Mary knew that she was alive. This was a shock for her as the last thing she could remember was a certainty that she had reached the end. Thrusting the curtains open she could see that the sun was high overhead. She had slept until late morning at least, but all the same, her body felt like it had been trampled by a team of horses. She needed to tap into those pressure-points and induce the trance that would refresh her.

She knew that she was still in Summerscale's house, in Richmond Upon Thames. She knew that when she had lost consciousness, she had been at the riverside. Who had brought her back? Summerscale himself? It was possible. Charles? Unlikely. George? Under the close influence of the creature, was he any more likely to help than Charles was?

Mary could not decide that one.

She unfastened the dress and lifted it over her head. She noted that the garment was ruined and guiltily reasoned that Margaret would not miss it. At the washstand she inspected herself in a dinner-plate sized mirror. Her abdominal wound had been expertly cleaned and stitched. As had her head injury. George.

Flashes of the fight at the top of the stairs returned to her. Wrestling for the revolver. Wrestling for the knife.

Charles' hands gripping her hair, hurling her against the wall. His startling strength. Her elbows smashing against his jaw, his temple, his nose. Her palms extended, thrusting into his face, desperately trying to drive his nose into his brain. The nagging in the back of her mind that she should have brought the poisoned dagger from her bag – she could have ended it all with one punch.

Next to the bed she found her bag. It had been

searched, nothing was in its usual place. Something extra was there, a note, from George.

Leave my father alone.

From the child, then, she thought. It had completely infiltrated his mind. It was at the reins – George himself a mere puppet. There were moments when the creature allowed him his humanity, but these moments were becoming fewer and further between. When the creature needed protection, when she needed food, she manipulated him. She could play on that paternal instinct of his, that healing nature, and make him act for her. Her hold exceeded the degree to which that paternal instinct and healing nature applied to his family, friends and patients, whom he had abandoned, hurt or even killed.

Mary reasoned then that George had kept Niamh at arms length. She wondered if this had been to protect her from the creature – minimising the need for her to be eliminated when the creature decided that it was time to run.

Had he recognised this, and left her behind, to spare the child what he knew would surely follow? His downfall.

His humanity still shone through. Those eyes could never change, she reasoned. Those beautiful eyes of his.

She closed her fist around the note and threw it on the floor. *Never*, she thought, in reply to the message.

She put the torn dress back on, despairing slightly at the rip across her midriff, and the crust of blood that had stiffened the velvet. She would attract some attention on her journey back to London.

Mary put on her shoes and picked up her bag. She tried the door. It was locked. She peered into the keyhole and could see that a key was still secure in place. She quickly found her picklock and fitted it to the aperture. She tried to nudge the key free so that she could operate the tool properly. Her fingers were shaking. She needed to eat.

Mary knew there was a quicker way out. She opened the sash window and peered down. She was on the second floor. Looking to the left she saw there was a drainpipe within reach. Easy, she thought.

A minute or so later, she was making her way along the streets, heading for the train station, London and whatever lectures Doctor McEwan had in store for her.

Had Mary managed to open the door, she may have found that Edward had left the key in place in haste after locking her in upon detecting an intruder, to protect her rather than imprison her.

On the other hand, his motivation may have remained unknown to her even if she had found Edward, being as he was, unconscious on the kitchen floor, with six severed fingers lying next to him.

Thirty-one.

There was no turning back. My transformation was complete. Doctor George Blessing had been discarded like old clothing, worn threadbare to the point of indecency. I had emerged from my chrysalis stronger than ever.

Three months before, in the dying moments of my old life, I had clung to regrets, to sadness, to guilt. Those things I had stored away, safe as Panacea in her bell-jar.

In clinging to hopes for improved medicine for mankind, I had succumbed to evil. Even if I could cure every disease in the world, there was no way to bring Margaret back.

My only hope for salvation was that Summerscale had carried out his duties as agreed, and had taken the adoption papers to Charlotte, and the financial instructions to Francis.

I imagined Charlotte receiving that letter. I imagined her haste to summon a driver, to rush to Niamh's quarters. I imagined her, eager to improve the situation of a new, vulnerable little girl – the ghost of me standing behind them, observing with pride. I could see them, even as I sat in the tent with tears in my eyes. I saw them, a picture together, shopping for dresses. I saw quite clearly Niamh listening attentively to a governess, as Charlotte beams, sewing in the corner of the parlour, her pregnancy more obvious by the day. And there they are in an afternoon, arranging ferns together and placing their displays on the mantle, with care.

This daily imagining never failed to dissolve some of my newfound strength, never failed to resurrect the sentimentality, the regrets, of Doctor George Blessing.

Once more, as was my ritual every time I felt the intense sadness at the death of my old world, I closed my eyes, breathed deeply and raised the revolver to my temple. Was this the only way to shatter the destiny thrust upon me by the creature in the glass?

I heard her scream for me to stop. Screaming at that part of my being that calls itself father. “Niamh?” I cried.

No. It is not Niamh, it is *her*.

“Blessing!”

“No!” a man’s voice.

My strength, the strength Panacea lent me, returned.

I opened my eyes. The brute was there, holding open the entrance to my tent. He was different somehow. His bulk had increased, and he wore the same suit, ragged and filthy, from months ago in Richmond. His eyes were ringed in black, his teeth were jagged and uncared for.

How had he managed to find me? The sideshow had moved by night every night for months! Every day we were in a different town, or attached to a different carnival, show or fair.

She told me what to do in an instant. The revolver in my hand turned and barked at Charles. His left knee exploded and he fell, quivering, grasping at his shattered leg.

I rose to my feet, and gathered my fur cloak about me against the chill of the autumn night.

Raising the lamp I drew the sheets from the looming objects behind me, one by one.

Charles gasped at the horrors he witnessed. There, the remains of a dog, frozen in time and preserved with its seeking eyes and distorted mouth craving blood, or appearing to, even months after death.

Here a glass case teeming with slavering, clawing hairless, eyeless white rats, rolling over each other like waves.

There a cat, hairless, eyeless, feeding on an uninfected kitten.

Screaming in another tank, dozens of vampiric mice, the mutated progeny of a male mouse infected with the secretion of my daughter.

All of them baying, ready to feast.

Finally, I exposed the central tank, ten-feet tall, reaching the very top of my tent. And there, in the lamp light, amber in her murky fluids, was the mother of them all, her palms pressed against the glass, row upon row of teeth scratching and chattering silently in the gloom. An eight foot tall machine of blood-drinking vengeance.

"We have been waiting, Charles," I growled, reaching for the wheel with which to release the pressurised lid, keeping *her* secure in her home. "We thought you could never find us. But we are so glad you did."

"Blessing! Don't do it!" Charles begged.

"Oh, but she is hungry," I said, chest heaving with satisfaction at this happy turn of events. "And she so enjoyed the taste of you. How could I deny her?"

Charles squirmed, trying to claw his way from my tent. His increased muscle mass had failed him, overcome as he was by terror.

I knew the nature of what Charles had become. I knew the gifts he had inherited. I knew that his knee was repairing itself even then.

Others gathered, alarmed by the report of the revolver, Smokey himself among them, accompanied by the French girls born joined at the head, only three eyes between them.

A dwarf played an accordion, wheezing out a cheerful little ditty to suit the occasion.

Charles looked about the freaks and horrors.

The wolf-man, all covered in hair, with his teeth filed down to points.

The tree-boy, his skin so encrusted with scabs and seborrhoeic warts so as to give his flesh the appearance of tree bark.

"My God, Blessing! What pack of demons is this, that you have summoned to carry me into Hell?"

I levelled the revolver at Charles and smiled, ready to prepare a meal for her, the main attraction, the *star* of our sideshow.

I mounted the steps at the side of her tank and reached up with my free hand. Turning the brass wheel, the vacuum was released and the rubber seals sighed as they peeled apart.

Her hands grasped the open top of her glass tank and she hauled herself aloft, this movement no effort to her. Controlled, she doubled over the lip and scaled down the outside of the tank and padded to my side, pressing herself against my legs as I descended the steps.

I ran my fingers down her white head and caressed her slick back.

Charles screamed and howled, surrounded by our new family, unable to escape.

She tilted her head towards me, showing me her gratitude as I had shown her my loyalty and my love. She stalked across the ground to the entrance of the tent, to where Charles lay, where he clawed at the ground, clawed at his own face, trying to tear his eyes out, desperate to extricate himself from this beautiful inevitability.

I looked forward to the dissection I would perform later; keen to learn what changes had occurred in Charles. I expected perhaps a swelling of the parietal lobe and sensory cortex, resulting in enhanced perception and greater sensory awareness. Had he been able to form an extra-sensory link with the child that enabled him to track us?

Setting aside my plans for the evening, I watched her feast, brimming with pride, for she is my greatest discovery, she is my daughter, she is my master... And I am her doctor.

End of Part 2.

Part 3:

A Christmas Blessing

In which, five months after the events of Dr Blessing's Rapture, we find London in a terrible state, and horrific events about to befall several persons of interest.

Niamh.

"Why not let the child away from her books, Nanny?" Giles Burton asked as he entered the parlour.

Niamh looked up from her studies and smiled at the man she had learned to call Grandpa. His generous smile beamed across the room and he added, "We have many preparations to make before Old Christmas arrives."

Since becoming a resident of the Burton household, Niamh had enjoyed, or as she saw it, *endured* lessons from her new governess Miss Pinchstaff.

The widow Burton, Charlotte, had invited Giles to spend the Christmas season at the Burton household and hoped that he would decide to stay. Her late husband, Henry, had left her with a fortune and a thriving shipping business, as well as an unborn child due any day. Giles Burton, Henry's aged uncle, was the last remaining Burton relative that the baby would have; Henry had been very fond of the man and it seemed only natural that the surviving members of the Burton name should unite, even if only for Christmas.

Giles was a round man with a mischievous look in his eyes, with red cheeks and grey sideburns. Despite his large frame, he was more than capable of keeping up with Niamh at play, and it seemed that being in close proximity to someone so young gave him a new vitality.

"Please, Miss Pinchstaff," Niamh pleaded, widening her eyes, not quite daring to close her book until permitted by her governess to do so.

Miss Pinchstaff suppressed her amusement at the old man and his mischievous ways. A thirty-year old spinster, Miss Pinchstaff had learned her life lessons among other families, and knew that Giles enjoyed playful distraction as much as any child she had taught in the six years she had spent in her chosen field. "Well, Mr Burton, you certainly make a compelling case," Miss Pinchstaff said, only just managing to keep a look of stern detachment on her face. "And Old Christmas is coming soon, as you say. There are so many preparations to be made…"

"So many," Giles added.

"So, so many," Niamh added, her eyes darting from Grandpa to governess, to Grandpa and back to governess.

"Well then, young Niamh. It seems that we could leave our studies there. But the day after Christmas, you must promise to study twice as hard."

"I promise, Miss Pinchstaff, I promise!" Niamh exclaimed, leaping to her feet. She flung her arms around her tutor and thanked her profusely before running to Giles' side.

As Giles and Niamh left the parlour and stepped into the domed reception, they became aware of another person at the top of the stairs to their right.

"Mrs Burton!" Niamh called, cheerily. "Miss Pinchstaff has let me go with Grandpa to prepare for Old Christmas!"

Charlotte, still dressed in the black of mourning, was leaning against the banister as though she had not the energy to keep herself entirely upright. "That's nice, dear. Wrap up warm. Wrap up for the cold outside."

Charlotte descended the stairs as Niamh busied herself. She had been thrust into motherhood early when, in July, Dr George Blessing, Niamh's unofficial guardian, had fled London. Blessing had made arrangements for the child – he was recorded as a legal guardian on paper, but custody of Niamh had been signed over to her.

Both her feelings on the responsibility, and the circumstances in which she had taken it on, had been complicated. She had met Niamh the same night as did Dr Blessing. They had met the girl when she was eight, three years earlier. She had summoned Charlotte and the doctor to a doss where a prostitute was struggling in childbirth. That night had changed everything.

What Charlotte had not known at the time was that the child born that night was not human, and among its mysterious ways, the creature drank blood and could control minds. For three years Dr Blessing had hidden the creature, sharing the secret only with her husband, Henry.

The subject had been the ruin of Henry's close friendship with Blessing – they had grown ever more distant. Then one night, Henry disappeared. He was fished out of the Thames, drained of blood.

At Henry's funeral, she was approached by a man who introduced himself as Charles. He had been a police constable, who had become a private investigator. He had claimed to have information on Henry's death and Charlotte had believed him.

Charles had suspected Dr Blessing. Charles said that Henry and the doctor had removed something from the prostitute's body that fateful night. Charles revealed he had been one of the constables at the scene and that he had witnessed them stealing something away.

Charlotte had had her doubts about Charles, but time proved that he was right. Unfortunately, Charles had been a brutal, violent man, who had lost control before he was able to conclude his investigation. Dr Blessing had left London in July, and Charles disappeared in his wake.

Another tragedy had struck at that time. Mrs Margaret Blessing had been found drained of blood, like Henry. Charlotte had not seen the body, but she was told that Margaret had been found in her marital bed.

Charlotte had been approached by a remarkable woman named Mary Brigham, who helped to make arrangements for Margaret, and the whole matter of the poor woman's death was put to rest quietly, almost secretly. It was Mary who had helped Charlotte to make sense of the doctor's murderous insanity, and the power of the creature that had enslaved him.

And as terrible a tale as that had all been, worse than the death of Henry, worse than the death of Margaret, London had suffered terribly since Dr Blessing left the city. Not only had he harboured the creature, but he had been experimenting with it. The cost of his secrecy and his curiosity had been immeasurable.

As it was, taking Niamh in had been no trouble at all, but the child's grief at the loss of her second makeshift family had been turbulent. That was where Miss Pinchstaff had come in handy and, unexpectedly, Giles had become indispensible.

Charlotte's mind returned from her review of the past, to note that Niamh was dressed in her favourite coat and scarf and waiting at the door, with Giles hot on her heels.

Charlotte reached the bottom of the stairs and was struck suddenly with a great swell of sadness that Henry was not there with her to enjoy the scene. The tears came and she tried to conceal them. Niamh turned to face her, beaming. She saw the tears; her smile faded. Charlotte did her best to smile and wave her on. "Go ahead, child! Have your fun! Have some for me!"

Niamh hated to see Mrs Burton like this. "Grandpa," she said, as Giles stepped out of the front door.

"Yes, my flower."

"Grandpa, do people only cry when they are terribly sad?"

"Not always, my flower. People can cry when they are happy, I suppose. Some people cry when they are feeling poorly." Giles closed the door and locked it, then turned to look out past the gates of the mansion. Two men bowed their heads slightly and touched the peaks of their caps in greeting. Giles gave a short wave and the two men returned their attention to the world beyond the gates, small puffs of steam rising from their mouths in the chilly air. Giles knew the men to be armed, and knew that more men were stationed around the mansion and worked shifts to secure the property all day and all night.

Giles pulled a brown bottle from inside his coat, popped off the stopper and took a quick sip of the golden, syrupy liquid within.

"Grandpa, what is that you are drinking? It is like wine?"

"This is no wine, my dear, it is… my medicine!"

"I tasted wine once, and it was awful, it made me want to be sick."

Giles laughed at the bitter face Niamh pulled at the recollection of the taste. "Wine is an acquired taste, my dear."

"What does that mean, Grandpa?"

Giles thought of a simple explanation and offered, "It means that when you are older, you will learn to like the taste."

"Grandpa?"

"Yes, my flower?"

"I thought only sick people had to take medicine. That is what Father used to say. And he is a doctor."

"Well yes, I suppose that he is right. He is after all, a doctor."

"Well then Grandpa, if only sick people have to take medicine, how do you take medicine?"

"*Why* do I take medicine?" Giles corrected her.

"Why do you take medicine?" Niamh asked. "You do not look sick."

"I am well *because* of my medicine, my child. I am an old man and my medicine staves off my aches and pains; it keeps me young."

"Then how does Mrs Burton not take medicine?" Niamh asked.

"*Why* does Mrs Burton not take medicine," Giles corrected her.

"Why does Mrs Burton not take medicine?" Niamh asked. "I think she might be poorly. I see her crying sometimes."

The pair walked the pavement across the front of the house, making a leisurely pace. Giles made long-reaching stabs at the path with his cane, letting it *clack* loudly as he went. "There are lots of ways in which a person can be poorly, my flower petal. Sometimes it can last a moment and then go. And we must remember that Mrs Burton is with child."

"If Father was here, he would fix her," Niamh said slipping an arm around Giles'.

"Yes, child. Perhaps he would," Giles agreed.

"He would know what to do. I think that Mrs Burton is very sad because she misses Mr Burton… perhaps she needs a special medicine that nobody knows about."

"You are very wise, little one. This is a time of year for family to be together."

"We are family now," Niamh said, squeezing up close to Giles.

"We are, my darling."

"I should very much like Father to be here. But since he can not be here, I am glad that we are all here. Perhaps if I could get Mrs Burton a gift, the likes of which only a daughter would get for her Mama, she would forget about Mr Burton for a while and feel better."

"Now listen to me, little flower," Giles said, his tone deepening to one of caution. He knew that Niamh had been raised on the streets of London at night and that there was a fearless streak in her. "There are bad goings-on out there in London these days."

"You mean the monsters. Miss Pinchstaff said that it was all nonsense."

Giles cleared his throat.

Niamh tugged at Giles' sleeve. "It is not, is it? The monsters are real. I always knew it."

Giles nodded his head. "Well, perhaps your Miss Pinchstaff did not want to frighten you."

"I am not afraid, anyway. I saw horrible things when I was just little."

Giles smiled at his young companion and said, "I know, flower. You are a very worldly little thing. But you must stay here at the mansion where it is nice and safe."

They rounded the corner of the house and continued down the path, which began to slope slightly. The side of the garden was cold in the long shadows of the afternoon, as the hollow sun stole away.

"Grandpa, if the monsters are real, then there is something else that is real."

"What would that be, child?"

"I heard people, when they said there were monsters… they said my Father made the monsters."

Giles stopped in his tracks and peered down at the child. His normally jovial face strained, contorted into a look of concern. "Oh, you poor thing. What a terrible thing it is to be a child. Let people talk, little Niamh. Let them say their spiteful things. And let me ask you this, if your Father *did* make the monsters, would he have made arrangements for you to live in this wonderful house?"

Niamh considered this for a moment. It made sense. Father loves me because he is a good man. "I knew they were lying!"

"Now then!" Giles struck up into his good cheer once more. "Back to the task at hand! We must search the grounds! First, a good, stout yuletide log!"

Niamh ran ahead, shrouded in the shadow of the day's decline, running for the light of the terraced gardens to the rear of the property. Giles watched her, picking up his pace so that he could mind the girl on the terraces. The joy of a child such as Niamh was her enquiring mind. He suspected that same enquiring mind would bring her much pain when one day she learned the truth.

In the evening, Niamh was sat in the parlour, inspecting the flowers she had collected, positioning them one by one around the Yule log she had selected from the grounds.

Giles was present in the parlour, his great paunch supporting the book he was reading in between naps. He kept slipping into a snooze and his grip on the book loosened slightly and the book tipped, causing him to awaken with a start. Giles then invariably glanced around to see if anyone had noticed his slumber, commenced reading the book again and the whole process started afresh.

Miss Pinchstaff sat sewing a pretty hat that Niamh suspected was to be presented to her as a gift on Christmas Day. She had, on other nights, observed a dress, one which matched the hat, and which Charlotte had insisted was to be a gift for her niece who lived in Wales. Niamh had never heard mention of this niece before the dress had appeared!

Charlotte, swollen with pregnancy, struggled to find a comfortable position on her chair. She repeatedly rose to her feet and approached Niamh, admired her arrangement and encouraged her.

"Thank you Mrs Burton," Niamh said, wanting to sound grateful so that she would not betray how utterly bored she was.

Charlotte sighed and waddled back to her chair, hands clasped beneath her bulging midriff, attempting in vain to alleviate the strain on her lower back. Occasionally, Niamh saw Charlotte glancing at a portrait of Mr Burton. Charlotte dabbed at her eyes with an embroidered handkerchief before quickly tucking the handkerchief away, hoping that nobody had noticed. But Niamh had noticed, as she had on many occasions.

"Why do we not play a game?" Miss Pinchstaff suggested.

Niamh had other ideas and set aside her decorations. "If it pleases you, I would very much like to go to bed."

"Are you all right, dear?" Charlotte asked, leaning forwards, filled with attentive concern. "Are you feeling unwell?"

"A little. Perhaps I am just tired with excitement for Christmas."

Charlotte tutted sympathetically and offered, "Can I get one of the servants to bring you something, little one?"

"No thank you, Mrs Burton. I am sure an early night will make me well."

"Should I take her to the sickroom?" Miss Pinchstaff asked.

"Not at all," Charlotte replied. "She is not suffering from some terrible disease. She simply wishes Old Christmas would arrive sooner! Am I not right, my dear child?"

"I s'pose so, Mrs Burton."

"Then you sleep well, child. You will be busy again tomorrow, with Grandpa no doubt. We will need plums for the pudding, and I am not quite up to climbing trees!"

Niamh took her leave and hurried upstairs. She felt she needed to stretch her legs. It seemed as though the walls of the Burton house were closing in on her.

No sooner had Niamh moved into the Burton home, than it became apparent why the doctor felt he could not return. Since the hospital had burned down, a number of rumours began to circulate. Rumours of madmen roaming the streets of London at night, rumours of a disease infecting animals and humans alike. Rumours that Dr Blessing's hospital had been the source of the disease.

As the news of more deaths rolled in, so more rumours emerged. More accusations. Niamh and Mrs Burton had been openly derided in the streets, spat at and threatened.

Niamh had heard the coachmen and the servants discussing the state of the city. She had heard that certain parts of the city had become uninhabitable because of the monsters or the madmen or the disease.

Mrs Burton tried to protect her from the stories, and had acquired the services of Miss Pinchstaff to school her, to try to occupy her mind in this oasis, this sanctuary.

Niamh knew what they were trying to do, and she appreciated it, but it was not working. She craved adventure. She was a street-runner at heart. She had seen the horrible things that men could do to women of the night. She had lived in enough fear to last her a lifetime, until she met Dr Blessing. He brought the fear to an end, until she became fearful for him.

But she had not been afraid for herself.

She opened the drawer of the small dresser in her bedroom and pocketed the coins she had been saving. Anytime she was given a ha'penny she saved it in the drawer. Her plan was simple. Giles had taken her to a pharmacy in the city the day before, when he picked up his medicine. In there, Niamh had looked at lovely, coloured glass bottles filled with wonderful, flowery scents. She thought that perhaps something from the shop might make Mrs Burton happy. It would be both a Christmas gift, and a thank you for her kindness and protection.

Niamh peered out of the bedroom window, watching for the lanterns of the guards. She could see two glowing orbs flitting between the dark shapes of plants on the lower terraces of the grounds. Niamh knew that it would be cold, but her coat was downstairs – she did not want to risk being caught. She decided she would go without, like she had years before. Anyway, she thought, I need to be light and nimble for climbing, and a coat would only get in the way.

Silently she slid open the window and reached out to the creeping vines that grew on the trellis on that end of the mansion. Even in her cumbersome dress, she managed to scurry down to the ground, and broke into a run for the orchard, where she was safe from the light of the house. She knew that, within the orchard, she could easily hide from the guards' lanterns should they approach.

The chilly night air made her shiver as she pressed her back against an apple tree. For a moment she wished she had brought her coat, but then remembered the winters where she had shared the coats of the women who had protected her. Women like Judith Cloonan, the woman who had died on the night Niamh met Dr Blessing.

Those frozen nights suddenly came back to her. Waiting on the streets while the women worked, sneaking into baker's shops to steal the heat and a piece of bread if she could manage it. She thought of the end of so many nights, with six or seven of them huddled together in a doss, all together in a bed, or out on the hard floor. They were hard times, but not all bad times.

Niamh was pleased to commence an adventure as she feared comfort had made her soft.

The lanterns and voices approached. The guards were nearing the orchard. She caught the whiff of a sweet pipe tobacco. Inching her way around the tree she saw the lantern about ten feet away. She saw the two bearded men.

She became aware of her hot breath in the cold night and pressed her lips together, not wanting to release a jet of steam that would catch the light. When she could hold her breath no longer, she released tiny amounts of air through her nostrils and drew in only a tiny amount of air in exchange. The effect was dizzying after a minute.

Gravel crunched as the men began to move again, back in the direction from which they had come. Niamh knew she could breathe easily once more as the men had turned their backs on her.

Twigs glistened as moisture turned to frost. Niamh was careful to place each footstep where she could make the least amount of noise.

A vixen cried out in the grounds, or the grounds of a neighbouring mansion. The blood-curdling sound was like a woman being attacked - a sound with which she was only too familiar. The sudden cry had caused Niamh to duck, knees bent and head low.

The guards, who had also been startled by the noise, chuckled. One man chided the other playfully for showing fear. They moved on.

Niamh hitched up her dress to the knees and commenced to climb a sturdy beech tree close to the perimeter wall of the grounds. Midway up the tree, a hefty limb drew level with the top of the wall. As Niamh scampered along its length, she remembered a lady she had met during the summer: Mary Brigham, whom she had witnessed besting three men in combat and who had shown no shortage of athletic ability. That was a woman of interest to Niamh – a woman who could handle herself with assurance.

Perfectly balanced, Niamh felt the bow of the limb upon which she moved. It was then that she leapt, knowing that were she to continue, she ran the risk of snapping the branch, falling, and creating such a noise as would alert the guards immediately. Her torso hit the top of the wall, arms fully outstretched. The collision knocked some wind out of her. She kicked her toes to the wall, scraping her shoes terribly as she worked her arms and managed to rise to the top of the wall. She peered down at the pavement on the other side. The street was in utter darkness.

Niamh looked back at the lights of the warm,

comfortable mansion. She thought for a moment of the terrible explosions she and the others of the house had heard the previous night. Grandpa had told her they were mere fireworks, being tested in preparation for a huge New Year celebration, when the city would return to normal. Now that she had heard for a fact that the monsters were real, Niamh realised that the explosions probably had something to do with all of that.

She thought of the explosions and how frightening it had sounded. Thought of the safety of the house. Thought about Mary Brigham, and adventure. She thought about the cannibals or monsters or whatever was meant to be out there. Thought about how worried Mrs Burton would be if she was not back by morning. Thought about the good, bad old days, of slipping into the shadows of the city. She thought about how pleased Mrs Burton would be with a nice present on Christmas morning.

She hung from the lip of the wall for a second or two, then dropped to the pavement and broke into a run to get across the road. Niamh knew to pick a route past St James Park that would take her close to Buckingham Palace. She reasoned that if anywhere in London would be fortified, it would be there. She wanted to be close to the Palace in case she found trouble, but not so close to the Palace that the authorities guarding the Queen would find her and arrest her. Or worse, find her and take her home to face trouble from Mrs Burton!

The fringe of Hyde Park had been a frightening sight for two reasons. The first, the fence and trees had resembled great black claws and teeth. The second, there was nobody else abroad. This meant that either nobody dared go there, and she was the only person mad enough to pass, or that people had been passing, or attempting to do so, but had been dragged into the shadows, to be roasted and eaten in the park.

She imagined the Serpentine running with

blood, and her being able to walk from one side to the other on the backs of the dead who bobbed, swollen and green, in the murky water.

Along her way, Niamh began to notice that some of the Kensington mansions were guarded like the Burton house. When she had passed in daylight this had not been as obvious to her. The guards eyed her suspiciously as she scurried on her way.

Niamh finally saw Londoners on the move when she reached the turnpike at Hyde Park corner. A ragtag group of men had created a wide barricade of carts, crates, barrels and stalls. Through the barricade, they had made a narrow passage – the only way for Niamh to pass into the city proper, in this direction. The men stood by a fire, rifles by their sides. They challenged anybody who approached them from any direction. The only item to pick them out as a uniformed unit was the scruffy bandage of material they each wore around their foreheads.

Niamh observed the small militia, of about a dozen men in total, as they stopped men, women and children. They asked a series of questions, and as one man spoke, two others pointed their rifles. They let the people pass and then turned to the next group, then the next. The scene was one of organised chaos – dozens of men calling orders and instructions, scurrying about the barricade and dozens of travellers trying to pass, chattering with each other as they waited in line. Niamh hoped that in the darkness, her scuffed shoes would not give her away, as she sidled up to the turnpike.

Her keen eyes had spotted a well-dressed couple who were walking into the city, from almost the same direction as her. Their fine clothes marked them as Kensington people. Her fine clothes marked her as a Kensington child - *their* child, as she hoped to appear.

The first flakes of snow fell as she followed the couple into the opening of the barricade. Extending her fingers, she felt the icy droplets land, melting quickly. The thought of the cold and the snow had caused her, involuntarily, to stand closer to the lady and gentleman, wanting to share the heat of their coats, regretting once again that she had decided to leave her own at home.

"Visiting a sick relative," the man said.

"Who?" the guard asked.

"My mother in law, if you must know!" the man replied, his tone telling of his impatience. He wrapped an arm around his wife, and drew her closer to his side.

"The little girl with you?" the guard asked.

"Little girl?" the man asked, turning to follow the stained, crooked finger that extended past his shoulder, pointing straight at Niamh.

"Of course not! No child of mine would be out here without a coat! And with those *things* abroad! The very idea!"

Niamh was about to turn and flee from the barricade, when she heard a screaming whistle from over to her left. The guard's dirty face turned suddenly in the direction of the sound. He grabbed a whistle from the chain around his neck, placed it between his lips, and blew one loud blast. "Hurry, hurry through!" the guard ushered, patting the couple on their backs as they passed. "Come on, girly! Get yourself through!"

Niamh's eyes widened in shock as two other guards brushed past her. They grasped two crates and toppled them into the passage, forming a low blockade.

She could not turn back; there was only one way to go.

A guard shouted, "Over there! I saw two of them by the railings!"

A shot roared out into the night. A shiver ran down Niamh's spine, like cold water. She ran for the boundary of Green Park and could see the opening for Tyburn Lane to her left before she and the others who had fled the turnpike even dared to glance back.

Rifle fire crackled at the turnpike and a cheer

rose from the men. Silver speckles of snow drifted lazily to the ground like glitter in the gaslight. Again she caught some flakes in her hand. Some of the speckles melted, but then she noticed that some of the white speckles remained. She rubbed her palms together and noted the grey and black smears left behind. She realised that there was not just snow falling, but ash and soot.

Wondering why it would snow ash, Niamh hurried along Picadilly and saw Constables with their lanterns, moving with great caution among those who lingered on the thoroughfare. They ordered the Londoners to go home and insisted they were mad for even thinking of stepping out.

Niamh recognised that the best way to remain unnoticed was to move along, and so she did, hoping to reach the Charing Cross area before long.

The way was marked by small fires on the pavements, around which the lowly and frightened huddled. Her nicely made clothes, made scruffy from her climb, and the muck of the city roads, created an appearance that confused them and made them suspicious – she looked incomplete, a half-breed, both one of them and something else altogether.

The streets narrowed and the sense of being crushed by the buildings, and bodies increased as she moved ever closer to the riverside rookeries. Every now and then she noticed the ruins of buildings gutted by fire, or houses boarded up completely.

A woman selling oysters referred to Niamh as "Princess" as she passed. A gentleman in a top-hat, with a handkerchief pressed to his lips, referred to her as, "A stray bitch" to his friend.

She considered how easy it would be to dip a hand into his pocket and remove the pocket watch she knew would be connected to the gold chain the gentleman displayed so dangerously. Moving on, it was only seconds before she realised someone else had noticed the chain and the man cried, “Thief!”

Scuffling feet and fits of giggling rose behind her, then two boys in torn grey shirts and trousers brushed past, inspecting their stolen treasure.

Women called down from the windows of slums, trying to entice the lonely to come and part with their money. Drunken sailors pointed up to them and talked of giving themselves a little present from Old Christmas.

The snow began to fall more persistently, the flakes like feathers in the fog, perfect and white until they landed on the carpet of soot, manure and human filth at Niamh’s feet. She crossed her arms and rubbed at her little biceps, hoping to instil some warmth in them.

Hags and living skeletons, moving piles of rags and yellow-skinned children brushed past her as she continued down the ever narrowing streets, trying to recall the whereabouts of a little pharmacy she had once seen. She ignored the warnings and inquiries as she passed:

“You lost, little madam?”

“Nasty things, abroad…”

She recognised a lodging house near Charing Cross and turned left into a narrow lane, barely wide enough for two adults to pass each other side-on. She could hear the squeal of a pig further down the lane and could smell the hot, thick scent of wet faeces. She caught a glimpse of the two boys she had seen with the pocket watch, flitting in and out, between the legs of the night’s travellers.

A scream in the suffocating lane caused many around her to take flight, running against her. She changed direction to avoid the crush, turning on her heels on the slick ground as a wave of screams rose in the direction she had originally wanted to go. She bumped into the man behind her, excused herself and joined the row of bodies on the other side of the lane, moving with the flow once more. She was, before long, back at the lodging house she had recognised.

Niamh worked a way around, by cutting down two further lanes, taking her back in the direction she had originally intended to travel. She had to admit, in the three years that Dr Blessing had provided her with accommodation, her nose had become a little more delicate to the smells of the city. Her eyes had become less accustomed to the ugly scenes of London at night. She felt unclean and longed to bathe. Niamh intended to buy some rose soap or floral cologne for Charlotte, but wondered if the little money she had on her person would allow her to buy a little treat for herself – something to take away the foul stench of the rookeries at night.

A man roasted chestnuts in a brazier and Niamh longed to buy a bag and warm herself a little by the hot coals, but she had no idea how much her gift for Mrs Burton would cost and so dared not even spend half a penny. The snow melting against her had made her dress damp and the garment clung to her skin, icy and heavy.

Whistles sounded in nearby streets, as constables raised the alarm of one incident or another but before Niamh could make sense of this, she noticed a sign indicating the sale of soap, and a green and red sign reading: Sacks' Pharmacy.

Niamh felt instantly warmed as she jostled through the throng to the shop door. She darted inside. A wall of fragrance welcomed her, saving her from the malodour of the streets. The candlelight reflected off the jars and vessels around the room like a thousand eyes watching her.

It was then she noticed the two real eyes that watched her and the tall, skeletal man to whom the eyes belonged. His thinning fair hair and hooked nose added to his overall appearance which was scarecrow-like, and he wiped long, bony fingers on a scruffy apron as he asked, “Can I help you, my child?”

Niamh was startled at the deep, rich voice. She had expected a much more sinister tone from the man, not the warm, gentle sound she heard. “Errr… yes. Yes. I have come for a present for… my Mama.” She felt the lie was easier than trying to explain her situation. The lie was easy, was comfortable and a spark of yearning presented itself in her heart; she wished the gift was truly for her mother.

“Your Mama? How lovely. And what gift would you give to your Mama?”

“I was thinking of perhaps a perfume. Or a rose soap.”

The pharmacist frowned at Niamh and looked her up and down, tapping his long, discoloured fingernails on the counter. “You must be frozen, child. With no coat, I can assume that your Mama is unaware of your being here.”

Niamh felt her heart pounding and drew in a short breath. Her back straightened. She was immediately aware of her error in stealing away into the city. This strange man caused her more discomfort than the darkness of the park and the shouts, screams and gunfire did together.

“Do not fear, child. I shall keep your secret. I promise,” the pharmacist said, moving to the edge of the counter. His long fingers pushed up the hatch, opening the path from behind the counter, to the shop floor.

Her nerve broke. “I have made a mistake. I must return home immediately!” Niamh cried, turning to the door.

A gunshot roared outside, echoing up and down the lane. The echo mingled with panicked screams and cries.

Niamh’s fingers reached the door handle, but as she pulled, a weight kept the door in place and she was instantly aware of the long, dirty fingers outstretched, holding the door closed. Bolts slammed into place, locking her inside.

"Let me go!" Niamh screamed as the long arms and fingers snaked towards her, snatching her up, dragging her away.

"Shhhhh, child! Be quiet!" the man hissed, dragging her with one arm loose around her neck. He blew on candles as he passed, extinguishing them, casting the shop into darkness. "Shhhhh!"

Niamh shrieked as one of the windows banged and a woman's face appeared pressed against the glass. The woman's head whipped away into the darkness as suddenly as it appeared. Hands, arms and shoulders scraped along the windows as the frightened citizens of the night pushed past each other, fighting to escape some unseen threat in the lane.

The pharmacist pulled Niamh down behind the counter with him and the two of them listened to the chaos of the street.

"Sometimes the constables fire a shot to warn them away," the pharmacist whispered, "to make them run home and bolt their doors. And sometimes they are firing at the vampires."

"Vampires?" Niamh rasped, pressing her fingers against the flesh of her neck. She was not in pain. The pharmacist had moved her quickly, but without applying much pressure. Her movement had been an unconscious one; protecting her neck from imagined vampire bites.

"Yes, child. Devils of the night, I have seen them. Some of them nest near here. The cannons must have missed them last night."

"Cannons?"

The pharmacist pointed into a doorway that led to his private quarters. "Go through there," he said. "We will be safer there."

The back room was sparsely furnished and contained a desk and chair both littered with papers, an unlit stove and an untidy bed that looked to Niamh neither comfortable nor warm.

"Move the papers, child, take a seat," the gangly pharmacist insisted. He lit a candle in a vain effort to make the room seem less imposing.

Niamh did as she had been instructed and did her best to block out the screams and shouts on the street.

"Do not be afraid. We will be quite safe here. The creatures hunt the crowded streets when it gets dark. Fortunately for us, there are plenty of men with guns out there who keep them at bay."

Niamh nodded, and asked, "Did you say they had fired cannons?"

"I did my dear. It must have been the navy. I thought the world was coming to an end, let me tell you!" the pharmacist laughed at the memory of his fear.

Niamh chuckled too, feeling slightly easier about the unusual looking man before her. To think, that she had been afraid of a man so ready to admit his own fear! She began to think of him as some woodland creature in clothes, who had made a little burrow for himself in the middle of the city. She observed that even the candle he had lit resembled him: skinny and tall and looking as though it would break any moment!

"What do they call you, young lady?"

"Niamh. Niamh Blessing."

"And I am Stanley Sacks. And you said earlier, Niamh, that you had come here for a gift for your Mama?"

Niamh nodded.

"What a strange time of day to come calling for such a thing. One so little as you should be tucked up safely in your bed."

Niamh was about to agree when the noise from the street intensified. The twin plate glass windows rattled in the shop front once more. She felt certain that the glass would shatter any moment. Her shoulders hunched up and her fingernails felt as though they would cut through her palms.

Stanley frowned as the frantic banging persisted. "Here, Niamh," he said, passing her a blanket from his bed. "If the glass breaks, you must dash for the back door, throw the bolts and flee into the night."

He rose to his feet and blew out the candle before tiptoeing out of the room. The banging was ceaseless; a loud cracking sound followed some of the impacts.

Niamh rose to her feet and positioned herself by the door.

The banging intensified. There were many hands, many more, more joining the throng all of the time.

"Niamh?" Stanley called.

"Yes?"

"Run for your life!"

It was then that the windows exploded inwards. Niamh raced for the back door. She threw the bolt at her feet, threw the bolt by the handle and reached for another that secured the top of the door. Her fingertips reached the lock, as she stretched onto the very tips of her toes.

Stanley screamed from back in the shop, as what sounded like a pack of wild animals ran amok.

Niamh heard glass cabinet doors shatter, and jars break against the walls and floor. She glanced over her shoulder for only a moment and could see shapes darting about in the darkness. She heard a sniffing sound as a shape shifted through the gloom, stalking into the passage where she stood.

With only a second to decide, she abandoned the door and dashed for the stairs to her right. It seemed foolish to enter the first floor of the building as for all she knew, escape was impossible from there, but it seemed even more foolish to remain, with who knew how many creatures in the shop.

Bounding up the stairs, Niamh heard the chattering of teeth close behind her. Her heart pounded all the quicker, pumping her precious blood through her limbs, urging her on, faster, faster.

From the street she heard a whistle and a man call, “Sacks! Your windows are put through!”

A rasping voice replied from within the shop, “We know it!”

“My God,” came the reply, “they have murdered Stanley Sacks! Fire at will, men!”

A rattle of gunfire filled the air as Niamh rounded the head of the stairs, up onto the passage. To aid her turn, she swung around the wooden stair post to try to maintain her speed. Before she managed to snatch her hand away, icy fingers tore at her skin, opening up her skin with savage speed. The blanket had been discarded somewhere on the stairs and she was able to run as free as her dress would allow.

Ignoring the pain in her hand, she pressed on past two doors that she assumed were normally storerooms. Ahead there was another door. The room beyond must have been directly above the one Stanley appeared to sleep in.

Niamh felt the hot breath at her neck, which sent a shiver from the top to the bottom of her spine. She heard the screams and howls from the shop below. She prayed the door would open. She extended her fingers, grasped the handle and turned it.

Her pursuer crashed into her back, knocking her through the open door and sending her sprawling across the floor. Instantly she scrambled to her feet, unable to see around her. She kicked at the bedroom door and knocked it shut, scrambling to find a lock she could throw to lock the creature outside.

Then she heard the chatter once more; she felt the breath on her neck.

“I have tasted your blood, pretty. And now I will have all of it.”

Heavy footsteps sounded up the stairs.

"They come for you! They come to save me!"

"I will have another taste," hissed the creature.

Niamh shuddered as jagged, cracked teeth scraped her neck. She cried, "They will find you before you even spill a drop!" Knowing there was no reasoning with the monster, she screamed from the top of her lungs.

A voice came from the landing, "In here! Stanley said there's a child up here!"

A Scottish voice called out, "To the floor, child!"

Niamh dropped to the ground immediately, feeling the back of her dress snag and tear in the creature's hand.

Revolvers popped from out on the landing and the door thudded and splintered as the bullets whizzed above her head. Shafts of light appeared through the gloom, cast by the lantern her saviours carried.

The creature moaned in pain and staggered backwards.

Niamh heard a window shatter, and cries rose up from the lane below. It was then that she turned and stayed low, moving for the broken window, hoping to catch a glimpse of her attacker. "He is gone!" she cried, knowing that the men outside were reloading their revolvers. "You blasted him through the window!"

She looked down into the lane that ran alongside the shop and could see several bystanders pointing up at her, shouting.

The bullet-riddled door burst open and two large men in suits entered the room, one of them holding up a lantern. "Are you alright, lassie?" came a Scottish voice.

"Yes. He managed to escape, I think."

The other man, the man with the lantern, spoke with an educated accent and barked, "Get away from the window!"

Niamh was about to comply, when an arm

swept around her from through the broken frame and she was yanked out into the freezing London night.

Her cheeks stung in the bitter cold as her tears ran and mingled with the snow that clung to her face as her captor hauled her over the slippery roof tiles. If this creature was worried about the slick surface beneath his feet, he did not show it, using the sloping roof to gain height before shifting his weight to turn and spring back, vaulting over the gap between the pharmacy and the next building.

He landed running. His feet clattered on the tiles as he scrambled forward with Niamh tucked under one muscular arm, his other arm probing and grasping, seeking out ways to support his flight – a chimney pot here, a rafter there.

Niamh felt sick. She heard shouts and gunshots from the street below. She heard the *whizz* of the bullets as they cut past, inches away from her ears. The authorities were no longer worried about saving her life – to them she was clearly already dead, food for their enemy, or another enemy in the making, perhaps. All the same, Niamh thought, it seemed to be their opinion that a bullet was preferable.

They took off again on another leap from one roof to another. The landing was not as graceful, the roof not as stable. The tiles cracked under the weight of both of them and down they tumbled, into a crooked, dirty lodging house.

Niamh hit the floorboards hard. There was no carpet, no rugs to warm or cushion the wood. She lay still. Her battered body ached if she even thought to move. How easily she had become accustomed to the comforts of a proper home. She thought angrily about how soft and foolish she had become. Her life was to end and all because of the silly notion of a kindness. Any happiness she could have brought to Mrs Burton was undone a hundred times by the fact that by morning, she would be dead and Mrs Burton would have a reason to continue wearing black.

The sound of sniffing made her more alert. Her instincts bristled at the strange, ragged sound.

"No, stay away from her!" her captor roared. "She belongs to me!"

The sniffing became more pronounced and was joined by the occasional chattering of teeth, much as she had heard during her flight in the pharmacy.

A broad, thick, strong hand appeared in her vision. The fingers wrapped around a broken tile, brandishing it as if it was a blade.

"Stay away!"

Niamh remained silent, she turned her head slightly. The effort was monstrous. The sight she saw even more so, but trumped even by the consuming stench of death.

The lodging house attic was lit by only a few stubs of candles. The intrusion of the night air had disturbed the flames and made them so weak that they would die any second. She knew that the moment the light went out, the murdering would start.

Lurking in the light were a dozen withered bodies. Some of them lay still, lifeless, naked. Others crawled like the lowliest of creatures, bony, sunken, putrefying, but somehow alive. Each of them showed livid bites on their torn, papery skin.

"Vampires," she thought.

Her captor stood close to her, his back turned. He was unconcerned with her at that moment. He was occupied with the others in the room.

"Stay back! Keep your disease to yourself!"

"Sick vampires," she thought.

A glance at her captor's leg revealed why he had not pounced on his enemy immediately. A chunk of wood had become embedded in his calf muscle. Flesh and blood waxed and waned at the site of the wound, wanting to heal but unable to do so with the foreign body in place.

Two of the slithering, diseased creatures moved from the shadows to her left as one. Their skin was so corrupt with lesions and pus that they seemed to have melted together. Drawing closer to her, they peeled apart, rending open the unhealed wounds. They moved to attack the vampire who threatened them with the tile shard. She could smell the overpowering scent of decay from their open sores as though a foul fog had descended upon her.

The candles flickered as a breeze drove spiralling snowflakes through the gaping cavity in the roof.

Niamh knew that she had perhaps one chance, if she had any chance at all. Willing her body to fight the pain, she twisted her head to the right, lifting her shoulders slightly.

"Jusssst a little drink!"

"Stay away!"

Her eyes searched the floor, hoping to see a handle, a pull ring, anything.

The two creatures on the floor pounced. They tore at her captor's legs, dislodging the wood from his wound. The vampire slashed wildly with the tile shard, his muscle mass allowing him to cause devastating damage to the emaciated bodies of those who clawed at him. Others joined the scramble, though, crawling over each other, their skin peeling off across the floor, tearing as they reached out to attack the outnumbered vampire.

Niamh recognised that moment as the time to move. She urged her muscles into action, drawing up her legs. She noticed the hatch, but winced when she realised that it was pinned shut by a decomposing body. Scrambling to her right, she reached beneath the sweaty, slimy corpse, her fingers slipping over the metal ring. Trying not to vomit, she pressed her shoulder against the cadaver, desperate to shove it off the hatch.

Her shoulder sank into the putrid flesh. As her

cheek met the oozing, festering mass, Niamh could not tell if the body was moving, or if she was simply moving *into* it.

One glance at her captor told her she had perhaps a minute, perhaps more. His arms swung in wide arcs, the creatures he battled clawed to stand upright. Teeth sank into his legs. He cried out, terrified of their disease. The vampire stabbed downwards, slashing into a neck. With his free hand he grasped a clump of thin, straw-coloured hair. The hair tore free, bringing with it a chunk of scalp, exposing a portion of skull.

The body was moving as Niamh heaved further and further. Her fingers slid over into the flesh. It felt like the skin on custard.

Teeth chattered, close to her. Niamh looked beyond the corpse, expecting to see another of the diseased, wasted creatures coming to ambush her, but there was nothing there.

The corpse slid more easily, moved further. She could see the hatch was free of obstruction.

That was when the corpse turned its swollen head towards her. Teeth appeared between strings of saliva and the webbed flesh of rotten lips.

Her hands found the ring of the hatch; the slime prevented her from gaining a solid hold.

Fingers reached for her, torn skin hung loose, exposing the bony knuckles and every muscle and tendon in the hand.

A rattling chuckle broke free of the creature's monstrous mouth.

Niamh squeezed the pull ring and heaved the hatch open. Beneath her, there was nothing but darkness. She did not know how far she would fall, or what awaited her in the gloaming. The room could be filled with more creatures and more danger than the attic in which she stood, for all she knew.

The mouth surged forward, homing in on the open scratches on the back of her hand. Saliva and scum slid across her skin.

Niamh decided in an instant.

She dropped through the hatch.

Into the darkness.

And then came light.

“Look! The lassie!” came the Scottish voice.

“That smell!” came the local voice.

“Grab her! Grab her! Let us get her clear and burn this damned place doon!”

Giles.

"Where can she be?" Charlotte sobbed as the coach came to rest at the steps of the Burton household. "Why would she desert us? Was I unkind to her?"

"Try not to worry too much, my love," Giles said, reaching for the coach door. "She is a most resourceful child. She would not do anything stupid. Of that I am sure."

"Nothing stupid? Nothing stupid?" Charlotte exclaimed. "She is nowhere to be found on the grounds. She has left without even taking a coat with which to keep warm! If she would do nothing stupid, then why must you now search the city for her?"

Miss Pinchstaff hugged Charlotte in close, trying to mask her own upset and offer some consolation.

Giles could think of no answer. "Look, my dears, go back inside. We shall search all night, if we must. Never fear. She will be safe and sound. I have no doubt." Giles climbed into the coach with the two guards from the rear of the grounds. The men at the gate bade them good luck in their search as they passed into the night.

"So, where do you think we should look first?" one of the guards asked.

Giles produced his medicine bottle from his pocket and took a long draught. He turned to the guards and replied, "I have told the driver to get us to Sacks' Pharmacy. I am almost certain she is heading for there."

"What makes you say so?"

"She said something earlier about a present for Mrs Burton," Giles said. His eyes moistened; his face showed no trace of his joviality.

The coach raced towards the Hyde Park turnpike. Giles and the guards rode with their heads outside the windows of the carriage, hoping to catch a glimpse of the child, praying that she had not managed to stray too far from the house.

Giles examined his pocket watch. It was shortly after 9pm. The pharmacy would still be open if she had made it that far – if that was, indeed where she was headed. He hoped at least she would be safe inside.

The snow fell steadily and had been lying, gathering. The coach jostled occasionally as the horses struggled to find purchase on the icy stone. The driver wisely slowed the pace, although none of the men present wanted to sacrifice speed.

"These streets are dead," one of the guards commented. "It still strikes me after all these months."

Giles agreed. "There will be more life beyond the turnpike. But I agree, the city is not meant to be this way. Her soul is gone."

"Do you reckon it will ever go back the way it was, Mr Burton?" the other guard asked.

Giles felt some relief at the appearance of the turnpike and fortifications there. He turned to the guard who had spoken. "Go back? The city has been destroyed as surely as if it was the end of all days. The destruction is not entirely obvious from the outside, but thousands are dead, and the survivors are changed, decayed, tainted somehow. It would take a miracle for London to come back from this."

"They say the Grenadier Guards were almost wiped out," the first guard whispered.

"Shhh, the coachman's brother…"

"I know. I know."

"Shhh lads, please," Giles warned, turning from the window to give both guards a reproachful look for their gossip.

The coach slowed for the approach to the turnpike barrier. Giles leapt from the carriage, slipping slightly on the icy ground. He peered up at the array of rifles that pointed out at him from the fortifications.

"Good evening, gentlemen!" he called.

"State your business," came the dispassionate response.

"My name is Giles Burton. My fellows and I have an urgent matter to attend to. Have you seen a small child? A girl. She is 11 years old, a mere slip of a girl. She wore a dress, probably no coat."

One of the men stood tall among the barricade, lowered his rifle and adjusted the ragged bandage on his forehead. "I saw such a child. She walked in with a man and wife but they said she was a stranger to them."

Giles smiled at Niamh's cunning. That was her all right, passing herself off as the child of a couple so as not to arouse suspicion. "Did you let her pass?" he asked.

"I did. We had to get some business done with one of them things in the park over there to your back. We let her through and she moved on up Picadilly with the rest of 'em."

"Well, that child went missing from my house earlier this evening. She was believed to be in bed."

Another voice emerged from the fortifications, "What do you want us to do about it, my old fella? We already told you: the child moved on."

"I would consider it a great kindness if you would open a passage for my men and I to enter the city. I must find the child and bring her home safely."

"Are you mad, old man?" one of the guards called.

Giles watched as an oil lamp appeared on top of the barricade. "Watch this," called the guard.

The oil lamp hurtled through the air in the direction of the Hyde Park fence. When the lamp struck the ground the glass shattered, spilling burning oil. In the illumination afforded by the flames, Giles was able to see beyond the fence, glistening eyes and teeth. Dozens of creatures, which at first appeared human, stood at the fence, watching and waiting.

"The minute we open a passage for your coach, they will make a run for it. It has taken months for them to realise that if we put enough shots into them, they will eventually go down. Now they hold back awhile, and wait for the right moment to charge."

"Perhaps you need more guns," Giles said. He kept his eyes fixed on the huddled shapes in the Park.

"More guns, more men, more everything. They are just biding their time in the park, picking off anyone they can, beyond the range of our guns. In a night or two, they shall feel strong again and make another run for it. We will manage to pin a couple of them down, burn them, like many times before. It puts the rest off for a while. Then the whole sequence of events starts over once more."

"I thought they would be more determined than that," Giles said, staring at the creatures. It amazed him that this occurred every night, only streets away from his home. He had heard the gunfire, but had not realised that the creatures had amassed in such numbers so close to his home. Up until then, he had passed through the barrier without fully appreciating danger on his doorstep.

The guard sniffed. "These buggers are dying. Some sort of wasting disease. Like leprosy or something for vampires. If they *was* the real vampires, we would never stand a chance. Got to try and stop anyone going near and… feeding them, though. When they attack we try to take a few of them, they try to take a few of us. That is just the way it goes. We need to keep it that way until they starve to death, or a miracle presents itself."

"Well then, I wish you luck. And when I have found the child, I will have a mind in the morning to write a draft and you and your men shall have the munitions and extra manpower you need."

The guards seemed unenthusiastic about Giles' proposal. "The Government has been promising us men for weeks and weeks. Never send nothing."

"I am a Burton, of the Burton Shipping Company. I have access to money, and men, and guns. I will provision you and arm you. And from the day after tomorrow, from Christmas, you shall have enough resources to sweep that park clear of the demons who lurk there."

"What? All for us opening a passage for you?" one of the guards sneered.

"No. I would not put you so at risk now that I see the odds you are against. My coach will have to go back to the house. I will proceed on foot with my two men. The supplies are yours, because I admire your courage. The supplies are yours, because you need help to get the job done. The supplies are yours, because I would have no more good men killed by the evil that has torn the heart from this city!"

"Let him pass. Let him and his men pass!" the watch commander called. "Bear, take them over to Freddy, that drunk so-and-so you! Tell Freddy to get that horse and cart round. This gentleman shan't get his coach through, but we can spare him ours for an hour or two, while he finds that girl."

Giles turned back to the coach driver as his guards disembarked. "Godspeed, my friend."

The driver touched a finger to the rim of his hat. "Good hunting."

Once through the turnpike a large brute of a man, who walked with a heavy limp, led the small search party to a horse and cart. A thin, ruddy-faced man sat at the reins, turned to them and said, "Climb on, gentlemen. Tell me, where is ya headed?"

"Do you know Sacks' Pharmacy?" Giles asked, settling between a crate and barrel on the cart.

"I know it," Freddy replied.

"Get us there as quickly as you can," Giles said. "But keep your eyes peeled for a young girl out alone."

"Lot of orphans about, these days, sir. Lot more

than normal," Freddy said, cracking the reins. "But I shall keep a watchful eye out."

They carried on without further comment until one of the guards noticed the stench of burning flesh on the air. A column of smoke rose from the direction of Pall Mall.

Giles leaned forward to address Freddy. "Take us down St James's Street."

Freddy nodded. "No problem, sir. But beggin' yer pardon, it will be difficult to pass and even more difficult to see the girl, should she happen to be there."

"And why would that be?" Giles asked.

Freddy turned the cart and followed others down the street as instructed, preferring to wait a moment to let Giles take it in for himself, rather than explain.

Giles noticed the cart in front of them. A large square of ragged cloth flapped in the breeze, occasionally lifting high enough that he could make out what lay beneath. He saw feet, hands, grey faces, piled up and intermingled. He could not determine exactly how many bodies he was looking at, but he knew it was dozens.

"Every night, they take the dead to the pyres. St James's Square is one of the places they have been taking them. Lot of people head there at night."

Giles could see that Freddy was not mistaken. Trails of heartbroken Londoners poured away from the square, and scores travelled inward, bearing their dead. He had not been to the city after dark in recent months and had not heard of this custom. "Why are we burning our dead?" he asked.

"Problem is keeping 'em dead," Freddy sniffed.

Progress was slow as carts turned into St James's Square and, watched by armed guards, people took the bodies down and carried them into the square to conduct their dreary industry.

Freddy drove on, passing the carts with business at the square, but Giles and his guards managed to see into the square itself as they passed. They felt the heat from the pyres and wondered how anyone could stand to work near the intense, red flames. The whole square appeared to Giles to be burning at first glance, but when his eyes adjusted, he could make out dozens of separate mounds.

"We have truly arrived in Hell," he sobbed.

"They say it is best to burn 'em the night they die. Some say you have only an hour before they get back up. Others say if the vampires drain them completely, it's all right, they won't get up again. I don't know, though. I reckon burn them all, just to be on the safe side."

"Thank you, Freddy," Giles cried, wishing the man would stop talking. He turned away and saw other carts behind them, looked ahead and saw carts streaming in from the riverside. On every one of the conveyances he imagined the beloved child they sought.

By the Hay Market Freddy could take the cart no further, as the road was completely clogged with carts, coaches and pedestrians.

Giles and his guards disembarked and continued on foot, thanking the man who had managed to get them so far. They soon saw what had caused the traffic to stop. One cart had been so heavily laden with corpses that one of the wheels had buckled, then broken, turning the cart over and spilling the grim cargo across the road. The ensuing chaos had seen people trampled by spooked horses and several fights had broken out in which drivers were dragged from their perches and beaten.

"See how they turn on each other?" Giles called to his companions. "So divided they will, each and every one of them, and before very long at all, find themselves consumed by the flames in St James's Square!"

To the south, gunshots told of the riots outside

of the unfinished Parliament buildings. A surge of protestors broke out in a dash north. They slowed before ever reaching Giles and his men, recovering their nerve before idling their way back toward the police line to resume their protest.

More smoke and flames caught Giles' attention, this appearing to be a building rather than a pyre. "My God, I fear that fire is close to our destination. I pray the child is well!"

The snow fell ever harder and the men slipped on the marsh of waste, snow and ice that had become their path.

One of the guards, frustrated at being jostled by so many passersby, threw a man to the ground, causing others to topple over.

Giles rebuked the guard, who replied, "Why are there so many still out and about? Why must they roam the streets when they are so dangerous?"

Giles considered this. "Perhaps there is no hiding from this evil. Perhaps home is no safer for these poor wretches. If our Queen can be forced to leave her heavily fortified home, then surely the shacks and doss-houses afford no security."

"Safety in numbers," the other guard offered.

"Quite so," Giles agreed. "And like the wildebeest on the great plains of Africa, they swarm in great numbers. Predators can claim only one or two of them at a time and the others… they flee for their lives, moving onward hoping to survive the next attack."

The comforting smell of roasting chestnuts drifted in the air, permeating the stench of the ravaged city. Giles savoured the scent as he swigged from his medicine bottle. "Not much further to go, men. With any luck we shall find our girl desperately trying to decide which gift to buy for her mother!"

"Hope upon hope, sir!" one of the guards wished.

"And another hope upon that!"

A woman wailed as she emerged from the shadows of a lane, huddling a tattered bundle in her arms. A tiny arm hung lifeless from the cloth. The woman was walking to St James's Square, following the established order, defying her instinct in order to protect strangers. The sorrow of the scene caused Giles to feel like his heart would burst. He wanted to reach out to her, to hold her, and help her give the child a proper burial rather than burn the tiny body like a tribe of savages would. The woman was followed by a bleeding soldier and an old man whose face was charred ebony-black from a house fire.

Everywhere Giles looked he saw ever more needy citizens, more desperation, more loneliness, more suffering. "I can not bear this! Who could you turn to first to provide charity, without turning your head and seeing a more needy soul immediately afterwards? I have seen too much! Must the city be tortured so before it dies?"

One of the guards grasped Giles' shoulder. "Take heart, sir. We are close to the pharmacy. Like you said, we shall find her there and then we take her straight home."

A priest thumped a bible against his chest, tears streaming down his cheeks as he walked slowly toward Parliament Street, roaring for all to hear, "And again he shall walk among us! As foretold and promised, the risen Christ shall walk among us once more and smite the devils plaguing our city! Death, and rebirth as the Lord God wills it! On Christmas Day He shall rise again - not a redeemer, but an avenger, with the Lord's might as his sword and our prayers as his breastplate!"

Behind the priest followed a cloaked gathering whose fervent chanting almost drowned out the proclamations of their leader. People stood by and watched the procession and others ran into the middle of the road to join them, stirred by the priest's words.

"To prayer! To prayer, ye heathen bastards!

To prayer and temper the Almighty's armour with your devotion!"

Giles wondered what would happen when the crusaders met with the rioters at Parliament, and all descended upon the police gathered there.

In only a few minutes, Sacks' Pharmacy came into view.

"Looks like they have been attacked!" one of the men declared.

Giles broke into a run that astonished his companions. He weaved his way through the crowded lane and inspected the open shop front. Inside, the shop had been ransacked, with bottles and earthenware jars discarded or shattered completely, all over the floor. Shards glistened in the light of lanterns positioned about the place. Some militia men and police constables stood in the doorway and worked within the building, some holding handkerchiefs across their mouths, others sweeping the mess into piles with long, stiff brooms.

Giles overheard one of the constables at the door saying, "It is nothing short of a bleeding miracle, I swear to it."

"Well then, that would be two miracles in one night," another said.

"Perhaps this is the sign of things to come. Perhaps this is the turn."

Giles approached the constables and asked, "Might I ask what has occurred here?"

A constable turned from the shop and held up a cautioning hand. "Stand back, sir. There are all manner of poisons and what have you in here, all over the floor as you can plainly see."

"Please. Tell me what happened," Giles insisted.

The constable frowned, unable to understand the pleading in this strange old man's voice. He nodded to the two men who joined Giles, the guards who had managed to catch up.

"They are with me; do not concern yourself with them. It is vital that I learn what has occurred here this night."

"There was another nest of blood-suckers here. We thought they got them all around here last night, but obviously some slipped through the net."

Another constable offered, "Perhaps they hadn't risen last night. They might have just turned tonight."

"Maybe, who knows?" the first constable snorted, before turning his attention back to Giles. "Anyway, it seems they smelled someone was home here at the pharmacy and they smashed through the plate glass and started tearing the place to bits. They attacked Stanley Sacks, the pharmacist, before we got here. One of them took a girl off the street and made off across the roofs with her."

Giles raised a hand to his mouth and staggered backwards. The guards braced him and kept him steady. "My God! We are too late!" His hand found the medicine bottle and trembling, he pressed the brown glass to his lips. He drained the few sips remaining and the empty bottle slipped from his grasp into the slush of mud and snow.

"Too late? What do you mean?"

Before Giles or the guards could respond, a detective emerged from the pharmacy. "Aye, by God, I have never known a thing like it."

"Sir?" the constables asked.

The detective removed his black bowler hat and scratched his ear. When he spoke, it was with a broad, Scottish accent, "That man is breathing. After those bites, those horrific bites... He lives."

"Then we burn him?"

The detective shook his head. "Not at all!"

Giles noticed that the constables and militia had gathered closer to hear the detective. He wondered if they might not rise against their superior and take matters into their own hands.

"He's a blood-sucker! I say we burn him like all the rest!" one of the constables demanded.

The detective turned and shot each man a steely glare. "You will do no such thing! I will put a bullet into the guts of any man who dares to lift a finger against that poor soul." He paused and let his threat sink in. His fingers were at the butt of his revolver. "I am as good a shot as I am a piper and with God as my judge I wis the best piper in all of Dundee."

"Why should the pharmacist get any better treatment?" one of the constables asked.

"His wounds. They are not healing. These vampire creatures, when they turn a man, he heals, barring mebbe a wee mark oan his neck. This Stanley Sacks character is in a bad way, but he is speaking. I lay a silver bullet on him and he didnae even flinch. And that wee lassie, her cuts on her hand have only now stopped bleeding. He was bitten, she wasnae. But neither one of them is turning."

"Yet."

Giles grabbed the detective's arm. "There's a girl? Please sir, let me see her! I have come over from Kensington to find my granddaughter. She ran away to get her guardian… her mother, a-a present. Her name is Niamh Blessing!"

The detective's eyes narrowed. "Blessing, yeh say?"

"Yes. Listen, never mind that. Please, could I see her? She will confirm my identity."

The detective replaced his hat and looked Giles up and down. "Come on, then. But I must warn you, she willnae be confirming anything at all. The poor wee thing she's in an awful state. Breathing, mind, but unconscious. We can not bring her around at all."

Giles was led into the back room, where a doctor stood over Niamh's fragile, battered frame. Giles dropped to his knees, weeping, kissing the child's hand

and crying out her name. “I have found you, my dear, sweet Niamh! I have found you.”

The detective was joined by another of his kind, similarly attired in a black suit and hat. “I wish we could have found her sooner, sir. I fear there is little our physician can do for her.”

Giles kissed the child’s forehead and turned to his fellows. “I must take her home. It will kill her mother to see her so stricken, yet what choice do I have? If the Lord must take her, then let him take her from her mother’s arms into his.”

The Scottish detective stepped forwards and reached for a mallet and wooden stake that was set aside on a shelf. “Do you ken what this is?”

Giles nodded.

“Do you ken what it is for?”

Giles nodded again.

“Then I suggest you keep it close to you, near the lassie’s sick bed. And keep some chloroform handy. If you find any here take it with you. They seem not to like it. One broken jar in the shop slowed half a dozen of them enough for us to shoot them down and stake them. If she changes, sir, then she is not the little lassie anymore. That you must take from me as a solid matter of truth.”

The doctor cleared his throat and whispered to the detective, “Are you sure we should take a chance, sir?”

“You doctors are a bloodthirsty lot, at times. It was one of your kind that got us into this mess, eh?” the detective immediately turned to Giles and raised an eyebrow. “What was his name again, eh? Had that wee hospital oan Poland Street.”

Giles shook his head and feigned ignorance. “I am quite sure I have no idea.”

“Aye… I am quite sure, too. No matter. I had pitied this wee lassie. Look at the state of her; I had thought it maybe a kinder thing had she not made it.

But who knows? Perhaps it is a blessing in disguise, eh, sir? Take her back home with yeh. I bet her Ma's worried sick."

Stanley Sacks appeared at the door, using the doorframe to prop himself up. His neck was covered in bandages and a greasy lotion had been slathered onto wounds across his face and head.

Giles noticed that two militia men stood behind Stanley, watching his every move with great interest.

Stanley's voice was weak and his eyes were heavy, it seemed an effort for Stanley to even blink. "Before you take the child, I must give you this." Stanley extended his pale hand to give Giles a small bottle. "A perfumed water. The girl, she said her mother was in need of some cheering. I believe this is what she was after."

Giles was touched by the stricken man's thoughtfulness. "That is very generous of you."

"I hope she… I hope little Niamh makes a swift recovery."

"And I you," Giles said, shaking the man's hand. "What will happen to you now?"

Stanley looked at the men in the room and those behind him. "Hopefully I will stay alive long enough to prove that I am no vampire."

Giles inspected the glass bottle in his hands, turning it around to see the label and ribbon that decorated it. "I believe your kindness proves you to be no monster."

"I have ordered my men to stay their hands, Mr Sacks. You need have no fear."

"I have one thing to ask of you, Mr Sacks," Giles said, his gaze flitting between the floor and the man he addressed.

"Anything," Sacks replied.

"I was here the other day. I bought a medicine or elixir here the other day. Brown bottle, Chinaman's name on it."

"You refer to Hong's Blessing," Sacks replied. He tried to stand up straight to talk business, but was met immediately with pain and leaned against the door-frame once more.

"That's the stuff," Giles said, his face lighting up. "I wonder if I might purchase from you another bottle… perhaps two?"

Sacks sighed and gestured toward his destroyed shop. "I am afraid all stocks of that particular elixir were ruined. I bought it in, and unfortunately have not the recipe, myself."

"Ah well, there is nothing to be done for it," Giles said with a disappointed shrug of his shoulders. "I bought a good deal of it from you and have another bottle or so tucked away at home. I simply should not like to find myself without it."

Sacks' eyes lit up in agreement. "I could use some of it myself. I have been taking it for a couple of old complaints lately. The results are remarkable, are they not?"

Giles agreed. "It makes an old man like me feel young again!"

Edward.

Edward Summerscale arrived at the Burton house shortly after ten O' clock in the morning on a snow-covered Christmas Eve. He noted the armed guards at the gate who allowed his carriage to pass when they recognised him. Edward then noted a carriage bearing the livery of the Burton Shipping Company parked near the entrance to the house and wondered if Charlotte had called a management meeting, perhaps so that she could spend Christmas itself uninterrupted, what with the pregnancy and the little girl now living with her.

A guard appeared at a ground floor window, nodded to an unseen comrade, and the front door opened as Edward disembarked the carriage. Edward reached into the carriage and clumsily pulled a paper parcel towards him. He was glad of his housekeeper's foresight in wrapping the grapes and oranges fully as he would doubtless have spent half of the day chasing stray fruit around the carriage otherwise.

He clutched the package close to his breast, crossing his arms over at the wrist, hoping not to crush the delicious fruit within. A mournful wave swept through his mind. He missed his fingers – the six of them that had been taken by the madman. He was left with only the thumb and forefinger of each hand. His black gloves concealed plaster imitation fingers which at least stopped people from staring too hard.

Sometimes, he had noticed particularly when entering a warm house from the cold, he felt an itch as though the fingers were still there, begging to be scratched. Those occasions were torturous – the desire to scratch something that was not there – and a reminder of the brutality he had suffered.

Edward was shown through to a small reception room warmed by a log fire. It was there that he realised the Burton Company carriage had carried his old friend

Francis Flanders.

Francis leapt to his feet and took the parcel from Edward, setting it on the couch gently. “It is good to see you Edward,” he enthused.

The two men embraced briefly, slapping each other on the back. “Have you been waiting very long?” Edward asked.

“An hour. Something terrible has happened.”

Edward immediately feared Charlotte had experienced problems with her unborn child. “Charlotte?”

Francis raised an assuring hand. “You need not worry about Charlotte. Charlotte is fine. The problem is little Niamh.”

“Niamh?”

Edward released a heavy sigh. “She stole away last night. Henry’s uncle Giles has been living here. He and some of the men went into the city and found her, thank God. But she has suffered an ordeal.”

It was then that both men became aware of a commotion out in the lobby. The parlour door had opened and a doctor hurried for the front door.

Giles rushed after the man, followed by a guard and the heavily pregnant Charlotte, who was red-faced with fury. “Shame on you, Doctor!” she cried. “If you dare to call yourself a doctor!”

Giles added. “I shall see you ruined for this, man!”

The doctor turned as he heaved the front door open. “I will give no treatment to that man’s child! The ruin he has brought on this city, well it is only God’s justice that he suffers loss himself!”

“A healing man? A Christian? You sir, are the worst of the worst! The lowest and meanest of the low! To refuse a child medical attention is the greatest sin a medical man could commit!” Charlotte screamed. “That child is dying!”

Giles turned to Charlotte and noticed that she was clutching her prominent bump. He stepped to her side and held her shoulders. "There is nothing more we can do, dear. We must get you a seat."

Edward and Francis made themselves known as the front door closed and the doctor raced away.

"I am deeply sorry that you gentlemen should find us in such a shambolic state," Charlotte said, gasping for breath.

"Not at all, let us get you back to your chair," Edward said, pressing a wrist against Charlotte's shoulder, not wishing to touch her with his hidden, deformed hands.

Giles led the two visitors upstairs and into the sickroom, where Miss Pinchstaff was found kneeling by Niamh's side. The child was dressed in a white night gown, her skin ashen and gray. The governess acknowledged them briefly, before returning to her supplications to God.

The three men left the room once more, not wishing to speak of their fears in the same room as the child. In the safety of the parlour, Charlotte composed herself and explained to Edward and Francis that the doctor they had seen leave was the fourth to do so and that none would assist them, knowing that the child was the daughter of George Blessing.

"And they call *him* a monster," Francis muttered.

"What sickens the child?" Edward asked.

"She has various cuts and sprains around her body. Those would heal well enough. The problem is that one of her wounds, the one on her hand, appears to have become infected. She was seen by a doctor last night, who managed to dress her injuries, but who claimed he could do no more for her. She stirs only very occasionally, and then only to wretch, but she is completely purged, she has no more to pass. She can not take food, rejects water, she is simply wasting away."

The two visitors were visibly upset by this. "I feared she had been bitten by one of these creatures they keep talking about," Francis said.

"She shows no signs of a bite, but these creatures seem to be carrying various diseases," Charlotte replied. "I have spoken with some experts on the subject."

Francis straightened his back at this insinuation. Only he and Charlotte knew precisely who these experts were. Burton Shipping had been running what was referred to in hushed tones as 'the Black Book'. The Black Book included a number of secret supply agreements started by Henry Burton back in his early days. Some of the agreements had fuelled his rise to dominance in shipping and included arming the Chinese against Naval and Parliamentary restrictions. Another section of the Black Book involved transactions for a secret organisation that specialised in matters such as the creatures running amok in London – the organisation known to a very limited few, as De Omori.

Charlotte had met an agent of De Omori five months beforehand and only after that had she learned of the Black Book, and the fact that her late husband's company had dealings with that particular organisation. She knew that in the shadows of London, De Omori was fighting a silent war to free the city of the menace that held it in terror. Indeed she knew that a series of explosions heard in the city a few nights before had been caused by De Omori weapons. She hoped that the explosions signalled a turning of the tide, but either way, it seemed it was too late to save Niamh.

"The experts, with whom I conferred, were unfortunately not medical men; they were more like... soldiers, I suppose. They did explain that these bloodthirsty vampires seem to be a weaker strain than they have seen elsewhere. The problem is their sheer number. They noted that pureblood vampires have been evolving over the years and have built up a certain tolerance of sunlight – particularly in our smoky industrial cities where the sunlight is choked. Apparently, only when they tap into their otherworldly powers do they fall prey to the sun. The creatures infesting London presently, however, shy away from daylight completely, and hunt solely at night."

"Are you saying that is what Niamh has become? That she has somehow become infected?" Francis asked.

"Not in the way you think. The experts have said these creatures normally have a phenomenal healing ability, yet in London they are finding nests of disease-riddled creatures, wasting away, craving blood, some of them turning on each other, not simply hunting humans."

Edward shook his head at the sheer fantastical nature of what Charlotte was saying. "So for some reason, the vampire-kind has become corrupted?"

"Quite so," Charlotte confirmed. "Are you familiar with the term 'zoonosis'?"

Francis nodded and said, "Yes. The transference of a disease from animals to man. Smallpox from cattle, for example."

Charlotte nodded enthusiastically. "Precisely. They tell me that the disease that makes a human into a vampire was transferred in much the same way. It was a venomous secretion, specific to a type of animal long-extinct, but at some point it infected humans, making the vampires that I, until recently, believed were pure myth. The epidemic that has gripped London is similar, but it is thought that the change has occurred through different species rather than straight from human to human, or from that original animal to humans."

Edward raised a hand to his forehead. "Oh God! George!"

Charlotte smiled, knowing that the pieces of the puzzle had fallen into place.

"This is why they blame him!" Edward cried.

"They think somehow George infected some rats or mice with this disease – God knows how he managed to get a source for the disease in the first place. But they think the fire in the hospital released these infected animals into the city at large, where they passed it on from rat to rat, or rat to cat, cat to dog, dog to man, and so on and so forth."

"Zoonosis," Francis added.

"But not only that," Charlotte added, "this weakened vampire strain has collected with it some of the diseases carried by the animals of the city and warped them – at least, that is what my informant thought. He thinks that many of the vampire creatures in London are now passing on not only the vampire venom, turning more and more humans to their side, but they are dying of a horrendous infection, which they pass on as they feed."

"This defies belief," Francis muttered. "I mean, it sounds like the outlandish plot of some, madman's penny-dreadful!"

Charlotte continued. "I think that our poor dear Niamh has not caught the disease that would turn her into a vampire – by this I mean, not bitten, not exposed to the venom, but she has caught the disease that causes vampires to waste away."

"That poor child," Edward sighed, his head hanging low. "And no doctor will even look at her."

"There is one who will," Charlotte corrected him. "George."

Francis and Edward glanced at each other.

"Francis, I know you deal with his finances, as per the arrangements he left." Charlotte turned to Edward and paused, wincing momentarily as she raised a hand to her swollen abdomen. "And you, Edward, I know that he made a dash to Richmond Upon Thames when he left London. He saw you that night. I am convinced you have the means to reach him. Between the two of you, I must get a message to him. I fear that there is little he can do, but he should at least know that Niamh is dying. Perhaps he could be here at the end."

Francis mumbled, "The letters he sends, they are vague and have been sent from all over the country, with no return address."

Edward took a few paces and seemed to warm himself by the fire. He stretched out what remained of his hands in their gloves as if to catch the heat.

"Edward?" Charlotte called, trying to shake him from his reverie. "Can you get a message to George?"

Suddenly Edward turned on his heels to face her. His eyes were wet with tears. "I can do even better. I can tell him directly. Today. Right here, in London."

With Charlotte settled and satisfied for the moment, Giles, Francis and Edward made their way to the drawing room. Giles strode through the house ordering the staff to make preparations as though the child was healthy and well.

"This house will be cheery, damn me! I promised that child a wonderful day, and so it shall be! Miss Pinchstaff, dry your eyes and set about making the best plum pudding you can. Edward has brought us prized treasure; grapes and oranges. They are the centre piece for tomorrow's feast!"

He ordered two guards to collect the goose he had ordered at a nearby butcher's shop. Charlotte protested, not wishing to send two men and two guns, at that, away.

"Those creatures come out at night. We are quite safe for the moment. And when night comes, let them come. Let them find a house that is as prepared for Old Christmas, as it is for them!"

Once in the drawing room, Giles distributed cigars which he lit for each man. He poured three glasses of an excellent brandy, and bade them all take comfortable chairs, which they did. Before commencing to drink his brandy, Giles took a swig from a small brown medicine bottle.

"Feeling under the weather, Giles?" Francis asked.

Giles glanced at the bottle and tucked it back away behind his waistcoat once more. "Me? No, I am in rude health. Never better. This is merely a little fortifying tonic that I have taken a liking to. I have heard a great deal of things called a cure-all to date, that never cured a damned thing, but this stuff… well, there is simply nothing quite like it."

Edward and Francis glanced at each other surreptitiously, each man's eyes confirming to the other that they suspected that the bottle, like every other cure-all they had heard of, contained mainly an opium derivative and alcohol.

"Back to business, gentlemen. Before we take the coach into the city, I must ask, Francis, if you could spare me an advance on my allowance from the Company."

Francis sipped his drink and frowned. "Giles, you barely take a penny. You have funds available for you to draw upon, as would make King Croesus weep with envy."

"All right then, very good, very good indeed. I would use my money to equip a local militia unit with as many of the rifles and bullets as I can buy from our warehouses. I want to pull as many of our hardy young lads as we can into this city; I want to arm them to the teeth." Giles' face was as stern as either man had ever seen. Edward and Francis knew that something had changed him.

"A noble enterprise," Edward said, using the thumb and forefinger of both hands to raise his brandy to his lips. "Francis, I wish to make a contribution to the cause."

Francis thought about this for a moment and smiled. "You know, I think Annie and I might just have a spare shilling or two we could put to the cause, too."

"I saw this city's folk burning their dead like heathens. Men, women, children, stacked high. I can not bear it. I will see this child restored to good health, or if God sees fit to take her, then so be it, but when her suffering ends, I will be out there myself with a rifle until the city's suffering ends." Giles had become very red with anger. "I would have little or nothing said to Charlotte on the matter. She would worry too much. I want none of the Company money involved, you understand, simply my own allowance. I want to make sure the men of this city have the tools for the job."

"Then as Edward seeks out George, so we shall set about our business," Francis agreed.

"Let us not waste another minute," Edward insisted, finishing his drink.

When the men left the drawing room and made for their coats and the front door, they interrupted one of the house maids who busied herself tying bundles of seasonal foliage she had collected from the gardens, holly, ivy and mistletoe.

Giles was delighted with this and called, "That is the spirit! This *must* be the most cheery house in London!"

The housemaid continued as encouraged by Giles, whom she believed had completely taken leave of his senses and who was entirely inappropriate given the gravity of the little girl's health in the sickroom.

When the coach approached the turnpike, Giles muttered, "What on Earth is going on here, now?"

As they drew closer, they could see unarmed Londoners, wrapped up warm against the chill of the winter air, dancing about and slapping the white-bandaged militia men on their backs. A vendor proclaimed that he was giving away roasted chestnuts in celebration, but of what? The passengers of the coach could not tell.

Giles barely registered the deliciously sweet and earthy mix of smells from the chestnuts as he brushed past some of the revellers, one of whom offered him a drink from his small silver flask.

"No, thank you," Giles growled. "What is the meaning of all of this?"

One of the militia men pointed into Hyde Park. Giles' eyes followed the man's finger and it took a couple of seconds to register what he was seeing. At first he wondered why people were celebrating the park becoming another ghastly pyre site, then he realised that it was a collection of the ragged creatures stacked up by militia men, ready for the flames.

"How is this possible?" he asked.

"Two strange men came last night. They brought us some supplies and stood to fight with us. We went on the hunt and put bullets into as many of them as we could find."

"You hunted them in the park at night?" Giles asked.

"Yes. Those men were fearless, so some of us went along with them. Those we didn't shoot dead crawled away and were found lying dead this morning."

"The tide *is* turning," Giles muttered, staring into the snow-covered park.

The militia man handed Giles a bottle of brandy. "It *has* turned. Drink to it."

"A miracle," Giles whispered, taking a swig of the brandy.

"'Tis Christmas, good fellow. A miracle we needed, and one was delivered."

Freddy, who had driven the cart the previous night approached with his large friend, who was known as The Bear. Both wore the tatty, ragtag uniform of the turnpike militia and had been drinking heavily. "Ahhh, Mr Burton," Freddy slurred.

"Freddy. I am pleased the day finds you well."

Freddy slapped Giles on the back, his drunkenness causing him to overestimate their affiliation. "I saw you come back through last night with the little girl, Mr

Burton. How is she?"

"I am sorry to report that her condition is quite grave."

"Sorry to hear it, Mr Burton. Right sorry to hear it."

"I appreciate your concern, Freddy. I came here to talk to the watch commander. I said last night I wanted to supply your men, but it appears I am too late."

The Bear spoke next in his deep, rough tone, "Not necessarily, sir. If you go through the barricade there you shall find the commander. He is talking to the gentlemen who assisted us last night. It appears they have grand plans."

Giles did as The Bear suggested, and weaved his way through the merry throng. He hoped the commander would help him to guide the coach through the crowd and gates as those assembled around the turnpike wanted to revel, rather than press on into the city as he and his companions wished.

A young boy passed Giles, pattering to sell his penny-blood pamphlets of 'The Battle for Hyde Park'. It amazed Giles that no matter what the event, the ink was always dry before the blood.

The watch commander and his two benefactors conferred at a makeshift table formed of a plank and two barrels. Stretched over the plank was a map of London. The men marked various locations on it and discussed each one. Giles recognised one of the men almost immediately as the detective from Dundee he had met at the pharmacy the night before.

"Well, look here, it is our friend, Mr Burton," the Scotsman announced. "How is the wee lassie?"

Giles noted that the Scotsman's attitude was a happier one than the previous night. "It pains me to say she is in an appalling condition. No doctors will treat her."

The Scotsman frowned. "And why wid that be, now?"

Giles shrugged and feigned ignorance. "Perhaps they are afraid she is to become a creature of the night. A vampire. Who knows? I just pray I can find her some help before it is too late."

"If the doctor you met last night, was not so busy himself, I would have sent him to you, to see if there was anything more he could do. But things being as they are," the Scotsman gestured behind him toward the rest of London and trailed off.

"I appreciate the thought anyway," Giles replied, remembering that the doctor in question had been plain in his opinion that they should not take a chance. Had the doctor his way, Niamh would have been a pile of ashes. "Do you know of Stanley Sacks? How is he?"

"Ahh, the pharmacist. He is *remarkable* well. Yes, *remarkable* well."

Giles was concerned at the use of *remarkable*, not in that he used the word instead of remarkably, rather the insinuation that the Scotsman was suspicious of the pharmacist being quite *so*well. "Did he… turn?"

"Not at all. In fact, he is plying his trade for us now, hoping to perfect some sort of elixir or tincture for the plague."

"Good luck to him," Giles offered. "Now, let me explain why I am here. Perhaps, Commander, you will remember my offer last night?"

"I do indeed. And a generous offer it was."

"Is, Commander. For I still extend it to you. I see the Battle for Hyde Park, as it were, has been won. I wanted to ascertain if your fight continues."

The Scotsman turned to the other two men and smiled. The third man, a man in a suit similar to the Scotsman, whom Giles had not met, and who spoke with a crisp, educated London accent, said, "Our fight continues, sir."

"We aim to hunt the creatures down wherever they nest in the city, and bring about their end," the

Commander added.

Giles smiled with relish at the blood-thirsty notion. "I am right pleased to hear it. All I would ask, Commander, is if we could allow my coach to pass, this being daylight, and things having taken a turn for the better, and I will make arrangements as promised."

The Commander yelled out immediately for two of his men to come to attention. "Get this gentleman the help he needs, lads!" he turned back to Giles, approaching him with his hand extended. They shook hands vigorously and laughed. "A true man of your word… a true man of your word, indeed!"

Summerscale rode the carriage all the way to the Priam Theatre. It was slow going, but it gave him plenty of time to consider what he would say if and when he saw George. The last he had seen of him, and the last he had heard of him directly, was in Richmond, where he was pursued by a sympathetic woman - an agent of some sort, and a brutal thug of a man whom he had learned was a disgraced policeman. It was this man who had severed his fingers when torturing him for information.

He had, in the delirium of the torture, somewhere between the third and fourth finger let slip the name of Smokey's Rolling Sideshow. Charles, his torturer, had continued to sever fingers, seeming to suck blood from each digit in his madness, before moving on to give chase.

The only saving graces Edward could consider when he emerged from unconsciousness, were that he had locked the sympathetic agent (who had been badly injured) away, hidden from Charles, and that the sideshow's movements were unknown to anyone but Smokey.

Smokey gathered beautiful performers who could not, for whatever reason, make a big name for themselves on the stage, or who were shunned or disgraced, and provided a safe haven for the deformed and misshapen. He offered all safety, and money, at the price of a thick skin.

Edward had seen some of the members of Smokey's freak show. He wondered how they had not killed themselves, having been born so hideously distorted. There was not a day went by that he did not consider ending his life, and he had not been born with a disfiguring mark on him. The loss of his fingers had been a cruel and unnecessary turn for him.

It was then that he realised that there was a day he had not considered suicide: *today*. He had a mission. He had started out with the intention of giving gifts, and planned to end it with the reunion of Dr George Blessing and his child. If only for a short while, he thought.

Edward had received occasional letters not only from George, but from Smokey. Smokey had always given the impression that George was well - busy, wrapped up in his work, but well. The creature, too, seemed to be thriving. There were times when George would ask Smokey where they were headed next, and he and the creature would remain in a town for a day or two, as he tended to a sick family, only to catch up with the sideshow shortly afterwards. Smokey had remarked that George had been fitting in well and was a remarkable healer. He made various concoctions and medicines to hawk at fairgrounds, always to an eager crowd who would lap up his wares. George had commenced to work with an old Chinaman who had no shortage of skill as an apothecary and the pair were quite a success, from what Edward had read.

"Wouldn't be surprised if all of them are bloodsuckers," a sailor muttered to his companion, leaving the Priam. Edward assumed they had taken in Smokey's freak show.

A woman in a grey coat and blue dress clutched her husband's arm and drew him close, shivering at either the cold, or the memory of something she had just witnessed. "Did you see that creature? No eyes, that skin… I thought I was able to see right through it to the intestines!"

"Those teeth!" her husband gasped.

Edward made his way around the side of the theatre and picked his way through the tents. All around him, performers were taking off makeup, warming soup at fires, pouring hot tea, chattering and joking. Their dark red skin told of a hard life out in the sun and the elements, but they were happy.

"Dr George Blessing?" he asked a young woman with dark brown, curly hair.

She turned to him and fixed him with beautiful, sparkling blue eyes. Edward could think of a time, not so long before, when he would have been in that woman's tent with her at a moment's notice. He could try again, but if she was not horrified by his destroyed hands, and if she unfastened his trousers as he barely able to, then the lack of vigour within would surely fail to impress her.

"The doctor?" she asked, her voice heavily accented. Austrian, Edward thought. She pointed the way to a tent further up the lane.

Edward thanked her and pressed on, momentarily startled as a strapping porter appeared, carrying a rod upon which was tied three fat, plucked geese. Edward knew that Smokey and his performers would enjoy a real feast for Christmas.

He noticed a large, tall tent further along the lane and made for it. Two more bulging porters emerged from the tent, one of them pushing a low trolley.

Edward entered the tent, calling for George. The sight that welcomed him was less than encouraging.

George was indeed present. Whereas five months earlier, George had shaven all of his hair and moustache off, he presently lay on a bed of wood, straw and blankets, his head still shaven but with a bushy moustache and beard. Edward thought that George, wrapped as he was in his heavy blankets, looked like a fur-coated Russian Tsar.

An elderly Chinaman was knelt next to George and was in the process of removing a long opium pipe from George's lips. A moment later there issued forth a great plume of grey smoke from Blessing's mouth.

"George!" Edward cried.

George shifted on his bed slightly, but remained settled, with his eyes half-closed.

Edward shook him and called for him again.

"Too late," the Chinaman said. "He has gone to the land of dreams."

"Land of dreams? I need him awake and alert!" Edward demanded.

The Chinaman placed the pipe into a long, wooden box with a sculpted inlay into which the pipe fit perfectly. "Impossible. The doctor is a haunted man. He must escape, or face madness."

Edward gestured towards the door of the tent. "Madness? There is plenty of madness out there, and we must all face it. Who granted him the right to escape it?"

The Chinaman glanced at a shrouded object at the back of the long tent. The object, covered in a grubby white cloth, measured around ten feet tall and about three feet across. Edward noticed a small set of wooden steps before the object. A chill ran through him. He knew what he would find there, but longed to see what the creature looked like in its present state and requiring such a spacious container. He began to walk slowly towards it.

"Leave alone. Not safe for you," the Chinaman warned.

"I have met the creature before," Edward said, never taking his gaze off the obscured tank. "She was a baby then. It appears she has grown."

"Stay back. She sleeps!"

Edward reached out with a gloved hand, making to grasp a corner of the drape between his thumb and forefinger.

A searing pain tore through his brain, seeming to slice it in half. He fell to his knees with one eye open and one closed. Staggering on all fours, he crawled away from the glass tank, the plaster fingers breaking with a soft, popping noise as he moved. White froth spewed from his lips, where it mingled with a stream of blood from his nostrils.

"Warned you," the Chinaman sighed, moving to help Edward put more distance between him and the tank where he had more chance to recover.

After a few minutes, Edward had cleaned his face with a cloth offered by the Chinaman. His senses seemed to have returned fully. "What happened to me?"

"She does not trust you. She will not let you see her, unless she trusts you."

Edward stared at George's prone, slumbering form for a long while. "It is all right for him. Vacant. Unaware of the horrors out there. When he wakes, give him this."

Edward then curled his thumb and finger around a pencil and scratched out a message for his old friend. "Tell him that this is a matter of great importance. It concerns Niamh. Did he tell you about Niamh?"

The Chinaman's face was overshadowed with concern. "The girl. Yes, he mentioned her. Sometimes, when he is in the land of dreams, he talks to her."

"She is gravely ill. She may not survive. Tell him to leave his bloody pipe here."

The Chinaman nodded as Edward rose to his feet and left the tent. His heart sank. There was not much chance of saving Niamh, he had already accepted that. But he knew that George loved Niamh, and if this was to be her end, then he would want to be with her, not be laid out insensible.

Silently, Edward prayed there would be enough time, at least for George to say goodbye.

George.

Were it not for the pipe, I might have found it impossible to rest in London. The child, on the other hand, seemed as settled as ever I had known her. At first I had assumed that perhaps she knew she was home, and that this somehow brought comfort to her. By comfort, I should specify that her hunger seemed to temper, she was not as desperate as she had been over the months we had been transient. Her mind still scoured my thoughts, however and suggested actions – *willed* me to do her bidding.

Which brings me back to the pipe. The purpose of me commencing to take the opium was to numb my senses when not at my work. I seemed to disconnect from her when under the influence of the drug. I had made the discovery while experimenting with various opium-heavy tinctures. From there it had been only a short hop to the pipe.

Overall, what it had meant was that for the time being the people of London were somewhat safe. Smokey had brought his travelling sideshow into the city for the winter. It made the bitterly cold months more bearable, although we were still situated on a camp of sorts. The yard and lanes behind and around the Priam Theatre had become something of a village, made up of our tents and bonfires. We were safe from the chill of the wind from the Thames each night at least, and our three shows daily at the Priam brought in more than enough money to keep us well-fed until spring.

Hong brought me a cup of his beef and herb tea. It tasted foul, but brought me around most effectively. I sat up and smiled through my beard at the wise-looking Chinaman. He smiled back and stood dutifully ready.

"What is it, Hong?"

Hong handed me a note. When I opened the

scrap of paper, the scrawled handwriting was difficult to make out at first. Then I realised that the note read simply:

Come Home - Edward

At first, I almost laughed at the idea. Home? It had taken Smokey a fortnight to convince me to join the show in London, so afraid was I that I would be arrested. I had been busy out there in the countryside, desperately avoiding news from travellers or the papers, but I was aware that the city was in the grip of an epidemic. The desire to know more was quelled by the fear that in picking up a newspaper, I would finally see in writing that I was a wanted man and that a rope was waiting for my neck. It was easier for my mind not to have the fear confirmed, but safer for my life to assume the threat was there.

You must remember that at the time all of this was happening, I believed my culpability for my wife Margaret's death, for Henry Burton's death, and the deaths of dozens of my patients, had become common knowledge. At that point, I was unaware that I was responsible for much, much more.

Visitors to the shows had muttered and complained something about monsters in the city at night. The only monsters I saw out there were the Londoners themselves, rioting, looting, attacking each other, attacking strangers, attacking sailors, attacking Chinamen, attacking Jews. We had only been encamped in London for eight nights and on three nights deputations of various sizes had come to 'burn the freaks'. Smokey feared that if the situation did not calm within the week, we would have to move on and take our chances in another town or city.

I had been in a deep, opium-induced sleep when Smokey had been forced to bribe some sort of militia group on the outskirts of London to let us enter the city at all. Even after the money had changed hands, Smokey had been forced to carry two wounded mercenaries with him into the city. Hong had tended to their wounds early in the morning, *gratis*, before sending them on their way.

The beauty of the opium, however, was that the sleep it gives allowed me little time for gossip, less time for reading papers and no time in which to wander the streets. I simply put on the show then returned to my tent, to attend to Panacea, and to work on my medicines with Hong.

I should tell you a little of my work with Hong, and my work in general. Hong was a brilliant assistant, a skilled apothecary in his own right and coupled with my discipline as a physician with some surgical experience, we were very close to perfecting a true cure-all. Or, at the very least, a cure-*many*.

The venom issued forth from Panacea's mouth was a dangerous and powerful substance. I had discovered, however, that in various concentrations and at various ratios, mixing the venom with blood before consuming it could deliver some of the benefits of the vampire condition – chiefly the enhanced ability to heal. Blending this with other substances had disguised the blood-venom mixture as a patent medicine.

My experiments with the animals had shown me the pure venom's function as a colonising agent – converting infected creatures into an almost cannibal state, essentially, creating a vampire variant of any species.

The venom caused physical changes within animals and humans, but these were more pronounced the more the host consumed blood. It seemed that there was a way back, but only in the early stages and it was a painful starvation, a near-death experience. If the host consumed enough blood, the transformation, and as a result, the benefits and hazards therein, would be permanent.

The animals in my experiments had shown

great variation. These included variations in conversion time from 'normal' to vampire depending on the volume of venom discharged at the initial exposure, coupled with the amount of blood consumed in the time shortly after the exposure. It was simple, but crude and I had not been able to calculate an exact ratio. Simply put: less venom delivered, more blood and more time required for the transformation to be completed.

I had felt first-hand, the rapidity of the change and the painful return from the precipice, in the days following my flight from London. The child's venom had reacted with blood in my shoulder, which had been wounded with a gunshot. Shortly after this, I had fed upon the blood of one of the child's victims – an act, I might add, quite out of character for my person. As a result, my recovery had been rapid and thorough, with no signs of infection at all. My physical state on the whole improved, and I found that I could fight for survival against the most deadly opposition – me, of all people, *fighting*! Never a fighting man in my life, but under the influence of the venom, I had become a warrior!

Following that fateful night, I was struck by the overwhelming thirst for blood. It was one hundred times worse than any morning that followed my debauched outings with Henry! One hundred times worse, at the least! I had to avoid daylight for three whole days as the combination of the venom and the woman's blood worked out of my system. Somehow, the child strengthened my will, and helped me overcome the cravings. After all, if I became a creature of the night, how could I protect her by day?

That was my own limited exposure. What was clear from my body of research was that an animal infected directly by the creature (or from the samples of venom I had extracted from her) would bite and infect other animals around it. If a rat bit a mouse and the mouse survived the initial attack, the mouse may not have the strength and vitality of its fellows who had been infected by another mouse. Cross-species infection does not always create a fully functional vampire – there are mongrel weaknesses that quite often appear. These mainly revolve around the enhanced healing ability and the ability to fight disease.

Mice who had been infected with the venom and who encountered a female at a point where it would mate rather than attack seemed to produce offspring like the male; that is to say, would spawn a mouse who would feed on its own kind, usually killing the mother minutes after birth. That instant kill and feed sustained the vampire offspring for a considerable period and grant a great surge of growth and development.

This second generation of mouse would impregnate females who would invariably, whether infected or not, birth vampire progeny. It seemed to me that if both parents were vampire at the point of copulation, no offspring could be spawned. I planned to study more complex animals to pursue this theory. For the truest reflection I needed to study infected humans for more than one generation. I feared I would never have the opportunity to complete my research.

The most interesting variation I discovered was when the first mouse infected by the venom, the prime mouse, as it were, would elect to mate with a female. The prime mouse would appear normal and behave as its vampire kin, but the offspring of the prime mouse would display strange mutations. They were, without exception, born without eyes, without hair, and would hunt in packs, as though highly communicative and predatory. Their instincts seemed almost precognitive.

The sub-prime mice would bite and infect others, converting those mice into vampire mice, which would bite and convert others creating generations of vampire mice. Where the sub-prime mice mated, however, their offspring shared the sub-prime mutations and carried on a lineage of animals that reflected, quite simply, in mice, what the child in the bell-jar represents when compared to humans.

From these findings I could deduce much about the child in the bell-jar. I could state with confidence, that the child's father was a man, who had been converted by some sort of creature like her, with the most potent form of the venom. He himself had become vampire, but in mating, his offspring had carried the mutated appearance of the origin creature. My theory was that if the child's father bit me, and I went on to impregnate a woman, then that woman would bear a vampire child. However, if Panacea's true father mated with that same woman directly, without infecting her first, I was certain the child produced would be exactly like the one in the bell-jar.

The human vampire, therefore, was a diluted version of some primary creature, something that resembled the child I harboured. If a human was converted by that primary creature directly, he or she would produce offspring which was either that primary creature, or some sort of hybrid. Without seeing the primary creature, I could not know for certain. I had, however, heard that there was an island off the Northumberland coast, where these creatures dwelled in great number.

Any human infected by the primary creature, or the hybrid would further procreate and bear more hybrids, yet that same human vampire's bite would create only human vampire converts.

All of that was theory, until I could meet the child's father or at least learn about him. Having met Mary Brigham, a woman so skilled in the art of combat, and trained to aim those skills toward the extermination of vampires, I could only wonder if the child's father was not long dead, and the opportunity of learning the true story of the child in the bell-jar long passed.

I snapped out of my mental review of all my research and found that Hong was still standing before me.

"The child's father is not dead," Hong said.

"What?" I asked.

"You said you wondered if the child's father was not long dead. But the child's father is alive. It is you," Hong insisted.

"Hong, what is your deranged Chinese tongue babbling at me now?" I snapped.

Hong shook his head, causing his long, pointed grey beard to wave from side to side. He seemed disappointed that one as intelligent as I should stoop to the level of making crude remarks about his people. Or his tongue, for that matter.

I shuffled to the edge of my palette bed and glanced at the concealed tank at the rear of the tent. "So, Edward was here?"

Hong shrugged.

I sighed and tutted. "Really, Hong? All right then, I am sorry. I am sorry that I insulted your Chinese sensibilities. I can see you have every inch of you the national pride and, of course, intellect, of your average English gentleman... and dare I say, almost the intellect of your average English doctor."

"I think you should stop now, Doctor."

"Better?"

Hong rolled his eyes up and nodded.

"All better, then. So, Edward was here, was he?"

"I did not conjure up the note with my 'Chi-nee' magic," Hong snapped, exaggerating his own accent.

"True enough. True enough," I replied, casting a glance around the tent. "Hong, you could soften your replies... I am, mainly thanks to you, I should add, quite hopelessly addicted to opium, and at this moment am still not quite back from the.... Land of dreams, shall we say?"

"Hopeless, yes I think that is the correct word you use."

"Thank you, Hong. Now, listen! Edward did not

chance to look under that cloth, did he?" I asked, pointing at the shrouded tank.

Hong shook his head. "No, he was going to, but the child... she defended herself."

"He recovered, though?" I asked.

"If he had died, he would be lying right here in front of you, no? Let us say that curiosity made the cat vomit and have nose bleed."

I sighed with sheer relief. The corpse of another friend was the last thing I needed on my conscience.

"Did you hear nothing I said before, Doctor? I told you it was the girl – the little girl you sometimes talk about."

"Niamh?" Suddenly I was all ears. "What of her?"

"She is unwell, she is most unwell, he said. That is why this man wants you to go home. I think she needs your help."

A crushing weight seemed to descend upon me all at once as I grasped for my heavy bearskin coat. A protest. *She* was angry. Wherever Niamh was, whatever was wrong with her, I knew that I would go; I did not require the use of the opium to help me overcome Panacea's control on this particular matter.

Of course, that meant confronting Charlotte. I wondered, would she have me arrested? Would my letter of months ago, and my provision for her and Niamh have softened her at all? Would she accuse me of Margaret's murder, or had Edward gone some way to explaining things?

There was no way that I could take Panacea with me. She would have to remain in her tank under the guardianship of Hong and Smokey. The very moment I had completed that thought, I felt a mental projection of claws being scraped down the inside of my brain.

I glanced at Hong, he stood with his eyes closed, fingers poised at his temples, breathing heavily and deeply through his nose. The expansion and contraction of his chest continued in an unbroken rhythm – he seemed to have overcome the pain she tried to inflict on him. I was able to tell the very moment her attack on Hong ceased, for he snapped out of his trance and began to ready my Gladstone bag. "Wait outside. I bring your things."

Still reeling from her psychical tantrum, I managed to sweep aside the flap of the tent door and step outside. I could see that it was early afternoon, and the sun, wreathed in the city's smoky breath, granted no heat to the earth. I was glad of the bearskin coat and wished I had managed to obtain my hat, hoping that Hong would notice it as he gathered my supplies.

"Doctor!" one of the show children called. "What do you think of our tree?"

I checked my nose to see if the child in the tank had caused my blood vessels to rupture again, as she had on many other similar occasions. She had not. I turned to the child who had hailed me and smiled at her.

"It is marvellous, my darling!" I exclaimed, moving towards her. I ruffled her hair and encouraged her younger brother who had helped her to decorate an evergreen branch with coloured tatters of paper, and flower petals, emulating the German tradition that had caught on in England thanks to Prince Albert's lineage.

I reached into my pocket, produced two three penny coins and handed one to each child. "I must say, I have never seen a more beautiful tree than this."

"Thank you, Doctor!" the children chimed, marvelling at the gifted coins, before returning their attention to their little makeshift tree.

Hong cleared his throat behind me, loudly enough for me to hear over the clamour of our camp site. "I take care of her for you until you come back. Never fear."

I took my bag from him and silently forgave

him for not thinking to bring my hat. It stood to reason that a man so small would have a smaller brain, with a reduced cognitive capacity, by comparison to the Western mind. I outstretched my fingers and touched his forehead, taking a crude estimate of size. I made a mental note to take an accurate measurement on another occasion.

"That is strange, Doctor. I would really rather you shook my hand," Hong protested with as much dignity as he could muster.

Privately, I marvelled at him, looking at him there. Little. And Chinese. How could he possibly think to bring me the hat when all of his cognition must be fixed on retaining all he knew of medicines and potions, as well as desperately clinging to every word of the English language that he could. I knew that I should not remonstrate with him, should not send him back into the tent for the hat, further angering *her*. I focussed instead on all that was remarkable about him.

"Doctor, must you stare at me, so?"

What must his eyes have seen on the way to this great nation?

"Doctor, you have business to attend to."

This jewel of an island.

"What jewel? Doctor, what are you muttering about?"

"Precious to me, Hong."

"Doctor?"

"You. The child. Niamh."

"Please, Doctor. Let me teach you how to meditate. It blocks out her attacks most effectively. You need to leave the pipe alone."

I scowled at Hong. "Those are easy words for you now. It was you who introduced me to it!"

"A sad day."

"And besides, I am a man of science. Your, what is it? Meditation is a mere fiction. You have doubtless been raised on fairy stories and superstition; your primitive mind is, of course, open to all manner of suggestions. Your belief in this meditation serves simply as a distraction, causing you to stand there while her mental attacks do Lord knows what kind of damage to your brain. Were you a rational man, such as I, you would reject such notions and simply flee her attacks or, as I do, protect my mind in a cloud of opiates so dense that she becomes confused and ultimately relents."

"Superstition? You house a vampire in our tent."

"And furthermore," I continued, barely noticing that he had spoken at all, "as you insist on presenting your flanks to each barrage, Panacea will leave you, quite soon, I fear, a gibbering husk on the ground of our domicile. Or worse, leave you stone dead. And when that day arrives, I will, for the betterment of mankind, remove your destroyed brain and study it."

Hong sighed. "I have no idea how I have managed to work with you for all of this time."

"Anyway. Do take good care, Hong. I shall be with you once more before very long at all. Tomorrow, or perhaps the day after. I bid you a merry old Christmas," I announced, before chuckling to myself. "Christmas. Haha! What would the yellow man know of Christ?"

"You realise that I can hear you talking about me this way?" Hong asked.

I shuddered and focussed on his face, realising that my gaze had drifted off at some point. I cleared my throat, tapped him on the shoulder and said, "I thank you, Hong. Take care, my good friend. I shall see you soon."

"When you do, we shall talk again about this pipe."

"Nonsense!" I declared and moved off between the tents, out onto the road to rejoin my fellow Londoners, quite disguised by my beard and heavy fur coat.

The streets were clogged with carriages and wagons, with men offering to lead the horses through the throng for a shilling or two – and drivers willing to pay! – so that the travellers could get to their destinations a little earlier. I knew that I was as well to continue on foot rather than pay inflated fares for a journey that would take more time.

All the same, it took only a short while of my walking along the familiar streets, amid the hustle and bustle of a capital preparing for Christmas, for memories to strike up and play out before my eyes.

I could see Christmas morning with Margaret, and our exchange of gifts and kisses, the recollection fond, but tainted by other images – a gift of poison, of laudanum used to keep her docile after the goose was eaten, so that she spent the rest of Christmas alone while I busied myself in the study, hunched over books and journals with my sleeves rolled up. The first year, the work in the study was professional curiosity, an attempt to understand the creature more. Then I saw the second Christmas, and the third, where my time spent with the creature was obsession and in favour of spending time with my wife. Even my visits with Niamh were crammed into the mornings so that I could get back to the study, leaving Niamh alone for the rest of the day. Leaving everyone alone except *her*.

By utilising opium to mute the creature's hold over me, and by achieving some physical distance between it or *she* and myself, I was able to analyse my past behaviour as I walked to my former home. I could see that when I was physically close to the creature, I was compelled to protect her, to obey her at the cost of all else. The very fact that I was beginning to slip back into thoughts of Panacea as an *it* and a *creature*, was testament to the change.

I wondered at the fits Margaret used to suffer and pondered; had I used a greater strength tincture of opium, I might have prevented Panacea from inflicting those attacks on her. I had caused my wife to become so sedated that she had been trapped in the vortex with me, her only release her untimely, horrific death. The paradox of this - the idea that I had poisoned my wife too much and at the same time not enough - was crushing.

A trio of carol singers beckoned me to join them. I declined and moved on as they struck up another verse of 'Hark! The Herald Angels Sing'. A child ran before them as they moved on down the street in good voice, the child selling sheets of verse for a penny a time.

Tendrils of fog crept through the streets, from the river, mingling with the tiny crystals of snow that swirled in the air around me. For a moment, I was transported back to the destruction of the hospital, when the currents of heat sent burning paper and ash swirling around me. I thought of Mary – that lovely, mysterious creature. She had sparked a lust in me I had thought dead – a lust that Margaret, ravaged in her addiction, had been unable to provoke in years.

Once again, the weight of guilt pressed down on me. Panacea may have stopped Margaret's heart from beating, but it was I who had killed her, three years earlier, by sedating her to a point that I drowned everything in her I loved and found desirable. I had damned her to a half-life, and then judged her as though I was not single-handedly responsible for her ruin.

Before long, I had reached my destination, the grey, terraced house. Home. But it was not my home. It was not anybody's home, it appeared. There was not a window intact on the façade. The battered front door was marked here and there with the holes of nails, where the house had spent some time boarded up. Perhaps it had been boarded up by the police. Paranoia crept over me in a flash as my palm pressed against the door.

Was it a trap? Would the police be waiting for me inside?

The door offered no resistance. I entered my former abode.

No description I give can conjure for you the smell, as it was the smell that hit me first. Strong, stale urine and evidence of faeces smeared there on the floor, here on the wall. Such a terrible sight it was, to see one's former happy home so defiled.

I recalled warm red and green Christmases in the parlour, but the memory flickered into view only for a moment, as the present state of the room, as I saw it, extinguished the vision. The furniture was long gone. No pictures, no rugs, no gas fittings remained, only filth and decay.

On the chimney breast was written in blood:

MONSTER

I walked onward, upward, heading for the study. The room in which I had whiled away so many hours. The room in which I had caused the death of two of my friends.

The house seemed to me to be colder than the city outside. All of the windows had been shattered and boarded over, but the boards had been broken, partially pried away, or removed completely.

I turned from the study, looking up the stairs towards the bedrooms. I could see my old bedroom door, smashed apart, only fragments of wood clinging to the hinges. Nausea pumped my stomach, and I managed, but only just, to hold down the beef broth I had consumed in my tent.

I saw Margaret's cold body in the bed, drained of all life...

"You are returned, old friend," Edward called from the reception.

"Edward! Edward!" I cried. "Jesus Christ, Jesus Christ, Edward! This house... Why did you summon me here?"

Edward was already striding up the stairs towards me. He could see my panic. Perhaps he knew what I felt – creeping fuzz, a moss, colonising my brain, turning my limbs to jelly. His arms wrapped around me, but he was urging me to find my feet.

"I can not hold you, George! I can not hold you up!" he cried.

"It is all right, Edward! I will be all right."

I lowered my body and crouched, steadying myself on the floorboards with only my fingertips. "Niamh. Tell me of Niamh. Please, tell me it was a ruse to bring me out of my stupor. Tell me she is safe and well!"

Edward cleared his throat. "She is safe. That is all I can say."

I had to admit, Edward was nothing if not honest with me. He would not dress truth in a lie to spare my feelings.

"She lies in the sickroom at the Burton house, and Charlotte and her household attend her well," Edward said, raising both of his gloved hands in a gesture of reassurance.

"Thank God!" I exclaimed.

"As per the instructions you left with Charlotte and Francis, arrangements have been made for Niamh and your money has been used well. But things have… well… things have changed here in London, George. It is better that you see for yourself. But the real concern is Niamh, of course. She left the house the other night, for God only knows what purpose. She was attacked and lies in a state that I can only describe as… well, I am sorry to say it, but she would appear very close to death. You are asked to come to her, to heal her, or to say goodbye."

The words stung me, burned in me. I could not decide whether I was happy to have returned or not. It is strange, is it not, that my first instinct was not that I would without doubt make the child well again? I feared that by returning to her, I would only cause further harm and had I not returned, I would have been unaware and she may not have been safe entirely, but safe from *me* and the chaos I bring.

Even to this day, the fact that my feelings varied so, that I did not recognise a chance for redemption, is a mark of shame on my conscience, rivalling any other of my many shames acquired before or since.

I noticed something in Edward's gloves then. Four fingers on each hand seemed not to move. I asked Edward about it. It was then that he removed the gloves and I saw the work of that brute Charles.

"He tortured me, George. I stayed my tongue for as long as I could, but he made me talk eventually. That bastard, George, he kept licking my blood, sucking it from my fingers."

I pressed my hands into my eyes and wept a few hot tears. "Edward! Edward I am sorry! My friendship has brought you ruin!"

Edward quickly replaced his gloves, conscious as he was of the horrific scars and disfigurement of his hands. He smiled a sad smile and said, "My hands certainly have more character than they did before. Besides, you did not do this to me. He did. And your letters said that you saw him, and you are still alive, from which I may deduce that you, by default, avenged me. Am I correct?"

I nodded and rose to my feet once more.

Edward wrapped an arm around me. "Come! I have much to show you. It is not safe for you here, anyway. I feel sure that someone must enquire with the neighbours to see if you return."

The next thing I knew I was bundled into a coach bearing the Burton Company seal and we were off. The driver was expert, aggressive and a man who took advantage of every inch afforded on the dirty streets. I heard him yell and roar at other drivers nearby.

Edward pointed out the huddled militia men,

standing over their fires in the midst of makeshift fortifications. Whatever horror had struck the city, it seemed Kensington was prepared, but I could see from the fearful faces and the sheer number of weapons on display, that they had not been spared tragedy altogether, despite those preparations.

"What the hell has happened here, Edward?"

"London may still be standing, George, in that bricks and timber still cling together, but let me assure you, old friend: this city has been destroyed."

"Destroyed? What on earth do you mean?"

"The London you left is gone forever. The people scurry around like terrified cattle. The Queen resides in Scotland - they say she may never return."

I told Edward, "When we were in the North, on the East coast, I heard rumours of Catholic riots in Edinburgh."

"Indeed. They are more than rumour. Apparently there were plans to declare Edinburgh the new capital city of the Empire."

I frowned in disbelief and gasped, "Surely not."

"I swear to it. What with the new Parliament building set back due to nightly riots here in London, the government and Her Majesty have all but abandoned us."

"The Queen would never… I do not dare to believe it!"

"Believe it! The city is plagued each night by creatures not dissimilar to your discovery, George! Blood-drinking animals carry Londoners off to nests in the rookeries and parks all across the city. The East End is at war. They say there are even vigilante squads outside London policing the roads, summarily executing any person whom they suspect to be carrying this vampire plague. I am surprised that Smokey and the sideshow managed to enter the city at all."

The driver slowed at some sort of makeshift checkpoint and we were allowed to pass. I could see some sort of celebration in Hyde Park and men were firing rifles into the air. "What is that all about, Edward?"

"They must have reclaimed the park."

"Reclaimed it. Jesus, Edward. Are you aware that what you are saying is quite insane?"

"I am aware of how it must sound to you. But I can not for a moment imagine that when you ended that monster Charles, that you did not... inspect him."

I cleared my throat.

"I suspected as much. And your discoveries?"

"Some transformation had occurred."

"I had no way of knowing where you would go with Smokey, did I? I only knew where you would meet him."

"Yet still he tracked me. It took him three months, but I suspect he would only have been able to move by night. The transformation I noted in him corresponded to my previous findings... it would appear that Charles had become almost entirely vampire."

"Almost?"

"From what I understand, Edward, these things like to nest together, at least in the early stages of transformation. Normally an experienced vampire will lead his converts until they have grown in strength and confidence. Without that guiding hand, perhaps he was unable to hunt effectively and to a sufficient level to make the final leap into the animal kingdom."

"Animals?"

"Yes, animals, what of it?"

"The way you held that mysterious creature of yours, George... she was no animal to you. She was your child."

"Is my child," I corrected. It seemed my connection was not quite entirely severed by my safeguards.

Edward nodded and stared at the floor of the coach, which slowed as we approached the gates of the Burton house. The nausea returned. I squeezed the handle of my bag until my fingers felt as though they would burst.

I shifted in my seat. The temptation to leap from the coach was almost overwhelming. "They destroyed my house, Edward. If the people of London blame me for all of this, then they shall surely tear me apart."

"They will never find out that you are here, George."

"Why did you take me there? Why lure me there, eh?"

"Calm, George. Please. I had to show you your house, or else you might not have come to help."

"I would always have helped that girl! I love her as though she was my own child!"

"That is not what I meant."

I felt my face burning as the coach rolled through the gates. "Then what do you mean, Edward?"

I saw armed guards. A trap!

"I mean, George… if you could help Niamh… or even, God forbid, if it is too late for Niamh… then perhaps it is not too late for you to help this city."

"Impossible!" I wiped beads of sweat across my forehead and clawed at my beard. "Impossible. How can I help a whole city? The city, by your own admission, was destroyed over the course of months! If even the Queen and government are powerless, then what more could I do?"

Edward pressed the side of one of his hands down on my knee and whispered into my ear, "You had the power to destroy the city! Now save it!"

I said nothing more. I kept my thoughts to myself: that Edward was beyond insane; that London was dead; that Niamh would be my sole mission and in the morning, I would be gone.

To stay in the house of Charlotte Burton was suicide – she knew perfectly well that her husband's death was my fault. She would allow me to tend to Niamh, or commend her spirit to God if that was to be the case, but she would not hesitate for one moment, once Niamh's condition found a resolution, to plant the kiss on my cheek and mark me out to the mob.

I would never even make it to the gallows, never! They would behead me in this very courtyard, I knew it, and Edward had to know it too!

But despite my fear, my apprehension, my sense of self-preservation, the armed guards I had noticed at the gates were soon at the side of the coach and they were smiling, wishing me well. They opened the coach door for me and assisted me with my bag.

"We hope you can help her, Doctor. She is a lovely child," one of them offered.

A barrel of a man, who introduced himself as Giles Burton, Henry's uncle, raced from the door, embraced me and ushered me toward the house.

I looked over my shoulder and Edward raised his eyebrows, I imagined in hope. And the fact that he remained my friend, even with his hands so mangled as a result of our friendship, gave me hope. And what transpired in that house transformed my life, and may have changed the fate of London.

The late afternoon's wintry light cast a stark white glow over everything it fell upon; the clean linen tucked in neatly around Niamh's little frame took on an otherworldly aspect.

To complete the whiteness of the scene, Niamh's face was as marble – she was like a Greek statue in Athens. I challenge any man alive to keep a dry eye at seeing his child in such a state.

And if that vision had pulled my heart apart, leaving only a thread to bind the two pieces together, then surely the sight of the governess, introduced to me as Miss Pinchstaff, at the bedside was enough to sever the connection and shatter both parts of my heart into fragments. Miss Pinchstaff's fingers were wrapped around Niamh's right hand.

My shoulders juddered, wracked as I was, with

sobs. I moved to a spot just behind the governess with such a slow and deliberate movement, it was as if I was afraid to wake Niamh from some long-needed slumber.

I had no idea how to assist, or where I would work, it being better to work away from the afflicted person's bedside.

I turned to leave the sickroom, and found at the door, Charlotte Burton, her midriff swollen in pregnancy. Her cheeks seemed to radiate warmth and life, but her eyes observed me with icy suspicion.

"Charlotte. My dear Charlotte, you are the very cure for sore eyes," I exclaimed, suppressing my apprehension.

She smiled faintly, with a blend of fear, distrust, and relief that I had arrived. "It is good that you are here, George," she said at last.

"I must look to Niamh and commence my work. We shall talk, but later, yes?"

"That would be… satisfactory."

I nodded in agreement and stepped aside as Charlotte and Miss Pinchstaff took up positions beside Niamh's bed. They stroked her hands, her cheeks, her forehead and spoke in soft, soothing tones. I could hear my own thoughts, "Women! It was remarkable to think that despite my involvement in some matters of a dark nature… that Charlotte had kindness enough in her to grant sanctuary to my child, that she and the governess and Henry's uncle had formed a family of their own in this mansion, with a fatherless child on the way to complete the picture of bizarre domestic arrangements." I then turned and cast my eyes on Giles, who stood overlooking the ladies, a concerned patriarch. A guardian. A stronger man than I.

I stifled the nausea that came upon me suddenly, a reminder that I had abandoned my pipe. The sensation passed, but I knew that it would return, with more vigour, and within the hour.

To my shame, I wasted several minutes more, openly weeping over Niamh's sickbed. Giles was soon by my side, and he squeezed my shoulder and patted my back. Edward joined him and the pair issued a dozen platitudes and consolations.

"I must gain purchase once more," I exclaimed, springing to my feet. I strode across the room, putting distance between myself and Niamh. I rummaged with vigour just short of violence, through my bag and returned to Niamh's side, not as her father, but as a physician.

At the time, I had only a single ear stethoscope. I pressed a finger to my redundant ear, muting the sounds of the house. I heard Niamh's heartbeat. The pulse was steady, but faint. Her breathing was slow and shallow, but it was clear. I pressed my palm against her forehead and found that the child was clammy and hot. I glanced at my pocket watch and jotted down the time. I had not brought a thermometer with me, mine having broken in transit between one site and another on my travels with the sideshow.

I inspected the wound on Niamh's hand, removing the dressings that obscured it from view. "The wound, well tended, clear of debris," I remarked.

Giles wore a concerned face, but allowed himself a shallow breath of relief. I assumed from this that he had helped to manage the cleaning and dressing of the injury. Edward too, showed visible concern.

I realised then that they thought my mutterings were intended for their ears, when in fact I was talking to myself in an attempt to marshal my faculties and focus on the presentation of Niamh's condition. In essence, I was trying to mute my body's rising cry for the pipe.

"Signs of an infection, however," I muttered, and knowing that those assembled may have thought I judged them, I added, "unavoidable in the circumstances." I probed gently at the angry red tissue within the lacerations. I extracted a sample of the custard-like pus that had settled in the wounds and scraped it into a small vial.

Giles showed me to a guestroom, as the others left the sickroom to give me space to work. Charlotte had instructed her staff to furnish the guestroom with some tables and a chair to give me a makeshift laboratory. The gas lighting allowed me to work unimpeded, despite the rapidly fading day.

The gentle hiss of the gas took me back, back to my study. Back to Henry, back to Father Haddon, back to their screams… I shuddered, and returned to the matter at hand.

With my equipment set up, I began to inspect the mucous in close detail. The cell structure of the infectious material was curious in that it was both unusual and at the same time only too familiar. The structure showed a bonding of germs I recognised as the seeds of rabies, typhoid, yellow fever, cholera and typhus. In the magnification, the cells looked like some malevolent snowflake.

The elements of these diseases in one person would suggest someone living among putrid dead bodies and stray dogs in a sewer beneath the streets, emerging only to sup the filthy water of the Thames! Yet Niamh had been missing only hours.

Looking again at the sample revealed another piece of the puzzle. The germs were locked into a structure only too familiar to me: Panacea's venom.

The germs were bonded; several diseases moving and behaving as a single unit.

I knew that venom to aggressively colonise the host's tissues and to promote healing, essentially the venom is the tool through which vampirism prolongs and preserves itself. Niamh's hand had not healed, and one could reason that this is simply because she had not fed upon blood, but I knew that was not the reason – the transformation had not even begun to occur. The venom and the infection were holding each other at bay.

I stared at the ceiling and pondered this. Niamh had been in contact with vampire creatures that had not, it seemed, bitten her. All the same, venom, from either the saliva or blood of a vampire, had touched an open wound. At the same time, presumably upon the same contact, she had been exposed to the infection which was some mixture of other diseases bonded and changed by the vampire venom. I reasoned from this that the disease that had made Niamh gravely ill, was one to which vampires are susceptible. For her part, she had succumbed to a collection of illnesses which had caused her physiological collapse, but which lay yet dormant, unable to run rampant through her body.

I cried out a long, anguished moan as a physical pain gripped my chest. The pain had nothing to do with the opium withdrawal; it was the effect of the moment that I realised it was all true! This was my doing! The people of London were correct, I was a monster!

I staggered to the sickroom. The other occupants of the house came to see what the commotion was, but stood stock still in fear as I raced along the corridor.

The mice, the rats, the dogs – it all made sense to me at that moment! Over the months since my hasty departure, the strays and vermin had bred and bitten and colonised so much that the venom itself had become tainted! The venom had melted into diseases most prevalent in the shadows of the city, and strengthened them!

The next thing I knew, I found myself at Niamh's bedside once more, on hands and knees, begging her for forgiveness.

But even through my hysteria, a theory was forming. It took God knows how long for me to collect my emotions once more, but when I did, I raced back to my makeshift laboratory, leaving Charlotte, Miss

Pinchstaff, Edward and Giles standing quite perplexed in the sickroom.

I quickly produced two vials from my bag and prepared two glass slides for my microscope.

My hands started to shake and I feared I would drop the vials and slides, and so quickly placed them on the table and tried to master my nerves. I could not proceed without satisfying my addiction. But I needed to keep my wits about me – no time for the Land of Dreams!

"You are quite taken with it, are you not?" came Giles' voice from the door.

"I beg your pardon?"

"Opium. I recognise the signs. Your body is crying out for it."

I steadied myself on the table and rose to my feet. "I assure you I am simply fatigued."

"Try this. It has a little laudanum in it, I think. Perhaps enough to satisfy you, but certainly the mixture is potent enough to grant you some vigour." Giles handed me a familiar brown bottle. The printed label on the front said 'Hong's Blessing'.

I chuckled and collapsed to my chair once more. My laughter rose and my shoulders trembled as I became hysterical.

"Whatever is wrong with you, man? Crying one minute, laughing like a fool the next!"

I uncorked the bottle and took a draught then handed it back to Giles. "Do you enjoy that mixture and find it effective?"

"It has taken years off me, I swear to it, with my right hand to God." Giles raised his right hand then tucked the bottle away again.

"How long have you been drinking it?"

"A week or so. It appeared at a pharmacy I frequent." Giles' face changed and he appeared to be defensive about his consumption of the medicine. "In fact it is the pharmacy from which I recovered dear little

Niamh."

"There have been many variations of that medicine. This last one appears to work well, eh?"

"I could not attest to knowledge of variations, but this agrees with me," Giles responded. Then his eyes widened. "It is you! Why, your name is on the bottle! I imagined some Chinaman with a mortar and pestle!"

"Hong is real, too," I assured him. "And he is rather useful with a mortar and pestle."

By then, the cure-all had taken effect and my tremors had abated. "Stay with me, if you like. Perhaps my work will be of interest to you."

With my first experiment, I observed that venom extracted directly from my creature could rapidly destroy the disease. In the second experiment, I used venom extracted from a converted vampire mouse. The venom was not effective and the disease destroyed it. I set about a third experiment, this time involving the blood of a converted mouse. I could see that the disease absorbed the blood cells, transforming them, colonising aggressively.

I pricked my finger and conducted a fourth experiment. The disease did not react with my blood.

The disease, I reasoned, was only truly harmful to vampire creatures.

Had Niamh been bitten, and the colonising process either begun, or completed, I suspected this new disease would have corrupted the colonised cells in her body.

I explained to Giles that the only treatment for Niamh was in the first vial. Giles began to celebrate the discovery.

"Do not celebrate for the moment. I must first fathom a way to introduce this into Niamh's body without causing her to become vampire."

"And if she becomes one of them… will she not then be susceptible to the disease?"

I nodded and said, “Basing a judgment on what I have just witnessed through the microscope, I do not doubt that the child would be dead within the hour.” The trick was to introduce the benefits of the venom in the right concentration and through the correct route.

Giles tapped the breast of his jacket, causing the glass bottle to sound a dull chime. “Does this have any of that in it?” he pointed to the vial in my hand.

“It does, but while perfecting this, there had been some… miscalculations.”

Giles looked more concerned by the second.

Edward appeared at the door. “How goes the research?”

“I am trying to ascertain if I am to become a blood-supping demon,” Giles said.

Edward laughed at what he assumed was a joke.

“I am quite serious! Dr Blessing here has been hawking a patent cure-all which has in it a quantity of what drips from the fangs of these creatures of the night!” Giles cried.

Edward smiled at me and said, “Oh dear, George. What have you done?”

“Has all of this started with a medicine?” Giles cried. “The city destroyed for you to line your pocket?”

“How dare you, sir?” I cried, leaping to my feet. “My medicine is not responsible for this.” Then I sat down in a hurry and added, rather sheepishly, “It is my months of meddling with nature in my laboratory that is the cause of this.”

Giles composed himself and grasped my knee. “I apologise, George. I am afraid, that is all. I am afraid for Niamh, I am afraid for this household, I am afraid for myself.”

“I understand. I understand, and I accept the facts. This is entirely my fault. Niamh, London, all of it. All of these deaths.”

“Now you have accepted your lot,” Edward said,

"perhaps you can stop the death today. Perhaps Niamh will be the first of many you save. But God forbid, if she is beyond saving, perhaps you can learn something of the nature of this plague."

"There are two problems."

"Two?" Edward asked.

"Two problems, because there are two plagues. To the ignorant eye, Niamh's problem appears to be that she was attacked by a vampire. This is the *plague* that is commonly recognised at present. Londoners are being attacked and transformed into vampires, who in turn attack and transform others. There is evidence to suggest that there have been creatures of this kind among us for centuries."

"I thought it impossible until I saw the city brought to its knees, George," Giles added.

"Vampirism is thought of as a plague in London at the moment because of the sheer scale of the attacks and conversions. This is not merely a handful of creatures killing to survive; this is the wholesale destruction and transformation of a city's population. It may be true that this particular epidemic stemmed from my hospital. However, I have also discovered that within this known, visible plague, another has emerged, once which kills even the vampire creatures we fear. It is that plague which has infected Niamh, but which can not yet take her completely."

"It can not kill humans?" Edward asked.

"Or it takes time to kill us... perhaps it is not used to us yet... acquiring a taste for us," I reasoned.

"Acquiring a taste. Like wine," Giles mumbled.

Edward cocked his ear towards Giles, attempting to hear him more clearly. "What was that, Giles?"

Giles turned on his heels and left the room with all haste, his face flushed and I am certain I saw tears on his cheeks.

Edward tightened his lips, his face showing sympathy for the likeable old man who, it seemed had become very fond of Niamh. Edward turned to me and asked, "What is next then, Doctor?"

"Next?" I considered the next move. "Next is goose fat."

Miss Pinchstaff was fast asleep on a chair in the corner of the sickroom. The sun had revoked its offer of light and so the flickering orange of the gas jets was the only illumination. The effect of this was that deep shadows were cast into the corners, including that in which Miss Pinchstaff sat.

Miss Pinchstaff woke in some distress. I imagined she had suffered a disturbing dream, or perhaps the awareness that I was in the room had been enough to cause her fright.

"How is she, Doctor?" Miss Pinchstaff enquired.

"Still asleep," I said, crouched at the bedside, not looking up from my work. "She has become quite cold. Perhaps you could ask Mrs Burton to arrange for the fire to be set and lit?" I asked, hoping to give Miss Pinchstaff something to concentrate on. Distraction had long been a technique of mine, as one can never tell who might faint at the sight of blood.

My technique, however, had been ineffective, as Miss Pinchstaff presently drifted over to my side, watching my work. "Whatever are you doing, Doctor?"

With my left hand, I squeezed Niamh's wounded hand and encouraged a steady stream of blood to flow from the lacerations I had agitated with my scalpel. "This is no business for a woman. Your attention is better suited to making arrangements for that fire."

I turned my head to see that Miss Pinchstaff was still present. Her eyes reflected the gaslight like two orbs of polished Whitby jet at a fireside. Her defiance quite disturbed me at the time, as I recall. At length she muttered her disapproval of my instructions and left me to my work.

I replaced the dressing on Niamh's hand and

returned to my station with the sample. I issued the same quantity of Niamh's blood into ten small dishes and commenced to offer one drop of Panacea's venom in the first, two drops in the second, three in the third, etc.

That Panacea's venom would defeat the infection was not in doubt, but my experiment would help me to gauge a safe quantity of venom to use so that Niamh's body would not be corrupted, would not become vampire.

Edward entered the room to say his goodbyes, and to wish me well. He feared that he would be unable to reach his lodgings if he delayed his journey any longer what with the militia groups along his route. He said that he would return in the morning to see the results of my labours. Edward assured me that he was convinced of my imminent success.

I considered for a moment how remarkable it was that Edward did not blame me for the loss of his fingers. The torture had only been inflicted on him because he had assisted me. I wished the world could be so forgiving.

Very few people know the secrets of Edward Summerscale. I am one of those trusted few, and I can confirm that some of those secrets would horrify you. However I was resolute in my opinion that the good in the man far outweighed the bad.

I saw him to the door, pleased for the opportunity to stretch my legs. The ground floor of the house was a hive of activity. Charlotte and Giles waved Edward off and returned to the warmth of the fires, the smell of burning pines, roasting chestnuts, hot plum pudding and goose.

A maid took hot tea out to the guards and enquired about Niamh as she passed.

It was then that Charlotte invited me into the parlour so that we could discuss matters of mutual concern.

That was not a moment I had been looking forward to.

"Truths, George. Simple, undeniable truths," Charlotte started. She seemed to have begun the sentence without me, but I was able to estimate the unspoken words.

I pretended not to follow her line of thought.

Charlotte's face seemed to take on the intensity of the parlour fire. "Do not play me for a fool, George. The fact that you are here, within my home, the fact that you are still alive, though I have armed men about me in every direction, tells you that you may speak plainly."

I cleared my throat and reasoned, "It simply tells me that I am useful for the moment."

Charlotte seemed to think about this for a long moment then blurted out, "You killed him. You killed my Henry."

I did not reply, but fear my eyes blinked several times, confirming her accusation. Oh, in that moment, I wished that my Panacea had been there to make a strong, cold, hard thing of me!

"You killed the priest, our friend Father Haddon."

I was gripped on a sudden by a terrible thirst.

"And you killed your own wife, Margaret."

I leapt from my seat, causing Charlotte to start with fright. I paced to the fireside and grasped the poker. I dare not tell you the actions I considered in that moment. I attacked the hot coals and logs in the fireplace, agitating the blaze, creating a crackling, spitting blizzard within the hearth.

"And the fire, George. You can not deny that you set the hospital alight. You burned down our last three years of work. Of all these charges I know you to be quite guilty. However, I know neither your motive, nor your method of murder."

I continued stabbing the fire. The heat singed

my knuckles, and grew into an irresistible, pleasant burning.

"You did not work alone."

The searing heat reached a crescendo and at last I withdrew my hand from the fireplace and clattered the poker back onto its brass stand.

"Charlotte, how am I to answer your charges? If I told you the truth, you would think me mad. If you believed me, you would think me evil. And I think... I think that I am neither of those things. I believe that I *am* a good man." I turned from the fire and met Charlotte's gaze.

"George. When you and I visited Judith Cloonan on that fateful night and I left the doss with the midwife... Something transpired in the time that I was unconscious. Something you hid from me. Something only Henry knew. And together you hid it. Am I correct?"

I nodded.

"Judith bore a child, did she not? One horribly disfigured, so disfigured you spirited it away?"

"No. The child... she was beautiful."

"Was?" Charlotte asked, shifting her position on her chair.

"She has grown somewhat in the last three years. She appears to be what I imagine is the juvenile to adult of her kind."

"Not a human, then?"

I shook my head. I was surprised that Charlotte did not accuse me of madness or lies then and there.

"She drinks blood, this monstrous child?" Charlotte stated this; it was not posed as a question.

I confirmed that she was correct, still amazed that she remained parallel with me in the conversation.

"She drank Henry's blood."

I nodded.

"She drank Margaret's. And Father Haddon's, I presume?"

"Yes."

"She drank the blood of some of our patients at the clinic, did she not?"

"She did."

Charlotte's eyes took on a sheen that keenly reflected the light of the fire. "She did the killing?"

"I think so. Most of it."

"The George Blessing I knew was a gentle man. A healer. He would never have hurt another living soul. Then came the time that I no longer knew you, and a secretive George Blessing came about. One who seemed heartless and who can not say for certain that he did not kill with his own hands. Yet here he stands before me, this man, *this* Doctor George Blessing. I can see he has the same face, those same beautiful, kind eyes and the heart… still there. Your heart is still there. Why else would you risk yourself to save that little girl?"

"Niamh is the child that Margaret and I could not have together. She wanted so badly to have a child – even to take Niamh into our home and I denied her that!" My voice cracked, tears flowed down my cheeks and I fell to my knees.

"They can control your mind, George! It is not your fault. She *made* you do these things. See how you behave while you are away from her? You have conscience! You are yourself once more!"

Charlotte rose from her chair at great effort and rested a hand upon my head as I wept uncontrollably, lamenting my part in the deaths of my wife, my friends and those strangers who had stepped out into the path of destruction.

"I feel as though I have been in a nightmare for the last three years, Charlotte. Some of it comes back to me in sleep; some of it has been struck from my mind completely. Some days I can not tell memory from imagination… I have been unable to tell anyone…"

Her fingers pressed my head to her swollen belly. I felt the movements, the *life* within. "I forgive you,

George. I forgive you. I wish you had told me all those months ago, before you ran away."

"It was impossible, Charlotte. *She* would not allow it."

"Had you been at the end of a rope, George, how could you have fed her? And in feeding her, you placed yourself in line with the hangman. She would have been forced out into the open without you. While you studied her, and thought that you were on the brink of a discovery, you were under her spell. She *used* you, George." Charlotte seemed to understand the situation remarkably well, but then I remembered Mary Brigham and wondered at the conversations they had enjoyed in my absence.

"It is too late, Charlotte. See our families… destroyed… see our city… fallen! It takes only a few rats on a few ships and I have wrought the end of the civilised world!"

Charlotte soothed me, as tenderly as if I was the child upstairs who lay at death's threshold.

I spent some welcome moments basking in the warmth of Charlotte's forgiveness. How good it felt to be in the company of an old and trusted friend.

Before long, I thought it best to check on Niamh to orientate myself to purpose once more. As I stepped out into the reception, a great commotion erupted. Giles was red-faced, pulling on a heavy coat as two armed guards held the front door open.

"Surely he would not have simply abandoned his station!" Giles cried.

"Is there a problem, Giles?" I called.

"We fear that one of our guards, Ernie, has taken his leave unexpectedly!" Giles announced, his face a picture of fury. He made for the door, and then turned to me once more, calling, "And if you should see Miss Pinchstaff, please ask her to attend Charlotte at once, Doctor."

"Certainly," I said, turning my attention back to Niamh.

The sickroom was cold. I tutted and shook my head when I realised that Miss Pinchstaff had neglected to request a fire as I had instructed. A sheen of perspiration glistened on the child's forehead. I checked her temperature with my palm. She was deathly cold.

I inspected the wound. Immediately upon removing the bandage, the smell of decay struck me. The wound had not only become septic, but Niamh's skin had begun to rot.

I raced back to the samples I had been working on, cursing my own negligence. Shifting the samples under the microscope, I found that the first three samples had been ineffective. There had been no significant change. The fourth sample showed signs of the diseased blood abating. In my excitement I reached for the last sample, with the strongest concentration of Panacea's venom. Immediately I could see that it was too potent, and that Niamh's blood had been corrupted – turned vampire like so many of those animals I had experimented on.

I picked up the sixth sample then compared it to the fifth and seventh.

The sixth was perfect. The disease was gone. Niamh's blood was cleansed and not corrupted.

Using the goose fat I had collected from the kitchen earlier, I prepared an ointment with the correct concentration of Panacea's venom. After a thought I added the sixth sample itself, where the reaction I desired had already taken place, hoping that it would spur on the process.

I hurried along the landing to the sickroom and almost collided with Miss Pinchstaff, who emerged from that room. I almost dropped the jar containing the ointment. "Watch where you are going, damn you, woman!" I cried.

Miss Pinchstaff scurried past me, saying not a

word. I thought her to be the most rude woman I had ever encountered and raised my voice to her, saying, "Did I not request a fire in that child's room?"

I then remembered Giles' request and called after her, as she descended the stairs, "Mrs Burton wishes to see you immediately!" Still there was no response from her.

Tutting my disapproval, I entered the sickroom. The room was in complete darkness save the light from the landing that followed me into the room. There was no hiss of gas, so I knew that the jets had been turned off rather than the flames alone extinguished.

I could not see well enough to carry out my work and so returned to the landing where I took a candle and matches from a side table. I lit the candle and returned to the sickroom when a series of gunshots sounded outside, giving me such a fright as I nearly dropped the candle and the precious ointment I carried.

Opening the curtains with some trepidation, it took some moments for my eyes to adjust to the darkness of the grounds. I realised that the gunshots had not come from this side of the building and that the shots had been fired to the rear.

I was about to close the curtains once more, when I noticed a shape, almost invisible in the blackness, flitting across the path below. The shape vanished, absorbed by the darkness of the trees and plants. I wondered if it was the guard Giles and his men were looking for. Perhaps he had become separated from his fellows, I reasoned. As I closed the curtains, a nagging doubt persisted in my mind; I was sure the shadowy shape had been wearing a dress.

The front door burst open and another commotion erupted in the reception.

Peering down the stairs I saw two armed guards ushering Giles back into the house. Giles clutched his neck, which bled profusely. "My God, Giles!" I cried, racing down the stairs towards him.

"What happened?"

"We found a vagrant… hiding in the wood-shed… bloody bit me!" he gasped. "Doctor, when you find yourself with a moment, could you grant me… your *blessing*?"

I ignored the request. "Let me see the bite, Giles."

He moved his hand, and hot sticky blood dribbled down his fingers, his clothes and onto the reception rug.

Producing a kerchief I wiped at his injury, fearing what I would see. With the blood momentarily clear, I saw two puncture marks, as of two sharpened, elongated canine teeth. Fangs. "Giles. I have grave news for you," I growled.

The front door opened once more, interrupting me.

Two more guards appeared, dragging a scruffy man between them. The man was either dead or unconscious. They dropped him on the rug and rolled him over. The gunshot wounds in his chest were fatal, of that I was certain.

"My God, it was Ernie!" Giles gasped. "Why would he bite me?"

The gathered guards evidently realised before Giles did. One of them tore at Ernie's shirt, exposing the scar on his neck. The mark of a healed bite.

The guard who had touched Ernie cursed and inspected his fingers. A string of mucous connected his fingers.

I knelt beside Ernie's corpse and pressed my fingers against his flesh. It was liquefying. "He is one of them," I muttered.

"We know it, see the bite!" one of the guards cried.

"No… he is one of these half-breed, diseased vampires that plague the city."

"A vampire all the same," cried the guard.

"But why did the bullets stop him?" I asked.

Giles smiled and gestured to one of the rifles. "Silver bullets, George. When I sent arms to the militias, I armed our men, too."

"Giles, but you have been bitten!" one of the men cried, not daring to finish his thought out loud.

I noticed that the men began fidgeting with their rifles.

"And yet I feel I am in rude health." Giles became aware then that others nearby were perhaps not as convinced of his condition as he was.

One of the guards raised his rifle so that it no longer stood with the stock against the floor, it was across his midriff. The others did the same.

Giles started to protest that perhaps he had not been infected. The guards kept looking at Ernie on the floor. I knew, and Giles must have known, that they avoided eye contact with Giles because they liked him, and they no longer wanted to see him as himself – they needed to depersonalise him, make him inanimate in their minds. That would make killing him easier. They also stared at Ernie so that they could associate Giles with *him*; a vampire, worthy of the same treatment as Ernie.

As Giles moved from man to man, touching coats, gripping hands, assuring them he was still one of them, something ticked away in my mind… The ointment I had prepared for Niamh, from Panacea's venom… it needed to bond with blood to be effective. Using it as a topical cream would work on her open wound, and it would be drawn into her bloodstream. My use of the initial sample would hopefully only speed matters up… but then I considered a similar process I had been using for some time. In every bottle of Hong's Blessing was a sample of Panacea's venom, but also a quantity of blood!

Those drops of human blood I added to every bottle were the element that triggered Panacea's venom and unlocked its healing properties... the venom was not in great enough concentration to cause colonisation... Panacea's venom was a class above the common vampire venom and, I thought, two classes above the venom of the diseased specimens, such as Ernie.

One of the guards' nerves snapped. He grabbed Giles and cried, "I am sorry, boss! I am sorry beyond words, but we can not leave this to chance!"

One of the other guards, with tears streaming down his cheeks, held the front door open. "We have to protect Mrs Burton!" he wailed, justifying his involvement.

The others grabbed Giles and started to move to the door with him, each crying out that they were sorry, but that it had to be done.

"Stay your hands, gentlemen!" I boomed.

The men stopped in their tracks and turned to face me.

I asked Giles, "What happened to the pharmacist? Edward told me the man Sacks was attacked. What happened to him?"

Giles sobbed, "He lives. He will take a while to heal fully, but I heard this morning that he makes progress."

"And Edward told me he was found bitten dozens of times."

"Indeed."

"But he did not change... And this is the pharmacist from whom you bought Hong's Blessing?"

"The same."

"Unhand him at once!" I commanded.

The men looked at me, confused.

"If you have any sense, unhand Giles at once. Giles, share your bottle of Hong with them!"

One of the guards stepped away from Giles, approached me and asked, "What are you talking about?"

"Giles has a medicine which makes him impervious to these vampires! He can not be turned. If you drink it, you will be immune, too!"

The men trusted my theory. One of them reasoned that Giles had been "swigging that stuff" every time he looked at him.

Giles produced his bottle, took a sip for himself, and then passed it among the men.

"Do you have any more of the medicine, Giles?" I asked.

"I may have a bottle or two somewhere..." Giles said, glad to be free of the guards.

"Doctor," one of the guards said, "what should we do with Ernie?"

I was, at that point, ascending the stairs, anxious to get the ointment onto Niamh's hand. I turned back to the men and informed them of the only effective way I knew of destroying such creatures, "Take him outside. Burn him."

Giles added, "You may wish to consider beheading him first."

"It might be prudent," I agreed.

I entered the sickroom once more, armed with a candle in one hand, and the jar containing the ointment in the other. I needed plenty of light in order to study the effects of the ointment properly and so moved to the gas jets to ignite them once more. It was when I approached the fireplace I noticed the smell of damp soot. I knelt by the hearth and used the candle to light the immediate area. Thick soot had spilled from the chimney and onto the floor. I had already stepped in it, and regretted that I would doubtless trail it throughout the house.

I thought it quite careless of Charlotte not to have her chimneys regularly swept. No matter, I thought, it will clean, but Niamh must be saved!

I ignited the gas jets once more and moved to the bedside. I expected to remove the dressing from her hand, but found that it was already gone. Niamh's hand was dark and glistening, and at first I had thought the whole appendage to be completely given over to rot. I held Niamh's arm so that her hand caught the gaslight better. The darkness was not rot, it was blood, and Niamh's clothes and bedding were marked with dark crimson spots.

Immediately, I knew that her wound had been agitated, opened up on purpose, and not by me. My mind leapt back. Before Giles entered the house injured, Miss Pinchstaff had left the room and her behaviour had been strange to say the least. I began to wonder if it had been her I had noticed wandering the grounds.

With all haste I applied the ointment to the child's wounded hand, certain that Panacea's venom would mend her, disease, wounds, everything.

I wiped at her hand to remove some of the blood staining, in order that I might better view the effects of the ointment, but I expected that it would take some time for any change to be discernible.

"Have you heard a word I said at all?" Charlotte cried.

"Charlotte, you are here!" I exclaimed, glancing about me to discover I was still in the sickroom. At the time I wondered if I had fallen asleep, watching over Niamh, but I was standing up.

"Your nose is bleeding," Charlotte said, thrusting a handkerchief in my face.

I took the handkerchief and dabbed my nose, inspecting the bright red blood. Blood. I was reminded of what I wanted to say to Charlotte. "Miss Pinchstaff… I believe she is in thrall, a servant to the vampire found hiding here earlier."

Charlotte appeared to be furious with me and shouted, "I have just told you twice! Miss Pinchstaff is dead!"

"In what circumstances?" I asked.

"*Suspicious* circumstances, George! *Most* suspicious circumstances!"

I was urged to the reception once more, which one began to think of as a mortuary, this being the second corpse to be seen there in a night.

Miss Pinchstaff had been left to lie on the floor, overlooked by Giles and several of the house guards. The indignity shocked me at first, in a way that it had not, with the man Ernie. Miss Pinchstaff's neck was angled at what appeared to be a merely uncomfortable angle, but the deformity of the bone structure, and livid bruising, told me that her head had been twisted to the point of breaking her neck. Someone, presumably one of the guards, had already checked her destroyed neck for bites.

"Bitten?" I asked.

"Not on her neck," Giles said. "But I could not swear to the rest of her."

"Then dismiss your men. I shall make a more thorough examination."

From the top of the stairs, Charlotte voiced her disapproval.

"I beg you, dear Charlotte, permit me. This may mean the difference between a proper burial, and a headless cremation."

She nodded her reluctant approval to me, and the guards left. Giles remained to assist me. I noted that his neck wound had stopped bleeding, and two small scabs were forming.

"Coagulation. A good sign," I said, unfastening the buttons of Miss Pinchstaff's dress.

"What is that you say, George?"

"Coagulation. That is to say that the vampires, in their bite, deliver an anticoagulant. It stops your blood from thickening as your body tries to heal the bite. This enables them to feed more freely, to bleed you more effectively. That your bite has a scab on it is a good sign."

After a brief examination, I was able to conclude that Miss Pinchstaff could safely be given a Christian burial. Giles showed me a small bottle that had been among the effects found on her person. I held it up to the light and could see that it contained a few drops of blood, but had likely been full until recently, as the blood was still liquid and dark red.

"Do not think ill of this poor woman, Giles. And do ensure she has the burial she deserves. Her mind was not her own when she took this blood to her master. See the reward she has earned, mangled and spat out like so much chewing tobacco. At least her master is dead." It was then that I cast my mind back to my arrival at Burton House. There had been several guards by the gate. Ernie had been one of them. And it had been daylight.

"Bloody Ernie!" Giles grumbled at my mention of him.

I turned back to the stairs and saw thick footprints of soot, where I had trampled the filth through the house. Without further hesitation I bounded up the stairs, telling Giles to bring a rifle. "Ernie is not the master, Giles!" I called as I reached the landing.

I heard a tumbling, rustling sound from within the sickroom and Charlotte, stepping back from the sickroom door exclaimed, "Another fall of soot!"

Particles of soot drifted to the sickroom door, cast up with considerable force.

"Stay back!" I cried and grabbed Charlotte's shoulders, drawing her back from the room before she could see what lay within.

I exchanged places with her as she cried out in protest that the sickroom was now no good for Niamh. How right she was.

My fingertips reached the door and I steeled my nerves, bracing myself for what horrors awaited me within. I heard a quiet creak from Niamh's bedstead, confirming my fear that someone was within the room with her, someone who was neither a guest, nor staff of the house.

I committed myself to the room fully. And there I saw it, blackened from head to toe with the soot from the chimney and dressed in blackened rags. The monstrous invader stood bent over the bed with only his white eyes and white fangs glowing in the gaslight.

I screamed for him to stop before he could sink his foul teeth into Niamh's neck. The creature turned to face me and hissed.

I did not know at the time, but learned much later, that this animal, with his torn ankle and calf muscles, with his corrupted skin mingling with soot, leaving a trail of black ooze behind him and upon every single thing he touched, was the same creature that had taken Niamh from Sacks' Pharmacy the previous night. When the creature told me that Niamh was his, and that he had followed her scent, it made no sense to me at the time.

I protested, "Listen to me! Her blood, no amount of blood, will save you! The disease you suffer can only be cured one way. I have that cure."

The black creature sniffed at Niamh and I prayed that if the child was to recover, she would not recover at that moment or else she might have died of fright. "Please, I beg you. You are fast enough, and strong enough to murder every person in this house if I lie to you. But see the wound on the child's hand. See the ointment that I have applied. I implore you to sniff at it. Tell me… is there an element to that substance that speaks to your animal nature? Something that calls to you?"

He sniffed her hand as I instructed. He licked his lips.

"You smell it?" I asked.

"I smell her blood," he growled.

"The healing element in that ointment is present in a medicine that I have perfected. I have a bottle of it here I could give you to drink. It will heal you. All I ask is that when you are healed, you leave this house and all within its boundaries, alive and well."

The vampire released Niamh's hand, and inspected the web of black slime that kept him connected to her. He knew that the slime was his skin. There was no way he could turn down my offer.

It was then, as the creature stepped clear of Niamh that I became aware of Giles at my side, hidden by the door from the creature's view. I turned to him. "Giles, please, give him the cure."

Instantly, Giles sprang into the room, raised his rifle and fired a shot that struck the creature above his left eye. Such gore sprayed across the bed and the poor child within as would turn a man's stomach.

I charged the foul creature and shoved him with such force that his brittle ribcage collapsed inwards, bursting his putrefying organs, as he tumbled back to the window, taking the curtains with him. I struck him again with all of my strength, all of my anger and all of my hate. In that moment, this monster represented *all* of the monsters, and he smashed through the glass and tumbled down through the darkness, amid the snowflakes and the smoke from Ernie's cremation somewhere on the grounds.

Shortly after the soft body of that vampire burst on the ground, there was little left to burn, but the guards did the best job they could.

We moved Niamh, still sleeping, into a room at the front of the house. It was not her own bedroom, as Charlotte did not want the child to associate her poor health with her usual sleeping quarters. I noted that Niamh's hand had sealed up with scabs and the black rot had receded, leaving pink, healthy skin. The fever had passed. I knew that she would live.

The guards were heartened by the news of Niamh's expected recovery and they returned to their watch with renewed energy, certain that they had seen the worst the night could offer, but vigilant all the same.

Giles and Charlotte had overseen the last of

the night's preparations for the festivities of Christmas morning and the Burton house smelled so good that when I retired to my room, exhausted as I was, I thought my rumbling stomach would never let me sleep without some goose and a helping of plum pudding.

The three of us had discussed the night's horrors, them scarcely believing it had all happened at all and mourning the loss of poor Miss Pinchstaff. Giles served me a good deal of drinks and a little of Hong's Blessing every now and then took the edge off my *other* appetite for a while.

"In the morning," Giles said, "what say we move in secret, George, you and I? Let us take off into London, to see your Chinaman, and my friend Sacks if he is well enough, and we shall come up with a plan to make this remedy of yours on an industrial scale, what?"

I agreed. "What better gift could we bestow upon London, Giles?"

"The gift is yours to give, my friend," Giles replied. "It is your ingenuity and nobody else's."

Charlotte smiled at me, but her eyes betrayed such sadness as she said, "We may not bring back those we have lost, George, but we can help prevent a great many more pointless deaths."

"And what with the weapons to destroy the creatures, and your cure to stop the others from being turned, why, we could restore this great city in no time at all!" Giles exclaimed, raising a glass in toast.

I joined him in his toast. The dream of my pardon was as warming as the whisky I sipped. Charlotte assured me that she was sure, following the horrors that London had survived, with people seeing their loved ones corrupted, that they would understand a doctor held in thrall in a similar manner, and forced to do the bidding of a monster. They may not have understood before, but she was certain that opinions had changed somewhat during the course of London's siege. "Of course," she added, "they would have to have the creature."

I knew that she was right. To save myself, I would have to serve Panacea to them. How else could I justify my actions? Without opium, I knew that I would be enslaved by her again, as soon as I was near her. But to offer her up, well, then it would be left to others to deal with her. With the warm glow of intoxication in my belly, I began to imagine the unimaginable, to consider the impossible...

At long last when I retired, I closed my eyes and fell into a deep sleep for some hours. In that time, the only dream I had, was not a dream at all. I heard screams and horses, I heard threats of violence, I heard Hong crying out warnings, could smell smoke, feel the heat and the panic and then I heard her scream. Her scream was silent to all others and bridged the distance between us in an instant. She was terrified. My other daughter. My Panacea.

I could no more ignore her plight than I had ignored Niamh's.

I woke up with the scream still ringing in my head. I wiped at my nose and noticed the smear of blood over the back of my hand. I dressed and packed and hurried down the stairs, away from little Niamh, away from Charlotte's forgiveness, away from potential absolution.

At the gates, I told the guards that I needed to collect my effects from my lodgings, as Mrs Burton had asked me to join them for Christmas. It must have seemed reasonable to them, even in the dead of night, as they let me pass. I huddled in my great fur coat against the biting chill and turned back to the Burton house. The building was a collision of the night's gloom and light from the guards' fires.

I gazed for a while at the window of the room little Niamh slept in and wished that I had peered in on her, just for a second, but it had not occurred to me to do so before leaving. I had been compelled to flee, without a word. Panacea had made me do that, I knew it. She made me abandon all decency and once again denied me any opportunity for my own pleasure or need.

I stood in the falling snow, staring at that window, waiting for Panacea to attack my mind again. I thought that perhaps I would blink and find myself in my tent once more, unaware of how I had travelled there, driven by Panacea's will.

I did not move, though. I thought that if only I saw that little face in the window, I would run back through the gate and burst through that front door. I thought about how picking that wonderful child up and holding her and showering her with kisses would be the greatest Christmas gift I could ever have.

Blessings.

When her eyes opened, the light creeping through the windows was the first thing she noticed. It was daylight.

The second thing she noticed was that she was alive. Immediately she thought that it might have all been a dream, but the third thing that came to her attention dissolved that, and that was the feeling in her hand.

She probed her hand and inspected it, and though a layer of soft, pink skin had grown, she could feel the throb of healing beneath. The injury had been real.

And because that was real, perhaps some of the other things that she thought might have been part of a dream were real too! She had heard a familiar voice, her father's voice.

"He is here!" she cried and leapt out of bed. She flung open the curtains and looked out at the snow-covered yard and street beyond, but was confused. The light had been from bonfires on the grounds and it was still the dead of night.

She saw a shape at the gates, a man. The man was waving at her. She waved back, her heart pounding with excitement. He had come back for her! Another man appeared and Niamh realised that both of them carried rifles. They were guards. They were happy to see her, and blew kisses to her and called Happy Christmas to her, not caring who heard them or if they woke the whole city. The men shook hands with each other and whooped and danced, making her laugh at their silliness.

Giles burst into the room, weeping and calling out, "My flower! My little flower, but I thought we had lost you!" And he showered her with so many kisses and spun her around.

"Do not over excite her, Uncle Giles! She must

still rest!" Charlotte warned, playfully, from the doorway. She looked very tired, but overjoyed to see that Niamh was well again.

Giles rushed out of the room as Charlotte took his place, smothering Niamh with affection.

"It is so good to see you, my child. Just wait until your-"

Giles coughed by way of interruption, returning to the room. Charlotte looked at him and he shook his head. "Gone."

"Who is, Grandpa?" Niamh asked.

"Errr, nobody, my dear. Just one of the guards."

Niamh's face glowed with happiness. "My father *was* here! He saved me, did he not? Tell me it is true!"

Giles shrugged at Charlotte, not knowing what to say for the best. "He was, my lamb. It is true. He had only enough time to make a miraculous cure for you, but he had to vanish before the sun rose!"

"Like Old Christmas!" Niamh exclaimed.

"Exactly!" Giles agreed. "Just like Old Christmas."

Niamh returned to the window and looked out to the road and the dark city beyond. "And now he is off to save everyone else, is he not?"

"He is, my pet. That is precisely what he is off to do!"

"I knew he loved me! I knew he would come back."

"And he shall return again, my flower. He will again. Now, let us see if Old Christmas did not leave a little treat or two for you!"

I wish that I had been there to see that, to see her wake from that sleep. As it was, however, I made my way from that gate. Not very far, but beyond the sight of the guards and the glow of their fires.

There in the darkness I felt an intense crack of pain through my skull and when my head smacked the road and I lay there, with half of my face freezing in the snow I thought at first that Panacea had assaulted me, psychically, from afar. The feet around me told me otherwise however and when darkness overcame my vision and I felt myself carried aloft I felt sure that I had died.

In and out of consciousness I drifted, occasionally feeling the movement of the carriage, and hearing the clattering hooves. I heard a Scottish accent; I heard a polished London accent.

When I woke, I found myself in the cold, with wind whipping around my head, which was covered in a sack or heavy cloth of some description.

My captors must have detected from my breathing or my struggling against the ropes bonding my wrists and ankles to my chair, that I was awake. I thought that perhaps I had been captured by the same parties who had caused Panacea her distress and I wondered then if she was alive or dead. I wondered what they would do with me.

My captors did not leave me to my wonder for very long, as my head was soon uncovered and I saw a great expanse of the East End of London laid out before me. Vast portions of it had been reduced to smouldering rubble. I realised after a short while that I was looking down from within the scaffolding at the tower of the new parliament buildings.

Then came her voice.

"Gaze upon your work. Look at the destruction you have wrought."

She stepped into my view, brandishing a slender blade which I knew she had probably kept concealed in the sleeve of her dress. "It is, however, lovely to see you again, George."

"Likewise, Mary."

End of Part 3.

Correspondence

Dear reader,

If you enjoyed this Dr Blessing collection, please take a few moments to leave a review.

If it pleases you to stay abreast of upcoming developments and publications from my own hand, then do feel free to join me, making full use of your electronic communication paraphernalia to locate my telegraphic presence:

Twitter: @JackRollins9280

Dr Blessing Facebook page: https://www.facebook.com/doctorblessing

jackrollinshorror.wordpress.com

Jack Rollins
January 2014

Dedications

In the original e-books these stories were dedicated as follows:

Dr Blessing's Curse, Or, The Baby In The Bell-Jar
dedicated to my good friend David Basnett

Dr Blessing's Rapture, Or, The Beast And The Bell-Jar
Dedicated to my brother Kevin

A Christmas Blessing
Dedicated to Mam and Dad

Dr Blessing will return…

Lightning Source UK Ltd.
Milton Keynes UK
UKOW04f0854020715

254436UK00001B/2/P